RESCUING ERIN (SPECIAL FORCES: OPERATION ALPHA)

A RED TEAM BOOK 5

RILEY EDWARDS

BEFORE YOU BEGIN

Thank you for purchasing Recusing Erin. I'm beyond thrilled to once again write in Susan Stoker's Special Forces: Operation Alpha universe. I've been a fan of Susan's for many years and have read every book she's published (multiple times.) While I've tried my hardest to stay true to her original characters (because, *hello*, they are already awesome) I am not Susan, I wrote them as I, the reader, experienced them.

I want fans of Susan to feel like they're visiting old friends when they see her beloved characters. I hope I've done them justice. But please remember, I've taken some liberties.

In Rescuing Erin, I use Susan's characters from her new Legacy SEAL series: Rocco, Ace, Gumby, Phantom, Bubba, and Rex. You don't want to miss this series. Securing Caite releases January 15, 2019.

You'll also see Susan's Delta Team: Ghost, Fletch, Hollywood, Beatle, Coach, Blade, and Truck.

And of course, The King of All Things Cyber, John "Tex" Keegan.

I hope you enjoy the world I've created for you as much as I loved writing it.

Sign up for the **Riley's Rebels** mailing list to receive a **FREE COPY of Unbroken** and stay up to date on releases, sales, and giveaways.

https://www.subscribepage.com/rileyedwardsfreebook

Dear Readers,

Welcome to the Special Forces: Operation Alpha Fan-Fiction world!

If you are new to this amazing world, in a nutshell the author wrote a story using one or more of my characters in it. Sometimes that character has a major role in the story, and other times they are only mentioned briefly. This is perfectly legal and allowable because they are going through Aces Press to publish the story.

This book is entirely the work of the author who wrote it. While I might have assisted with brainstorming and other ideas about which of my characters to use, I didn't have any part in the process or writing or editing the story.

I'm proud and excited that so many authors loved my characters enough that they wanted to write them into their own story. Thank you for supporting them, and me!

READ ON!
 Xoxo
 Susan Stoker

For Susan.

This book marks one year since I started writing in Special Forces: Operation Alpha. A universe in which I'm allowed to play with awesome characters. A universe that was born from all the creativity that is Susan Stoker.

A life changing year. Not only for me professionally but personally. It is an honor to call you my friend. Not only are you a brilliant author, but you are downright awesome. Humble, kind, giving, and did I mention brilliant. Oh, and funny as all get out. Thank you for allowing me to use your characters, I love them all. Thank you for encouraging me and helping me when I get stuck. Thank you for reading my first drafts (even though they are messy and hard to read) and offering your opinions. My books are better because of you.

And with Susan comes Amy. All there is to say about Amy is, she is one tough chick. Steely determination and courage—that is Amy. Thank you for putting up with me. (This book was delivered to her twelve hours before my deadline and on Christmas Eve.) And Thank you for all your help.

PROLOGUE

"You're a coward."

My carefully controlled temper was being tested. Erin Anderson had to be the most spoiled brat I'd ever met. However, my dick hadn't gotten the memo. She was too smart, too manipulative, too beautiful, too off-limits. She was the President of the United States' daughter.

Untouchable.

"Not a coward, Erin, smart," I replied.

She crossed her arms over her chest in annoyance, the movement showcasing the pristine flesh of her cleavage. In a moment of weakness my eyes lowered of their own accord, and I had to stifle a groan. The momentary glance had my dick stiffening and my resolve faltering. However, when my gaze met her smirk, I reminded myself I wasn't going to touch her. Not now, not ever.

She knew exactly what she was doing. It was all part of her manipulation. Erin knew how beautiful she was and she'd learned to use it to get what she wanted. And over the last few months, she'd made one thing very clear—she wanted me. That wasn't going to happen for a variety of reasons. Setting aside who her father was, I wouldn't be used; I wasn't any woman's boy toy.

As happy as I was for my team, I didn't believe in love. Not for myself anyway. Once bitten, twice shy and all that bullshit. I also didn't fuck women above my paygrade. Rich women who only wanted me on their arm because I was former Special Forces. Fuck that. My service was never going to be exploited.

"I know you feel it, too, Colin. You're either too stubborn or too stupid to admit it," Erin continued.

"Woman, the only thing I feel is annoyed."

"Colin—"

"Enough, Erin. I know you're used to the pansy, country club boys who kiss your ass, but I'm not them. You can throw whatever temper tantrum you'd like, and I still won't bend. I'm a man, not some punk who's gonna cave because you've begged enough."

"You're an ass!" she shouted.

"No, sweetheart, I'm real. I don't sugarcoat shit so I won't hurt your tender feelings. If that's what you're after, why the fuck do we keep having this same conversation?"

"Fine. I get it. You don't want me." The saucy grin she'd had earlier turned into a defeated frown. A look I found I didn't like on her pretty face, but one that was necessary. It was my job to protect her, and I couldn't do that if every time we were alone together, she was testing my patience and self-control.

"Erin—"

"No." She held her hand up, stalling my rebuttal. "Leave it. I have to get back downstairs. I have responsibilities to the charity."

She was right, she did. There were at least four hundred people here by her invitation, all waiting to be schmoozed by the first daughter. I had to hand it to her; she could work a room. All it took was an impassioned speech about the children she was helping and a smile, and people opened their wallets and money flowed.

Erin was almost to the door. I reached out and stopped her before she could leave. My first mistake was touching her, the second was savoring the way her small hand fit in mine.

"What?"

"Listen, I'm sorry. I didn't mean to be such an ass, Erin. You're a beautiful, smart woman." I opted to leave out what a pain in the ass she was. "But you have to know, I can't touch you. I was hired by your father to protect you. That's it. Whatever you think is between us is a case of wanting what you can't have. If I were some guy off the street, you wouldn't give me a second glance."

Her sexy, brown eyes narrowed into slits before she turned, bringing her closer to me. So close the flowery perfume she wore assailed my senses. When I tried to let go of her hand, her grip tightened and she leaned in close.

"You've miscalculated me, Colin. You presume to know me, and why I want what I want. Has it ever occurred to you, that I'm not, nor have I ever, been attracted to the ass kissers that chase me only to get closer to my father? I don't want a boy in my bed, Colin. I could have any number of them with a smile and a wink. I want you, not because I can't have you, but because I'm attracted to you."

When her mouth pressed against mine, I did nothing to stop her. When the silk of her tongue swept the seam of my lips, I opened for her. And when she invaded, I caved, then took over. The sexy mew she made fueled my desire, and I deepened the kiss, and, in an illicit battle I knew I'd lose, I waged war. It was wrong. I shouldn't have been devouring her like she was my last meal. I shouldn't have enjoyed the way her tongue felt against mine. But I did and I was. She pressed her body closer and there was no way she could miss my hard-on. The slacks I was wearing gave little by way of a barrier. Her hands roamed my back, and mine grabbed her ass and kneaded the firm muscles. Goddamn, she was sexy.

"More," she whispered against my mouth.

What the fuck am I doing?

"Stop, Erin." I grabbed her hands as she fumbled with my belt.

She kept her hands where they were but pulled back enough to focus on my face.

"What?"

"We can't do this."

"Why not?"

I pulled her hands away and stepped back, needing the space to gather my thoughts.

"I told you why. We can't do that again."

Her cheeks heated, and instead of embarrassment she looked pissed.

"If you try and tell me you weren't into that kiss just as much as I was, you're a goddamn liar."

I stood in silence, watching her get madder by the second. There was nothing for me to say. She was right, I *was* into the kiss just as much as she was, and had she not broken the spell by asking for more, there was a good chance she'd have my cock in her hand. But she did speak, her voice reminding me I couldn't touch her.

She stomped to the door and paused, looking back she tried one more time. "Come on, Colin, tell me you don't want me," she taunted. "I may be a virgin but I know a hard dick when I feel one."

A what?

A fucking virgin?

How in the hell does a sexy, beautiful, pain in the ass woman get to be Erin's age never having had sex? I was getting ready to call bullshit when her shoulders hunched just enough to tell me she was trying to be tough. Erin Anderson was a fake. All her bitchiness and attitude were a put on. A façade she hid behind.

Fuck me, what was I supposed to do with her now?

"I wasn't. And since you're a virgin and all, I'll explain to you that when a woman sticks her tongue in a man's mouth and rubs her tits on him, his dick gets hard. Hell, you could've been anyone and my cock would've been begging for attention." That was a lie, but it sounded like a good story to excuse my behavior.

"Fuck you."

In a move I would've been impressed by if the lamp she'd picked up off the side table hadn't been sailing through the air straight for my head, I ducked out of the way just in time. I have no idea how she'd managed to yank the cord out, but she had. The proof was laying shattered next to me.

"You're not only a coward but a liar, too." And with that parting shot, she walked out the door.

I was no coward—but I *was* a bold-faced liar.

"ANYONE HAVE A TWENTY ON SPARROW?" I ASKED INTO MY two-way radio about Erin's location.

"Negative," one of the secret service agents replied.

I waited for the other five men to report in before I left the main house and went in search of her. Her disappearing act was beginning to piss me off. I thought we'd gotten past her trying to ditch her security detail. Even though we were on a three-hundred-acre private estate it still wasn't safe for Erin to wander off. Movement by the guesthouse caught my attention and I slowed my step, waiting to see what it was. I saw it again, only this time it was a reflection from a lens. On silent feet I moved to the side of the guesthouse just as a man was lifting his camera, pointing it at the window. He was too interested in what was going on inside to notice me moving in behind him.

In a smooth, well-practiced move, one arm slipped around his neck and my hand covered his mouth. Five seconds later, he was choked out and on the ground. I picked his camera up and peered in the window. My blood instantly boiled. Erin was naked and there was a man in the room with her. What the fuck? So much for the blushing virgin act.

I quickly made my way to the door and was even more fucking angry that the door was unlocked. Anyone could've walked in.

"What the fuck?" I roared, and Erin jumped back and tried to cover herself with her hands.

"It's not what it looks like." The man put his hands up.

"Put your hands down, this isn't a fucking stick-up, asswipe. Give me your phone."

The man fished his phone out of his suit jacket that was neatly placed over the back of the chair.

"Here." He thrusted it in my direction.

"Is this your only device?"

"Yeah. That's all I have."

"Get gone." I took his phone and motioned to the door.

"Sorry, Erin," he said, picking up a large, spiral bound pad and bolted faster than a speeding ticket.

Pussy.

"Why's he sorry?" I asked. "Did he hurt you?"

"No," she mumbled.

"Put some fucking clothes on." I looked around on the floor trying to find her dress when I finally spotted it on the same chair the man had laid his suit jacket. I didn't bother looking for her bra and panties, if she had even worn them under her fancy gown. "Here." I tossed the dress to her and turned my back.

But it was too late. Erin's naked body would be forever seared into my memory. Every sexy inch of her.

Shit.

"It's not what you think," Erin said.

"It isn't?" I turned to face her.

"No."

"Funny, it looked to me like you were getting ready to fuck one of your country club boys, not even an hour after you were begging me to fuck you," I mocked.

Erin adjusted her tight-fitting, strapless dress and offered no further explanation. Not that she owed me one. She was no one to me, a woman I'd been hired to babysit. If that was the case, why did it piss me off so badly?

"Virgin, my ass," I mumbled and walked to the door. "Let's go. I'm taking you home." She didn't protest and followed me.

"It really wasn't—"

"Save it, Erin. I don't give a shit."

I heard something that sounded like a sob but I didn't dare ask her what was wrong. The last time I fell for her wounded doe act, she'd sneak attacked me and shoved her tongue in my mouth. That wasn't going to happen again.

"I know you don't. No one does."

It was on the tip of my tongue to ask her what she meant when I caught sight of the photographer I'd choked out running toward the woods, reminding me I had a job to do. Protection—nothing else. If she needed someone to unload her burdens on, she could hire a therapist. I wasn't that man.

CHAPTER 1

"WE'RE LEAVING," Colin announced.

I remained silent as he prowled around my apartment like a caged animal. He always did this when he was in my home. Every time we walked in the door, he searched the bedrooms, closets, and bathrooms as if someone might possibly be lying in wait. It was ridiculous. Hell, the last year of my life had been one big overreaction.

"Erin? Did you hear me? Get packed. We're leaving tonight," he grouched.

With each passing day since the charity event, he'd become more and more unbearable to be around. He barked orders, he gave commands, and he kept his distance. I knew I'd screwed up the night of the party. I never should've kissed him. And I really never should've used William to try and make Colin jealous. I should've made him listen to me that night and explained who Willy was and what we were doing. But I didn't, and the whole thing blew up in my face. Over the last few months, he'd put distance between us—both physical and figurative. He was never close to me unless we were in public and he was guarding me. No more sitting next to me on the couch at night. No more of the innocent touches I'd lived for. Nothing. He was distant and a complete ass.

I'd messed up.

"I heard you, Colin."

"Then what are you waiting for?"

"An explanation."

He was sadly mistaken if he thought I was going to pack a bag for places unknown and blindly follow. I had done that for the last seven years with my secret service detail. I was done being the dutiful first daughter. Done being told what to do instead of being asked. That's what had started all this nonsense to begin with. Now that I wasn't simply following orders, instead of living my life the way I wanted to, suddenly there was something wrong with me and I needed a full-time babysitter. It was beyond ridiculous. I knew my dad loved me and wanted me safe, but he'd gone way overboard ever since my friend, Olivia, had been kidnapped.

I was intimately aware of the limitations that were put on me because I was the first daughter. Being the only child of the President of the United States wasn't all it was cracked up to be. Colin thought I was a spoiled princess; he had no idea that was the furthest thing from the truth. Since my dad had been elected, I'd had no privacy. I was okay with most of it but never having a minute to just be me, had gotten old. It made me sound like a selfish bitch to everyone, including Colin. They all sat back and judged me. None of them had any idea what it was like to have someone always watching your every move. I'd been chastised by the media. Bloggers called me fat and ugly one week, and anorexic the next. Trolls on the internet made daily comments about everything from what I ate to what charities I supported. Everyone had an opinion—but no one knew me.

"An explanation? You've been briefed. Pack. We're leaving soon."

"Yes, Colin," I sighed in frustration. "I've been briefed. Which means I've been given the redacted version of what's going on. I want the truth. Why do I need to go into hiding? Where am I going? With whom? For how long? You know, actual information."

"I told you, there have been threats made. I don't know for how long, and you'll see when we get there."

"Yeah, that doesn't work for me. I think this is another overreaction. I'm not leaving unless you tell me what the threat is and who made it. I'm an adult. I get to make decisions for myself."

"If you're an adult, start acting like one, instead of a petulant child who's not getting her way, and go pack."

If he thought I was acting childish then, he hadn't seen anything yet.

"You can leave, Colin. I'm in for the night and Gerard should be in the hall by now."

I assumed the night guard was at his post by now; providing my father wasn't sneaking off the White House grounds like he frequently did. Gerard was one of my dad's personal protection agents. He was technically secret service, but my dad kept Gerard particularly close. He was also now my nightly babysitter, even though Colin had an apartment next door to mine.

"You can't dismiss me."

"I can and I did. I'm done with this bullshit. You're not going to tell me anything, and I'm not packing my bag until you do. So we're done, which means you can leave. Gerard will lock me in for the night and watch over me like I'm a toddler, and tomorrow I'll schedule a meeting with my father and tell him I've let you go."

"Is that what you think we're doing? Watching over you like a toddler?"

"Yeah, Colin. That is exactly what you're doing. I hadn't realized Zane Lewis offered adult daycare in his security site plans. You're nothing more than an over-priced babysitter. I don't need someone watching over me twenty-four seven."

"The hell you don't. And the fact that you're as naïve as you are about the threats surrounding you proves my point."

"I'm not naïve, Colin." I closed the distance between us and pointed my finger in his direction. "I'm in the dark because you won't tell me anything. It's utter bullshit. I've said it a hundred times, you're all overreacting and—"

"Someone was in your apartment, Erin. They tripped the silent alarm. By the time Gerard got here the person was gone. But they'd rummaged through your stuff."

"What? When? Why wasn't I told?"

"When you were at the Hope for All benefit."

"Why didn't anyone tell me?" Colin's unwillingness to answer pissed me off. "What else aren't you telling me?"

"A lot. Pack your bags."

"I'm not going anywhere with you. I'll go stay at the White House with my parents."

"The fuck you will. They've been there, too. I intercepted photos of you sleeping on the couch in the residence. Someone was trying to get the images to your father."

"What?" I hadn't meant to screech, but this was absurd.

A look of annoyance hardened Colin's features, and he yanked me forward. My body collided with his hard chest and he lowered his head to my ear and whispered, "We are not having this conversation in an unsecured location. Your place could be rigged with either video or audio surveillance. I need you to trust me. Go pack your bags now."

He set me away from him and stared down at me, daring me to disobey. Part of me wanted to just to see what he'd do.

But logic won out, and I turned to go to my room to pack. I tossed the bare essentials into the suitcase the presumptuous prick had already set out for me. Now that Colin had told me my apartment could be bugged, I was in a hurry to leave. The thought that someone could be watching or listening freaked me the hell out.

If this was all just a clever ruse to get me to leave with him, there'd be hell to pay.

CHAPTER 2

"Hey, man. Thanks for stopping by."

"Welcome to Texas, brother." Cormac "Fletch" Fletcher held out one beefy paw and nearly crushed my hand with a firm shake.

Fletch was an intimidating man to those who didn't know him. He stood about inch taller than me, but where I was toned and fit, he was bulk and brawn. Everything about the man screamed "scary motherfucker" until you got to his brightly colored tattooed forearms. Then you wanted to razz him about the cartoonish looking ink. Not that many people had the balls to say much of anything to the Delta Force Operator.

"I see you still haven't taken my advice and found a laser removal center," I said, poking fun.

"Yeah, when you find a plastic surgeon to fix your ugly mug, I'll remove my juvenile indiscretions. Besides, Annie loves them." The man's face transformed from deadly operative to loving father at the mere mention of his daughter. "You gonna invite me in or are we gonna stand on the porch sweatin' our balls off?"

I moved out of the way and allowed Fletch to enter the familiar house.

"Like what you've done with the place." His gaze searched the room. "I wasn't sure I agreed with the architect when in the rebuild they suggested taking out the wall to the kitchen. But it opened the whole space up. I like it."

I'd bought the house from Fletch only a month prior, and this would be my first time staying here. He and his family had decided to sell after the house had been severely damaged by an RPG. They'd rebuilt with the intention of staying but, in the end, they couldn't move back in. Not that I could blame them. Fletch had almost died when his liver had been nicked by the two by four that had punctured his side in the explosion. It was his teammate Ghost's quick thinking that had saved his life. Then there was Rayne's brother, Chase; he, too, almost died trying to protect his woman, Sadie. It had been a bad situation all the way around.

"So do I. When I heard you were selling, I couldn't pass it up."

"The security system up and running?"

"Oh, yeah. You had a great set-up, I didn't change anything. I thought Zane Lewis was an over-the-top bastard, then I met you. There's not an inch of land that's not covered."

"After what happened when I first met Emily, I upgraded to cover the street in front of the house, too. You'll be good here. Has Tex found anything new?"

John "Tex" Keegan was the go-to man for anything information related. If it was out there in the cyber world, he could find it. Hell, even if the intel was locked away behind the most encrypted system, he could still find it.

"The team is combing through security footage and traffic cameras now. Tex is also looking into it."

"Have you thought about asking Beth? You know she's the

one who found that asshole Jacks when he took Em and Annie."

I'd heard of Beth, she was making quite the name for herself here in Texas. What she hadn't known before she'd met Tex, he'd made sure she learned. I didn't know all the details of what Beth had done to find Fletch's then girlfriend, Emily, and her daughter, Annie. But from what I'd heard, the intel had come in the nick of time. Annie had already escaped the shipping container Jacks had locked the two in and she'd been making a run for it.

"We asked Tex about it, but he said she has her hands full. He didn't elaborate, just said there was a missing child."

"Shit, I hope she—" Fletch stopped talking, and I looked to the stairs to see Erin had come down.

"Erin, this is Fletch. Fletch, this is President Anderson's daughter."

"Nice to meet you, ma'am."

I almost laughed at his formal greeting, Erin was anything but proper. I was sure it drove her mother, Clarissa, crazy. Mrs. Anderson was a well put together, elegant woman. Erin was pretty much the opposite.

"Hi, Fletch. Please call me Erin." She pasted a fake smile on her pretty face and made her way over to us. "Sorry to interrupt."

God, I hated the phony persona she put on around people she didn't know. I much preferred the real Erin. The one I'd gotten to know before the night I found her naked in the guesthouse at the charity event. Since that night, I'd done my best to keep things professional with her.

"You're not," Fletch reassured her.

"I invited Fletch over so we could go over the security protocol while we're in Texas. Fletch and his team all live nearby and have offered to keep their eyes open for anything suspicious. We also need a contingency plan in place in case something happens to me, so you're covered."

"Don't you think that's a little overboard? I mean, no one even knows we're here." There was the snarky Erin she reserved special just for me.

"No, I don't think anything I do, when it comes to your safety, is overboard. And just because you think no one knows we're here doesn't mean that's actually the case."

"Come on, Colin. When we left D.C., you drove all the way into Pennsylvania before turning back into Maryland to fly from there. Not to mention, you drive like a lunatic, it's impossible someone could've followed you through all your speeding and weaving in and out of traffic. I thought I was going to die before we made it to the airport."

"You'd be surprised what people can and will do when they want something badly enough. And for some crazy reason, someone seems to want you. Though if they actually got their hands on you, I suspect they'd return you quickly once you started bitching."

"God, you're annoying."

"Right back 'atcha, doll."

Fletch's chuckle reminded me he was still in the room, witnessing my stupid squabble with Erin.

"Damn, you two sound like an old married couple."

"Did you get the email I sent with the new login info for the cameras?" I asked, ignoring his comment.

"I did. I passed it along to the team as well. They'll only be alerted if the alarm is triggered so don't forget to set it. You didn't say, has Tex found anything?"

"Not really, a side profile of the man, and not even a good one. Whoever was in Erin's apartment knew where the cameras were. What he *was* able to confirm was that the man entered using a key and had a toolbox. Gerard did a sweep, and it was bugged for audio but no video."

"What?" Erin shrieked. "When were you going to tell me?"

"I wasn't."

The less Erin knew the better, I shouldn't have been discussing this with Fletch in front of her, but I felt better when she was in my line of sight. The woman was practically Houdini the way she ghosted her security detail. I wouldn't put it past her to try to sneak away and go back to D.C. on her own.

"And why not?"

"For a lot of reasons, one being, you're not taking the situation seriously."

"Maybe I would if I had all the facts, but I don't. So, I think my father is being overprotective and I'm tired of being treated like I'm some national treasure that needs to be under lock and key."

"Do you have any idea how valuable you are?" Fletch asked. Erin's eyes widened in shock at his question. "You *and* your mom. If someone got their hands on one of you, they'd have the most powerful man on the planet in their back pocket."

"The US doesn't negotiate with terrorists."

"The US might not. But a father will. Your father may be a good president and have the American people's best interest always in the forefront, but he's still a man. A husband and a father. And knowing him the way I do, he'd do anything to get you back. So if you don't want to be the reason your father starts the next world war. I suggest you begin to take this seriously and listen to me when I tell you something is unsafe."

I could tell she wanted to argue more, but she wouldn't, not in front of Fletch. Sure, she'd throw me attitude with him present, but she wouldn't let me have it, both barrels, like she did in private.

"Please, thank your team for me, it might not sound like

it, but I appreciate you all keeping an eye on me. I think I'll go back upstairs and read."

"Remember, no cell phone."

She was halfway to the stairs when she spoke. "Not my first rodeo, cowboy."

Fletch let out a slow whistle once she was out of sight. "Damn. You've got your hands full."

"You have no idea. Tex had to refit all of her jewelry with tracking devices. She's good at giving the secret service the slip. The first few times I was pissed and actually called them incompetent. Until she did it to me at an event. The girl is a pain in the ass. I can't wait until this fucking op is over and I can dump her ass back in her apartment."

"Right." Fletch chuckled.

"What did the colonel say about me taking Erin on post to the firing range?"

"You're cleared. He'll leave a pass at the gate for you."

"I can't tell you how much I appreciate all your help."

"No thanks needed."

"You got a minute for a beer?"

Fletch looked down at his watch before he answered, "Yeah, just one."

I grabbed us two brews from the kitchen and joined Fletch on the back patio. Seeing him sitting, staring out over his old backyard made the hassle of having the new outside furniture delivered worth it.

"Lots of good memories in this house," he mused. "First time I met my daughter was in the front yard. I was working on my Charger." He chuckled. "And I'll never forget the first time Annie met Truck, it was right here on this patio." Fletch had a faraway look, as if he were replaying the actual moment in his mind's eye. "Em was sick. The guys and I were out here having a barbeque and Annie wandered over. She took one look at Truck, climbed up on a chair, palmed his face, and poked at his scar, before she asked him if it hurt. I think it was then, Truck, Hollywood, Blade, Beatle, Coach, me, and Ghost all fell for her. God knows, she's had Truck wrapped around her finger since then."

The story about how Emily and Annie had come into Fletch's life was widely known, but the tale about the barbeque was legendary. Truck was a big man with a gnarly scar that pulled one side of his face into what looked like a grimace. The fact that sweet little Annie had made her way to him said a lot about the goodness she had in her.

"She's something special," I agreed.

Annie also had to be one of the smartest kids I'd ever met, and pretty, too. Both inside and out. The girl had an old soul. Fletch was going to have his hands full with her when the boys start coming around.

"Then one asshole ruined it. Turned all the good into shit. My house was on fire, my wife and daughter were trapped upstairs, and there wasn't a damn thing I could do about it." Fletch turned to me and pinned me with his stare. "Do me a favor, yeah?"

"Anything."

"Make this place great again. Fill it with happiness and laughter. It fucking guts me our last memories are of smoke and carnage."

"I will. I promise. And when you're ready, we'll have a barbeque, just like old times."

"Damn, man, I must be getting old, sitting here waxing poetic about some old house."

He tried to laugh it off but he couldn't hide the pain. Now, more than ever, I was happy I was the one to buy this house. Even if Fletch and his family would never live here again, I could give them back some of the happiness they'd lost.

"So tell me about this epic wedding we missed."

Fletch went on to tell me all about the quadruple wedding his teammates had. What was supposed to be a double wedding between Ghost and Rayne and Truck and Mary had turned into a foursome. Blade and Wendy and Beatle and Casey had gotten married the same day, too. My team had missed the wedding when we were called away on an op. From the sound of it, we'd missed one hell of a party.

My mind momentarily wandered to Erin, and I wondered how she'd get along with Ivy and Violet. I knew she missed Olivia but for some reason she held herself back from rekindling their friendship. The women of Fletch's teammates, Rayne, Mary, Wendy, Casey, Harley, Kassie, and Emily were all as close as sisters. I'd never paid enough attention to know if Olivia, Ivy, and Violet were the same way. I supposed they were, but I'd missed a lot since I'd been spending most of my time in D.C. trying to keep one very exasperating, sexy woman out of trouble. I hoped like hell this was over soon. The faster we were away from each other the better.

CHAPTER 3

"Have you ever shot a gun?" Colin inquired as he laid his arsenal out on the blanket-covered, wooden bench in front of us.

I tried not to roll my eyes at his stupid question.

"You know I grew up here in Texas, right?"

"Yes."

"Well? Then why'd you ask?"

"Not everyone in Texas owns a gun, smartass. And, sorry to say, you don't really look like the huntin' type." My nose scrunched at the thought of killing a poor helpless animal. "I see I was right."

"I don't know what parts of Texas you've been to, that you'd draw that conclusion, but where I grew up, we all learned to shoot as soon as we could walk."

"Walk, huh?"

Damn, his laugh was sexy. I was almost glad he rarely did it because when he forgot to scowl at me, his smile made him even more good looking. And the deep rumble of his laugh made my girly parts wake up and take notice.

"Pretty much. Daddy bought me my first Mossberg .22

rifle for Christmas when I was ten. He always said, if there were guns in the house, we needed to know gun safety."

"Smart man."

"That he is."

I missed those days, when my dad was just my dad. When he wasn't the governor or the president. The man who used to give me piggyback rides, go on hikes with me, and take me camping in the back woods of our property. I guess I couldn't blame everything on politics. When I hit my preteens, I stupidly favored doing things with my friends. I'd thought my dad would always be there waiting.

"All right, Annie Oakley, pick which one you wanna start with."

I looked over the selection of handguns he'd laid out and I knew exactly which one I wanted. I picked up the Smith & Wesson M&P 9mm. The grip was a better fit for my hand than the Sig Sauer, and would have less recoil than the Glock .45 ACP.

"You wanna make a bet?" I asked as I slid my eye protection on.

"A bet?"

"Yeah. You know, a wager."

"I know what a bet is. What I don't know is why you'd think it's a good idea to challenge me."

"Cocky much?"

"Sweet cheeks, you ain't seen cocky."

He wouldn't be smirking for long, that was for damn sure. Colin had much to learn about me, one of those things being I was a damn good shot. I had the ribbons to prove I'd been the state 4-H shooting sports champion in both rifle and pistol.

"All right, Mr. Dead-eye-dick. Fifty bucks for the tightest grouping at twenty-five feet?"

"I can't take your money, Erin."

"Well, that's a relief because I'm not planning on giving it to you."

"You do realize I spend a good amount of time at the range?"

"I'm sure you do."

"Winner gets a five-minute foot massage."

"No way. I hate feet. If you're so worried about losing your money, we'll do a five-minute shoulder rub."

"You don't like feet?"

"Are you stalling?"

His head lolled back, and his deep, belly laugh filled the otherwise silent range.

"All right, Miss. Ladies first."

With a shrug, I pulled my hearing protection over my ears and loaded the magazine. I settled into a shooter's stance and brought the familiar weight of the Smith & Wesson eye level and lined up the sights. I slowly took up the slack on the trigger before I squeezed off the full ten-round magazine.

"Well, fuck me sideways."

"Eh. I pulled to the right on a few of those."

I had a fist-sized grouping, meaning that all of my bullets had hit within a two-inch diameter on the paper target.

"Went straight for the heart, I see." Colin shook his head and smiled. "Typical woman."

He picked up the Sig Sauer and moved over in front of his target. He, however, did not slowly bring the gun up eye level like I did. He pushed the barrel in the direction of the target and fired in rapid succession. When he was done, he had a silver-dollar sized grouping. From the distance we were from the targets, it looked like there was a big hole where the bullseye used to be.

"Show off."

"Warned you. You're not gonna renege, are you? My back

is killing me after sleeping on the too hard mattress last night."

"Glad I turned down the offer of the master bedroom then. The spare room's bed is nice and comfy."

I wasn't buying the story about the hard mattress. I'd seen the invoice for the new furniture on the kitchen table. It cost a bloody fortune. I'd furnished my entire apartment on what he'd spent on the bedrooms alone, and I didn't have cheap stuff.

"Guess you got lucky," he said, talking about my choice of beds.

"Right. I think you just want me to touch you."

"Maybe."

He removed the magazine and cleared his Sig before setting it back down on the bench and coming to stand next to me.

"You're aiming," he told me.

"Um . . . yeah. Of course I'm aiming."

"At twenty-five feet you don't need to aim. And if someone was coming at you and already that close there's no time to line up your sights. Pick up the Smith." I did what he asked, and he stepped behind me and wrapped his arms around me. His work-roughened hands covered mine, and he squeezed. "Tight grip. Keep your hands close to your body. Bring the gun up chest level and push straight at the target. Don't worry about your sight picture. This close all you need to worry about is grip and trigger control."

I was having a hard time concentrating on what he was saying. I'd forgotten about his hands covering mine and was more focused on the fact his very hard front was pressed against my back. Heat from his body was radiating through the layers of fabric separating our bare skin, but it did nothing to stop the warmth from penetrating.

"Are you listening to me?"

His hot breath was at my ear, and all I had to do was turn my head and we'd be face-to-face. I didn't dare move, or breathe really. For months, I'd tried to beat back the attraction. It hadn't gone over well the one time I'd given into it and, in a moment of unusual boldness, kissed him. It only proved Colin wanted nothing to do with me.

"Of course I am. What else would I be doing?"

"Daydreaming."

"Whatever. Tight grip, push the barrel toward the target, and trigger control. Got it."

"Last thing, you're anticipating the shot. That's why you're pulling high and to the right."

Now that my body had caught fire, I was anticipating a lot, however, recoil wasn't one of those things.

"Got it. Can you back away now?"

He let go of my hands and stepped back, and I immediately regretted my request.

"Go ahead and reload. I'll reset the targets."

Over the next hour we shot hundreds of rounds, and, by the end, my grouping, while still not as tight as his, was much better. All in all, it was a fun day. Much different than any day I'd spent with Colin thus far. Normally, it was him escorting me as my bodyguard to different functions around D.C. and Maryland. Or he was pacing my apartment like a caged beast on afterhours babysitting detail.

The drive back to his house was pleasant, albeit mostly silent. Until we pulled into his neighborhood and he asked about my relationship with Olivia Cox-Newton, now Olivia Gillonardo, since she'd married Leo. I was a little taken aback, Colin had gone out of his way not to ask me anything personal. Most of our conversations consisted of schedules, logistical issues, and my father's need to wrap me in cotton— especially after Olivia had been kidnapped.

"What about my relationship with Olivia?" I asked for clarification.

"Why haven't you accepted any of her invitations to visit?"

"We've both been busy. Besides, now that I have my own security force following me around, it makes it a little difficult to do anything."

"Right, because you haven't had the secret service around you for the last seven years." He called me out on my lie.

"She has Leo, and her mom's been sick, and she just found out who her dad is."

"All the more reason she needs her best friend."

I was fast becoming annoyed. He pulled into the garage and I debated asking if I could move into the apartment above it, even though Colin had already told me it wasn't furnished yet.

"What do you want from me?"

"The truth."

"The truth is," I snapped, "I was supposed to go out with her that night. But we got into a fight so I didn't go. It's my fault they took her."

"Your fault? There was nothing you would've been able to do to stop them."

"As you said, I've always had secret service with me. They stay in the background and try to blend into the crowd when we're in public, as if that's really possible. If I'd been there, she would've been protected."

I hated thinking about Olivia's kidnapping. I hated that I still couldn't face her. I missed her so much but I couldn't forgive myself. I let her down.

"Then they would've taken her when she went home, or the next day, or the one after that. She was snatched from the bar because they found their opening. She was being kidnapped one way or another. The plan had been set in motion, and no one, especially you, was going to be able to change the outcome."

The look on Colin's face told me he believed what he was telling me. And that was fine. But it didn't mean I had to. If I'd been there with my security detail, Olivia wouldn't have been taken from the bar, that was a fact. And it would've meant one less day in captivity, one less day being scared, one more day safe in her own home. I should've been there and given that to her. Instead, I was pissed at her and refused to go out. Then she was gone.

Colin, being the perceptive man he was, caught on that I was done talking about Olivia, and with a sigh you'd expect from a five-year-old not getting his way, he got out of the car. I knew better than to exit without him scanning the area first and then opening my door. I'd been scolded enough in the past I didn't think I'd ever open my own door again. Even if I thought he was being overly cautious, it wasn't worth another argument.

He led us into the house and went straight for the alarm panel before turning back to me.

"Hungry?"

We'd skipped lunch while on post, and I was starving. "Yeah. I'll cook tonight. You did it last night."

"Do you know how?"

"Why would you ask that? Do you really think I'm some spoiled bitch who's been pampered my whole life?"

I hated that he thought so poorly of me. I shouldn't have cared, but it rankled he constantly mistook me for a molly-coddled girl who'd never done anything for herself.

"It has nothing to do with me thinking you're spoiled and everything to do with being hungry."

"Sure, it does."

Not wanting to debate the state of his hunger, or how he'd placed me in this box of affluent indulgence where people waited on me hand and foot, I went into the kitchen. I searched the fridge and pantry and found both well-stocked. Figuring Colin was a steak and potatoes kind of guy, I pulled out everything I needed and went to work. The mundane task reminded me of my mom and the time we'd spent in the kitchen together when I was younger. She'd always told me the way to a man's heart was through his stomach and while she thought a woman should and could do anything she wanted outside of the home, it was still important to know how to run a household. When my father became president, our time in the kitchen was one of the many things that had changed. My mom had happily taken on more responsibility in my father's White House. She refused to become what the media had portrayed her as, nothing more than arm candy. It was true my mom was stunning, but she was smart, too, and played an active role in many goodwill trips overseas.

Unfortunately, that left me locked inside the confines of the White House grounds most of the time. Complaining about my upbringing or the luxuries I'd been afforded because of who my parents were made me sound like an entitled cow. But I wasn't. I was very aware of all the extras I'd received and the top-notch education. However, other than the grades I'd received while in school, I hadn't earned anything, it was all given to me, and I didn't like that. Even the apartment I lived in was well above what I could pay, but the building was chosen for me because the agents that guarded me deemed it safe. So my father paid for it. He also paid for my car. My college education was taken care of by them as well. I was an adult and still living off Mommy and Daddy. Most days I felt like a failure.

An hour later dinner was ready and on the table, and I went in search of Colin. I found him in a downstairs office, I scanned the space, noting there were no personal items in this room either. The whole house had been furnished but looked like it was staged to sell, rather than to live in. No part of the house told me about the man who resided there.

"Dinner's ready."

"Okay."

If he hadn't been so caught up in what he was looking at, I would've found his lack of attention rude, but when I got a look at the images spread out over the desk in front of him, I felt like I was going to vomit.

"What are those?"

"Pictures that were sent to your father today. They obviously didn't make it to his desk, but they were given to the secret service."

"They're of me." I knew my voice sounded shrill, but it wasn't every day I saw surveillance images of myself. "Who took those?"

"No clue. Zane and the team are analyzing them now."

I stepped closer, getting a better look. "Who in the world would want to take pictures of me getting in and out of a car?"

"To prove they can. Or to show how close they'd been to you. These were not taken with a high-powered lens."

"These are from a lunch meeting with the board of Hope for All." I pointed to three pictures grouped together. "There you are in the back. We were in the private conference room."

"Yes they were. Other than the men you were meeting with, the only other people in the room were the two waiters."

He was right. We'd been discussing donations and opted to eat lunch away from the crowded dining room of the hotel where our monthly meetings were held.

"Wait. A woman came in right at the beginning to give Mr. George a message. Look, there's no food on the table yet. These had to be taken before the servers came in to deliver our lunch, and my day planner is still in front of me on the table. I put that away when lunch was served."

Colin picked up one of the glossy, four-by-six images and gave it a thorough examination.

"Fuck, you're right. I totally missed the timing. Good eye."

Something that felt a lot like happiness swelled inside of me. It was nice to be on the receiving end of his praise for once.

"Maybe if you kept me in the loop I could be of more help. I'm not as stupid as you think I am."

His gaze shifted from the picture to me. "I don't think you're stupid, Erin. Far from it. I haven't told you everything because there's no reason to cause you unnecessary stress. It's not only my job to keep you safe, but to allow you to continue to live your life as normally as possible."

"Normal? You call having people following me all day, every day, normal? I don't even remember what normal feels like."

I had no control over my own life. I hadn't for the last seven years. At least when I was a kid, before we moved to Washington, I had the same freedoms all the other kids my age had. Then D.C. happened, and I wasn't just any other teenager, I was the first daughter, fair game for the tabloids and news outlets to take potshots at. My whole life was under the microscope. It fucking sucked.

CHAPTER 4

I watched Erin closely while we were eating. The good mood she'd been in when we were at the range was gone. I should've been happy she was no longer smiling and joking around. That Erin was hard to resist. Who the fuck was I kidding? The snappy and irritated Erin was just as hard. I don't know what the hell Tom Anderson was thinking leaving me unattended with his daughter after I'd told him she'd come onto me. Actually, I did know what he thought, he expected me to do my job and keep her safe and happy. It was the happy part I failed at, but at least when this was over, I'd return her in one piece. And just as pure.

"Who taught you how to cook?"

"My mom."

"She taught you well. Everything is delicious."

"Thanks."

The conversation continued to be strained through the rest of the meal. I asked her questions, and she kept her answers as succinct as possible. Her disinterest wasn't hard to miss. When I offered to clean the kitchen, she couldn't get away from me fast enough, going into the other room to watch TV. Again, this should've made me extremely happy, instead it was a kick to the gut. I didn't want her being so uncomfortable she couldn't stand being in the same room as me. With the dinner dishes cleaned and the counters wiped down I joined her on the couch.

She was mindlessly flipping through the channels. I couldn't take it anymore. I hated seeing her so miserable.

"I think you owe me a thirty-minute shoulder rub."

I lowered myself to the floor and pushed my way between her legs, sitting with my back to her.

"I believe it was five minutes."

"It was. But we shot five more targets after that, and I won each time."

I was pushing her buttons on purpose. I'd much rather see her full of piss and vinegar than forlorn and beaten down.

"Yeah. That's not how it works, friend."

"Friend? Is that what we are, Erin, friends?"

"Turn of phrase, smartass."

"You didn't answer my question. Are we friends?"

"No. You're my bodyguard. You've made it clear that's all you are."

"I'd like us to be friends."

Erin rested her hands on my shoulders, and my cock twitched. Yes, the simple touch made me react like a horny teenage boy. It was inexplicable and in no way should've happened, but my body was well aware of hers.

"Friends, huh?" Her grip tightened to near pain as she dug her thumbs into my shoulder blades, causing me to wince.

"Yep."

"So, what, like, you wanna gossip about past boyfriends?" She purposely clutched harder and gave up all pretense of an actual shoulder massage. "You wanna exchange stories about growing up, dreams, plans for the future?"

She was goading me, and I wasn't going to bite. She was shit out of luck, if she thought being a bitch was going to stop me.

"Why don't you tell me how you got into 4-H shooting?"

The shoulder rub was forgotten and her hands stilled. "What?"

"4-H? You were state champion, right?"

"You knew? Before we went to the range and you asked me if I'd ever shot a gun, you already knew I had."

"Yep."

Okay, so I was being a bit of a dick.

"What else do you know about me?"

"I think the better question is what don't I know about you."

"That's right, I forgot, there is a nice little dossier on me. A neat and tidy record of my life for anyone to peruse. I mean, why bother asking me anything? Just read the White House file on Erin Anderson and you'll know everything you need to know."

"Not everything, Erin. The file may list the facts and highlight your accomplishments but it says nothing about the woman you are."

"Accomplishments? I haven't accomplished anything."

I didn't like that she thought so little of herself. I'd studied her life inside and out and was impressed at what I'd found out about her. She was extremely giving of herself and her time. She was on the board of several charities and volunteered countless hours. I had to admit I'd judged her harshly before I knew her. I still thought she had issues with people telling her no, but maybe there was more to her rebellion than simple overindulgence.

"Who was the man in the guesthouse?"

"Willy?"

"Yes. William Shradder."

"If you already knew his name, why are you asking me who he is?"

"I want to know who he is to you."

"He's a friend."

"You get naked in front of all your friends?"

Simply thinking about that night infuriated me.

"No!"

"So? He gets special perks?"

"Don't be an asshole, Colin. Why do you care anyway?"

There was the million-dollar question. Why did I have a personal interest in who Erin got naked in front of? Why had I thought about William Shradder more than I cared to admit?

"I just do."

"Not good enough. If you want to be *friends* and you want me to answer your questions, I expect honest answers from you, too."

Well, damn, Erin had no problem calling me out on my lack of sharing. I'd have to reevaluate why I proposed a friendship.

"I care because you kissed me. Then you dropped the virgin bomb. Then I found you naked in a room with a man. I'm curious how that happened."

That was all the honesty she was getting from me. I wasn't about to tell her that feeling her lips on mine was an experience I wished I could repeat. Or that I'd liked how her body felt pressed up against mine. Or that the visual of her perky tits and toned body were forever seared into my memory. And there was no chance in hell I'd ever admit my dick hardened at the mere recollection. Lastly, I'd certainly never acknowledge there was something about her as a person that called to me so deeply, I did shit on purpose to push her away.

"I've known Willy for a long time. He's an artist and has

his first gallery show coming up soon and needed to finish one last pencil sketch he's displaying. It wasn't the best timing, but I figured we only needed about fifteen minutes and no one would notice I was gone. So, we used the guesthouse."

"I'm not tracking. What does that have to do with you taking your clothes off?"

"He sketches nudes."

"Come again?"

"Nudes. You know, he draws men and women without clothes. Nudes."

"What in the actual fuck, Erin? You cannot have someone draw you naked."

"And why the *fuck* not, Colin? I'm an adult, in case you've forgotten. I can consent to anything I want."

Was she insane? There were plenty of reasons I could give her. None of which would matter, but the biggest one was I didn't want anyone seeing Erin naked, let alone a gallery full of people. What if someone purchased the drawing and displayed her fully exposed in their home? Hell no!

"Your father for starters. You have a responsibility—"

"I'm aware of my responsibilities. They've been shoved down my throat so often, I couldn't forget them if I wanted to."

She sounded bitter she couldn't parade around with no clothes on for the world to see. That pissed me off.

"You obviously forgot because you posed for him."

"Whatever, think what you want. It never matters what I say anyway."

"Don't do that. It's not what I think, it's what you did. He drew you naked."

"He did. Numerous times. He also took pictures."

I was getting ready to blow my stack. Zane and Tom would have a shit hemorrhage. Zane had looked almost as angry as I'd felt when I'd shown him the pictures I'd confiscated from the man's camera who'd been outside the guesthouse that night. And now there were more.

I slowly stood up and tried to keep my temper in check. "You let him take pictures?"

"Jesus. Stop yelling."

I guess I didn't have as much control as I'd hoped.

"This isn't yelling, sunshine. Where are the pictures?"

"Hanging in the gallery, I suspect."

"I'm gonna wring his fucking neck."

"What? Why? Don't you think you're overreacting?"

"Overreacting? Have you lost your damn mind?"

"No. But you certainly have. What the hell is the big deal?"

"Let's see. The First Daughter of the United States posed nude for not only pictures, but drawings as well. I'm shocked the tabloids haven't gone crazy over the story yet."

"Maybe because I'm not an idiot. You can't see my face."

"What?"

"Yeah, Captain Drama. The pictures are from behind and I'm sitting so you can't even see my ass. Just my back. And the sketches don't have faces. No one will ever know they're me. How stupid do you think I am?"

"I don't think you're stupid. I think—"

"You didn't think. You didn't ask for details. You assumed. You do that a lot when it comes to me. I'm sick and fucking tired of it. You're no better than anyone else in my life. I can't wait for this to be over. For my father's last year as president to be done. I'm going to slink away into anonymity and finally live my life the way I want. I'm going to bed. Have a good night."

She didn't stomp away like I expected. She didn't say anything more about me being a presumptuous asshole, which I deserved. She simply walked away with her shoulders slumped forward.

Shit. I fucked up. I needed to stop making snap judgements about Erin. She'd proven time and time again she was an intelligent woman. Why the hell was I so irrational when it came to her?

CHAPTER 5

THE LAST FEW days had been tense, even worse than the preceding week had been, and I hadn't thought that was possible. I wasn't permitted to go anywhere alone, not that there was some place to go. At least I was allowed outside, and even that took some cajoling on my part. I swear, if Colin had his way I'd be kept in a windowless room with an armed guard at the ready.

I stepped on something in the dirt and looked down at the green, plastic Army men. Some were still standing, facing each other like they were in the middle of some sort of action figure combat zone battling it out. Story of my life, just like the toys, I was always locked inside some battle— only mine was internal. My love for my dad and how proud I was of him for all the good he'd done for the country, and the guilt and selfishness I had at wanting him all to myself. My mom, too. She was the best first lady. Supportive, altruistic, intelligent, and loving. And I wanted all of her attention. My mother was the very definition of class, a true lady. It was a pleasure to watch her work a room. Most would think it was all for show, but when my mother asked you how you were doing, she genuinely wanted to know. I missed her.

As I knelt down to pick up the toys, the back door opened. I didn't have to turn around to know Colin was scanning the area. He did it every time we went anywhere. It seemed a tad ridiculous to do it in the backyard, considering the man who'd lived here before had more cameras than the pentagon. Colin had shown me the monitor with all the different views of the property and explained Fletch was security conscious. I called it batshit crazy, but what did I know? Until I'd seen the pictures of me Colin had lying across his desk the other day, I'd thought all of them were a little nuts. Now, even I couldn't deny something creepy was going on.

"What'd you find?" Colin asked, stopping beside me.

"Little men with guns."

"Annie must've set them up and forgot about them."

"Guess so. What's going on?"

"I was wondering if you'd like to go out to lunch."

"Go out? Like, leave the house? God, yes."

Colin smiled, and I swear I'd never get over how the simple up tip of the lips could change his whole demeanor.

"Come on, we'll go anywhere you want."

"Anywhere?"

"You're gonna pick sushi, aren't you?"

One night, shortly after I'd first met Colin, he'd expressed his dislike for raw fish. I tried to tell him there was more to sushi than the raw stuff, but he'd refused to try it.

"Yep." I looked at the toys in my hands and asked, "Do you think Annie would want these?"

"Probably. I'll give them to Fletch the next time I see him." He reached out his hand, and, for a second, I was confused. Butterflies hit my belly, and I'd stupidly thought he wanted to hold my hand. Then I remembered the Army men. "Ready?"

"So ready."

I dropped the toys into Colin's hand, and, much to my surprise, he used his free hand to grab mine. "Let's go get you some uncooked fish and rice."

I was too shocked to answer. I simply followed him into the house. He dropped the Army men on the counter, grabbed his keys, and walked us out the front door to his car. Never letting go of my hand.

What the hell is this about?

On the drive to the restaurant he told me his team was still looking into who had taken the pictures and was trying to track down the woman who I'd remembered coming into the meeting room. Unfortunately, she didn't work for the hotel and had somehow avoided the cameras in the lobby. There was a street view of her, but she'd donned a baseball cap and most of her face was obscured. Colin explained that told them a lot. She obviously knew what she was doing, and it would help narrow down the suspects, of which there weren't any.

We were in a holding pattern waiting for them to make the next move. I hated there wasn't an end in sight, but Colin promised me everyone was working hard to figure out who was following me.

"What's changed?" I asked when we exited the car.

"What do you mean?"

"Suddenly you're freely giving me information about what's going on."

"I heard what you said the other night about not being in control of your own life. You were right, I'm no better than everyone else. I've kept you in the dark and I thought about how I'd feel if my life wasn't my own. I'd be just as pissed and fed up as you are. I was wrong. You not only deserve to know, but you need all the information. It's the only way you'll take these threats seriously. I can't protect you if you don't trust me."

"Trust, huh? Is this part of the whole friendship thing?"

Maybe I should've held on to my anger a little while longer, but holding a grudge wasn't going to make my time with him anymore pleasant. And I was tired of walking on eggshells around him.

"I guess it is. I'm man enough to admit when I'm wrong, and when it comes to you, there's plenty I've been wrong about. I'm sorry for that."

"Apology accepted. And I'm sorry for calling you a douchebag prick."

"You've never called me that."

"Sure I did. Hundreds of times, in my head."

"Good to know." He chuckled.

"You know, your eyes change color when you smile, or maybe it's when you're happy."

His smile faded, and I wished I could pull my stupid comment back.

"No, I didn't know that."

"They're a stormy blue, but when you forget to scowl at me, they brighten and become lighter."

"Is that what you think? I scowl at you."

"Normally, you do. Well maybe not scowl, but the look certainly isn't friendly."

A loud bang and crunching of metal sounded and Colin grabbed me around the waist and jerked me to his body, turning us so my back was against the car and his large frame crowded me.

"Shit. Sorry."

Car doors slammed in the distance and I could hear men yelling, but I was riveted by the man in front of me. He hadn't given it a second thought, he simply moved to protect me. Even though it was from a fender bender more than a hundred feet from us.

"Thank you," I croaked, overcome with emotion.

In all the years I'd had bodyguards and the secret service following me, never had I felt so safe. Which was strange because I knew those other men, like Colin, were all paid to watch over me. But this felt different, personal, and maybe even a little intimate the way his body was contoured to mine.

"You never have to thank me for keeping you safe."

He said keeping me safe, not doing his job. For some reason, in my mind, there was a clear distinction.

Colin brushed my hair away from my face, the touch sending chills down my arms. "You know, your eyes change color, too."

"No, I didn't know that." I used his words from earlier and tried not to smile.

"They're a pretty honey brown." His hand slid to the nape of my neck. "But right now, they have flecks of red. It looks like they're on fire."

God. If he only knew. My eyes weren't the only thing on fire due to his closeness.

"Is that a good thing?"

"Oh, yeah, sunshine. It's a very good thing." The arguing motorists' voices got louder, breaking the spell. "Come on, let's get you some lunch."

"Okay."

He made no effort to move, and neither did I. As a matter of fact, I was no longer hungry, not for food anyway. I could've spent the rest of the afternoon pressed against the car, cocooned by Colin, and been perfectly happy. I wasn't clear about what was happening between us, but there was no way I was alone in my thoughts. Not when I could feel his very stiff erection resting against my stomach.

Sadly, we hadn't spent the rest of the afternoon leaning against the car. We did, however, eat lunch, and Colin still refused to try sushi. He opted for a huge bowl of noodles and a double order of teriyaki chicken. Which led to a conversation about how much he worked out. There was no way any person could consume that much food in one sitting and maintain the body Colin had. Not that I'd seen it, but I'd sure felt it. He told me he normally worked out twice a day, a habit from his time in the Army. He hadn't said much about his service but he wasn't evasive either.

The conversation had been light and friendly, talking about favorite movies and the like. He'd asked me more about growing up and what it was like being the president's daughter. Now that I wasn't on the defensive and feeling like I was being treated like child, I told him about all the good parts about living in the White House—and there were a lot. Most of the time it had simply been home to me. But there'd been times when the gravity of where I'd lived and what I'd gotten to experience had struck me. Usually when I wasn't feeling sorry for myself because I couldn't have a normal teenage party, or have people over, or go to someone's house and sleep over. There were security checks, and background investigations to be done. It was invasive, and, unless the parents of my friends were already involved or wanted to be in politics, they frowned on the government digging through their lives. I'd lost more than one friend over it. I'd also learned that most people weren't truly genuine in wanting to know me. They just wanted an invite to my house.

However, there were times, late at night, my dad would walk me around the West Wing and the Oval Office. I'd seen the situation room. I'd peeked in on state dinners. I'd met princes and princesses from around the world. I'd cooked in the kitchen with world-famous chefs. Then there were the times my dad would have Gerard sneak us off the property and we'd grab a burger late at night and eat it on the lawn in front of the Washington Monument. Those were my favorite times with my dad. When he was just daddy, not President Anderson. And my mom had tried her best to be active in my life. More than once she'd cancelled an important meeting because I'd been in full, teenage-girl meltdown. Sometimes over boys, but most of the time because high school girls could be mean.

Throughout lunch my guilt had grown. I'd spent the last year perpetuating the notion my life had been horrible when it hadn't. One inconvenience didn't negate all the good. But after Olivia's kidnapping I'd allowed myself to make a mountain out of a mole hill.

"What has you thinking so hard over there?" Colin asked as he drove us home.

"Life."

"Life in general or something specific?"

"I'm trying to figure out when I became this bitchy, ungrateful person. I sure complain a lot about stupid things. I wasn't always like this."

"I don't think you're ungrateful."

"I'm not but I'm behaving like I am. My parents are great people. They've set an example of selfless service and duty to country. I've taken everything they've taught me and shit all over it. There are people who serve our country and make sacrifices every day, and I'm complaining I don't have my parents' undivided attention. I'm a selfish cow."

"A cow, huh?" Colin chuckled. "What made you think about all of this?"

"When you told me about all the time you'd spent overseas, and the holidays you'd missed with your family, and how there'd been times you couldn't call your mom on her birthday. It hit me how self-absorbed I've been. Here I am bitching to you because I have to have a bodyguard and my daddy has an important job running the country and doesn't have time to coddle me when I'm stomping my foot. Please tell me I haven't been as bad as I think I've been."

"I won't lie, you've been . . . challenging."

"I'm so embarrassed."

"You shouldn't be. I also recognize you've been through a lot in a short amount of time."

"Doesn't excuse my behavior."

Man, I owed my parents an apology. Not to mention, some secret service agents. Poor Gerard probably thought I'd lost my ever-loving mind. As soon as this latest situation was over, I'd make things right.

"Fuck!" Colin shouted, interrupting my thoughts. "Hold on."

But it was too late. My body jerked to the left, then the right, and Colin cursed again as he tried to regain control of the car.

Please, God, don't let this be it.

CHAPTER 6

SOME DIPSHIT HAD ROLLED through a right turn without slowing. I saw it out of the corner of my eye seconds before he took out the passenger-side back panel. The impact was so jarring Erin's head whipped left, then nearly smashed against the side window. I tightened my grip on the steering wheel and pulled left, barely avoiding careening into another vehicle. Fucking asshole thought he was a stunt driver on *Tokyo Drift*. I started to roll to a stop when, in my rearview mirror, I saw the car who'd hit us, maneuver around the cars in the intersection. The dick wasn't slowing down—he was speeding up.

"Hold tight." I hit the gas hard and quickly swerved back onto the road. "Grab my phone. I think it landed by your feet. My code to unlock is 0-7-3-0-1-9-9-8-0-0."

"That's too many numbers, Colin." It took her a minute to find the phone, which had slid off the center console in the near accident. "I can't remember all of that."

I repeated the numbers to her while trying to think of the best route to lose the car behind us.

"What now?"

47

"Hit the phone icon and dial pound one. Put the call on speaker."

She did as I asked, and ringing filled the car before Fletch answered.

"I have a silver Ford Taurus following us southbound on Cooper Road. No front plate, but the passenger-side bumper is fucked off from where he tried to run us off the road."

"Shit. You have an evac plan?" he asked.

"I do. Just need a few favors."

"Anything."

"Go by my house and do a walk through. I'm certain everything is in the safe, but I'd like for you to double check."

"Truck and I will head over there now."

"Also call Zane, tell him to check the traffic cameras from the area. Cooper and Freedom Highway."

"Anything else?"

"Yeah. Tell him, it's always best to be honest."

"Copy that. Be safe. Call if you need anything else."

"Will do. Out."

Fletch disconnected, and I glanced at Erin. Her hand shook as she held the phone, staring at a now blank screen.

"Everything's gonna be all right, sunshine."

"Who's following us?"

"No clue."

"Then how do you know everything is going to be okay?"

"Because I'll never let anyone hurt you. Can you do something for me?"

"Sure."

"I need you to trust me. If I tell you we're okay, we are."

"I'm not certain—"

"I am. The person following us is in a Ford Taurus for Christ sakes. I'm waiting until I can get on the interstate before I lose him. The last thing I want is to cause an accident and get someone hurt. Or have the police involved."

I checked the rearview mirror and the Taurus was two cars behind us. Other than the initial impact, he'd made no move on us. Something felt off about the whole situation.

"Where are we going?"

"California."

"California?"

"I need you reach over and take my gun out of my holster." I leaned to the left, giving her access to my right side. Her hands fumbled around the seat belt. "Just take it off."

"No way. What if he hits us again?"

She finally got my Sig free and settled back in her seat. "What now? Want me to shoot his tires out?"

"Easy there, cowgirl, this ain't the wild west. Just hold it. If something happens, and I'm hurt, use it. Whatever happens, do not let anyone get you in a car."

"I thought you said everything was all right."

"It is. Right now."

"What does that mean?"

Just as I merged onto an almost empty Highway 195, the Taurus gunned it, closing the distance between us. I swerved around the car in front of me, and so did the Taurus. Weaving through the few cars on the highway, I made a decision I hoped wouldn't cost us our lives. The driver of the Taurus pulled alongside us and a second car was on my bumper.

"Put your head between your legs and hold on."

I braked, causing the car behind me to slam into the back of us. Instead of the Taurus blowing by us like I'd hoped, allowing me to get behind him, he slowed as well.

"What are you doing?" Erin asked from her lowered position.

Before I could answer, the driver of the Taurus popped off two rounds, thankfully pulling high and hitting the top of the driver's side door. I jerked the wheel, my two right tires hitting the gravel of the shoulder. There wasn't anywhere to go, two lanes of traffic in either direction didn't give me a lot of options. If I were alone in the car, it would've been a different story, but with Erin beside me I needed to be extra cautious. If something happened to me, she'd be vulnerable.

"Fuck."

The sound reverberated inside the car, the ringing in my ears caused me to flinch in pain. I didn't have time to warn Erin to cover her ears as the car behind us got a shot off and took out the back window.

"Why aren't you driving faster?" Erin yelled, not lifting her head.

"Stay down and brace, Erin."

I jerked left, sideswiping the Taurus. Thank God for long stretches of Texas highways. The median between the north-bound and southbound lanes only had a couple feet of gravel before it gave way to a grassy embankment. Not so steep you couldn't pull off the side if need be, but a car traveling over eighty miles per hour wouldn't fare too well. We lurched forward when the car on my ass made contact again. I just needed a few more seconds to catch up to the tractor-trailers that were in front of us, and this would be done.

"Oh my God," Erin muttered, but thankfully hadn't sat up.

"Almost over. You're doing great."

Swerving left again, I hit the Taurus, harder this time, he didn't have time to recover before he lost traction on the paved road and went up on two wheels before spinning out of control. Pulling close to the bumper of the semi in front of me I waited until the very last second before veering back into the right lane as the two semis closed the gap, driving side-by-side, leaving no room for the car following us to pass.

"You okay?" I asked.

"My ears hurt. Are they still behind us?"

"One is stuck behind two semis at the moment."

"The other?"

"Non-issue."

"I thought Zane was crazy for renting you a Charger, now I'm thankful he didn't chintz out and rent you a Pinto."

"Years of experience. Never get behind the wheel of a slow car while on an op."

"Can I sit up yet?"

"Not yet."

The exit for State Road 2670 was coming up, and I merged right, taking the small off-ramp keeping my speed above eighty.

"Jesus, Mario Andretti. Warn a girl next time."

Erin's body rocked before she steadied in her seat.

"You can sit up."

The first thing Erin did was look over her shoulder and out the gaping hole where the rear window used to be.

"Holy shit. They shot at us," she said unnecessarily. "I mean, I knew they did. But, shit."

Erin's trembling hand was still holding my gun. Even though I knew she'd been scared, she'd held it together. I was impressed. I'd witnessed both men and women break down over less.

"You can put the gun in the glovebox." It took her a few tries to open the compartment, she was shaking so badly. With the gun secured, I grabbed her hand and placed it on my thigh and covered it with mine. "I'm proud of you, sunshine."

"Proud of me? I didn't do anything but keep my head down and silently freak out."

"You trusted me. And I don't believe you were freaking out. Hell, you offered to go all Lara Croft on the bad guys and shoot their tires out."

I was trying to make light of the situation, but now that Erin was out of danger the thought of her going full on badass was sexy as hell. And knowing she actually would've done it if I'd asked had my dick throbbing to life.

"What about all of our stuff back at the house?"

"Fletch and Truck will do a sweep and make sure there's nothing of importance left out."

"But we don't have anything with us. You said we're going to California."

"There's a go-bag in the trunk. I have everything we need. And what we don't have, we'll buy along the way."

"Okay."

Erin rested her head on the seat back but made no move to pull her hand away. Just like that, she trusted I'd take care of her even after I'd been mostly an asshole to her since I'd met her. I'd never had another woman have so much faith in me. It was a feeling that made my gut tighten. I wondered if this was what Leo felt when he'd saved Olivia. From the moment she'd laid eyes on him, she'd handed over her safety to him. I wasn't entirely sure what I was feeling toward Erin, but what I did know was I liked having her next to me.

CHAPTER 7

"Sorry the room is shit," Colin said as soon as we'd stepped inside the dingy room. "Not exactly what you're used to."

"What the hell does that mean?" I snapped.

I was exhausted and starving. We'd driven over eight hours, finally stopping in El Paso for the night.

"Whoa there, sunshine." Colin locked the top latch on the cheap door. I had serious doubts the safety device would actually prevent someone from getting in the room. "I didn't mean anything negative. Simply stating the obvious. When was the last time the first daughter was in a thirty dollar a night motel room?"

"Sorry I'm grouchy. Today sucked."

Colin tossed the backpacks on the bed and stopped in front of me, placing both of his hands on my shoulders. "Yeah, it did, and you've been great all day. I'm sorry the night has to end with a shit bed and fast food. In a few days, we'll be in California. I promise you a nice bubble bath and a home cooked meal."

I still hadn't set the drive-thru bags down, and the smell

of greasy hamburgers and fries drifted through the stale air of the room, making my stomach growl.

"Let's get you fed." Colin looked around the room before scrunching his nose. "Picnic on the bed?"

"Anywhere. I'm hungry."

He moved the packs onto the floor, took the bags out of my hands, and let me climb on the bed. With my back against the headboard, and in a very unladylike move, I tore off the wrapper of my cheeseburger and started without him. It wasn't until I'd eaten half my food that I really look around the shitty motel room.

"There's only one bed."

"Uh-huh," Colin mumbled around a bite.

"Do you think the guys from earlier will find us again?"

I'd had a lot of time to think about my brush with death and I was scared shitless. I was doing my best not to show Colin how freaked out I was, but inside I wanted to curl into a ball and hide behind him. I'd never been involved in a high-speed chase and while I was aware Colin wouldn't consider the ten-minute ordeal necessarily "high-speed," I did.

"No, Erin, they won't. I made sure we weren't being followed."

"They ran into us—"

"They did. Are you sore? How's your neck?"

He'd asked me about my neck and back no less than ten times during our drive. Every time he pulled off the road so I could use the restroom, he made me stretch and roll it, even though I'd told him repeatedly I was fine. Each time before we'd settled back in the car for the next leg of our trip, he'd kneaded and rubbed my shoulders and the back of my neck for a few minutes. He'd also done his best to keep my mind occupied while we were driving. He'd told me stories about growing up, the sports he played, and his high school shenanigans. I hadn't missed how he'd left out most of his military service and he'd only told me about the "bullshit" assignments he worked at Z Corps. Those were the cases where he followed cheating spouses or they assisted local law enforcement on investigations.

"It's okay."

We fell silent, and I shoved another handful of fries into my mouth.

Suddenly everything hit me.

Everything. All at once. The crash, the chase, the shooting. My apartment being bugged. Someone taking creepy pictures of me. My mom and dad. What a shitty friend I'd been to Olivia. Everything.

"Come here, sunshine." The container of fries was removed from my hand, Colin twisted, placing them on the nightstand, then hefted me up, and scooted down the bed, setting me mostly on top of him. With both of his strong arms wrapped around me, I did something I hadn't done in a very long time. I cried. Not a polite sniffle like a well-mannered, proper woman would. No, not me. The tears rolled, and the snot bubbled.

His strength never wavered, not in the time I took to cleanse my soul of all the fear that had bottled up. And not when I wiped my face on his tear-soaked shirt. He just held me.

"Sorry," I mumbled.

"Nothing to be sorry for."

"I thought I was okay."

"You were in shock. Most people go their whole lives and never experience what you did today."

"I'm really scared."

His arms tightened, and I desperately wanted to melt into him. "Nothing's going to happen to you. I promise, Erin, I will stand between you and anyone who dares to come after you."

"I'm glad there's only one bed."

"Why's that, sunshine?"

"Because I'm too afraid to sleep by myself, and this way I don't have to beg you to let me sleep next to you."

Colin pulled back and propped himself up on an elbow. When his brows pulled together, I worried I'd crossed a line. "I'll never make you beg for something you need." I searched his face and was shocked to find he looked so sincere, his eyes pleading with me to believe him.

"Thank you."

His hand brushed across my cheek, and he pushed my hair behind my ear. He was so close I could feel his breath on my face and, for a second, I thought he was leaning in to kiss me, but he stopped. "We'll only be in this shithole for tonight. Tomorrow we'll be someplace where you can feel safe."

I doubted a change in location was going to ease my fears but I agreed, "Okay."

"Are you still hungry?"

"No. I'm just tired and I want a shower but I'm afraid of what the bathroom looks like, so I'll wait until tomorrow. Where are we staying?"

"My buddy, Abe, has a cabin outside of San Diego. It's where Leo took Olivia when he was hiding her."

"Does he know we're coming? Don't you have to call and ask?"

"Zane's already taken care of it."

"When did you talk to Zane?" He hadn't called anyone since he talked to Fletch before we left Killeen. As a matter of fact, he'd taken the sim card out of his phone and smashed the rest of it when we stopped at a hardware store for a roll of plastic and duct tape. Which reminded me. "Are you worried someone will break into the car? It's not like the plastic taped to the back window is a great deterrent."

"It's a rental," he said by way of explanation. "Fletch called Zane and told him."

"He did?"

I thought back to the short conversation the two men had and didn't remember Colin mentioning Abe or California.

"He did," Colin confirmed. "Remember when I asked Fletch to tell Zane, it's always best to be honest?"

"Yeah."

I still wasn't understanding what that had to do with a cabin in San Diego.

"Abe's name is Christopher. His team nicknamed him Abe because he's always honest and has no tolerance for those who aren't. When Fletch called Zane and repeated what I'd said, Zane knew where we were going."

"What if Fletch didn't repeat your exact words? Then how will Zane know? Wouldn't it be easier to just call him?"

It seemed like a lot of work to pass secret coded messages when Colin could just call himself.

"First, Fletch repeated my words verbatim—"

"How do you know?"

"Because Fletch has been trained to follow instructions to the letter. He lives in a world where men die if they don't. He knew the situation we were in and the importance of my message. I wouldn't have said it, if it didn't mean something. And I didn't call Zane directly because I don't know how we were tracked. The only people who knew we were headed to Texas were your father, my team, and Fletch's team."

"Would Fletch—"

"Not only is the answer no, but a resounding, fuck no. Fletch and the men he works with are solid—a hundred percent."

"I'm sorry. I didn't mean to question their integrity."

It was a sad reality I didn't have anyone in my life who I trusted the way Colin trusted the men he worked with or

Fletch and his team. When Colin spoke about Zane and the guys, he was sure and confident they would never let him down. Even with Fletch, his answer was strong and quick. I loved that for Colin, but it reminded me how lonely I was. I had exactly one friend, and she didn't even count anymore because I'd stupidly turned my back on her.

"You don't know them and, right now, you should be questioning everyone. We are. Zane has Tex and Garrett, our in-house IT guy, combing through the lives of everyone you've come in contact with in the last few years. Friends, boyfriends, people who you worked with at the charities, anyone and everyone."

I was a little embarrassed at what they'd find. Not that I had anything to hide but the "friends" they'd check out would take less time than they thought. There were very few people I worked with who could even be considered acquaintances, and the boyfriends would be even faster. There had only been one since high school.

"Why do you think this is happening?"

"I don't know. But I promise we'll figure it out. Tomorrow, when we get to Abe's cabin, we'll have a secure line to Zane. There's a chance they've already started to put the pieces together."

"Thank you for sharing."

"I already told you, from now on I'll share what I can. But I want you to understand there will be things I can't tell you. It's not because I don't think you deserve to know or I'm purposefully being a dick, but I am bound by my word not to talk about certain things."

"What type of things?"

"Nice try, sunshine." He smiled and settled back on the pillow, pulling me back to his chest. "You should get some sleep. I wanna leave first thing."

"I'm not tired." His body started to shake with silent laughter. "What's funny?"

"You just told me you were tired and wanted a shower."

"That was five minutes ago."

"And in the last five minutes, you've changed your mind?"

"Well I changed my mind about three minutes ago when we started talking about super-secret coded messages."

He shook harder and chuckled as he said, "Super-secret messages. You're a nut."

For some reason Colin laughing warmed my insides, even if it was at my expense. In all the time I'd spent around him he rarely looked happy. I wanted to know why, then I wanted to figure out a way to change that. The closed off, silent but deadly side of Colin was sexy as hell. All it had taken was one look at his tough guy exterior and I was schoolgirl crushing. However this side of Colin, the softer, funny side where the fierce and gentle protector mingled—was swoon worthy.

"Thanks, I think." The hand that was resting on my hip squeezed and I liked that, too. "Tell me about your family."

"What about them?"

"I don't know. Anything. You know all about mine."

"I'm finding I don't know as much about you as I thought I knew."

I wanted to ask what that meant but I was too afraid of the answer. Too afraid he'd say something nice, and the infatuation I'd been harboring would grow. Lying next to Colin with my head resting on his chest, and his arms around me did crazy stuff to my head. As hard as I was trying to keep my distance, the pull was too strong. I knew it was too late, Colin Doyle was going to break my heart.

CHAPTER 8

I WAS PLAYING a dangerous game holding Erin in my arms. The most alarming part was how right it felt. I'd been wrong about her. Not only had I mistaken her as ungrateful, I'd also assumed she was a high-maintenance pain in the ass. I was wrong, she was anything but. I couldn't fault her for wanting her life as her own. And I suppose after repeatedly asking those around her to clue her in and being denied, she'd done what most anyone would do—she started demanding. I'd taken her ball-buster attitude as not liking to be told no, however, she simply wanted to understand why others were making decisions for her without consulting her first. That I could appreciate.

"There's nothing really to tell. We're just an average everyday family, I grew up middle-class. My dad's side immigrated here from Ireland. My mom's side is Italian. The mix always led to some fiery holidays when everyone got together. I have an older sister in the Navy. My parents still live in the house I grew up in. We really are a boring bunch."

"I don't believe there's anything average about your

family. It sounds like your parents raised two great, selfless kids. What does your sister do in the Navy?"

"She's a nuclear mechanic."

"Right." Erin laughed. "Nothing special there. So, you're telling me she's wicked smart."

"That she is. Keira got all the brains in the family."

"Does that mean you got all the good looks?"

I had to take a deep breath to stop the inappropriate comeback that was on the tip of my tongue. Somewhere in the recesses of my mind I'd known she thought I was attractive, she wouldn't have tried to kiss me otherwise. However I was finding it difficult to keep my body from reacting to her compliment.

"What made you want to be a Green Beret?"

Her question took me by surprise. At lunch we'd lightly touched on my military service, but when I'd steered the conversation to something slightly less personal like favorite movies she seemed to go with the flow and not push for more. I figured she was simply disinterested. I didn't have an issue talking about my time in the Army, however I didn't make a habit of getting into the details.

"I didn't set out to be special forces. I'd finished my first contract and decided to re-up, at the time recruitment numbers were down, and the military was trying to retain as many soldiers as they could, giving me the opportunity to write my own ticket, so to speak. I wanted to go to a special school, the Army wanted me to stay, so they sent me. I showed up in Fort Bragg for a ten-day assessment and selection course for Psychological Operations. Before I could start, a first sergeant I knew pulled me aside and asked me to go through the Special Operations Preparation Course. It was also held at Fort Bragg. He promised if I didn't pass SOPC he'd get me back into the PSYOP pipeline. After a few beers he convinced me."

"Wow. And just like that you became a Green Beret."

"Not exactly, just like that. I still had to go through about twenty months of training. But, yes, over beers First Serg Jenner convinced me my talents would better serve the Army as a Special Forces Soldier."

"That's incredible."

"I don't know about that. But it's a little different than most people's stories. I certainly didn't set out to go SF."

It felt a little weird talking to Erin about how I become a Green Beret. It wasn't that I was self-conscious, but it certainly didn't make me sound like a badass who'd dreamt all his life about kicking in doors and killing bad guys. Though ridding the world of scumbags was certainly one of the perks of being a Green Beret.

"Your parents must've been proud."

"Actually, they weren't happy. My dad, while proud at what I'd accomplished, was scared for me. He knew what was going on in the world, and what my new job entailed. My mom was pissed. You see, she comes from a big family, and my sister had already told her she didn't want children. That left me to provide her with the twenty grandchildren she imagined she'd have. Being frequently deployed, she knew her dreams of having grandchildren anytime in the near future was gone. There was no time for holiday visits, let alone dating or finding someone to spend my life with."

By the time I was done speaking, I couldn't believe I'd admitted all of that to Erin. I normally didn't share anything that could be categorized as touchy-feely shit. I didn't talk about my family or my mom wanting grandkids. Fuck, talking about kids with a woman was the kiss of death. Not that I'd ever been the one to bring them up, but if the woman I was on a date with did—I bailed. Quick, fast, and in a hurry.

"She wants twenty grandchildren?"

I could feel Erin's smile through her words, and, for some

unknown reason, it made me ridiculously happy she could relax enough in my arms to smile. Her trust in me to keep her safe after everything that had happened today was a powerful feeling.

"She wants as many as I can provide. My parents wanted more kids but after me, my mom had to have a hysterectomy. She's been waiting thirty-two years for a baby to bless her house again."

"I always wished I had a sister," she mused.

"Why don't you have a boyfriend?"

"Huh?"

Smooth, asshole, real smooth.

"You don't date."

Like that statement was any better than my previous lame question. When the hell had my balls shriveled up? Boyfriends? What in the hell was wrong with me?

"Because I've learned most men don't have any interest in me. They have their sights set on my father. And the ones who actually *do* want to get to know me get fed up with the background checks and secret service agents always lurking around."

"It sounds to me like you haven't found the right kind of guy."

"Sadly, that's not true. It's kinda hard for a man to get to know me, let alone give me a goodnight kiss when an armed guard is always within touching distance. I'm not worth that much trouble."

Before I fully understood what I was doing, I had Erin on her back and I was looming over her. Her shocked eyes looked up at me, but it wasn't fear I saw, it was excitement. The same excitement I felt. The same need I'd long ago shoved deep in a box and locked it away. The desire to have someone see me, the real me, and still find me worth the effort was something I never thought I'd have. So, instead of dwelling on it, I moved on. Convincing myself I didn't need anyone in my life.

"You are worth it. And any man who is worth your time would know it. They'd appreciate you were protected and see the necessity of it. They'd also move heaven and earth to get to know you better. They'd walk through fire if it meant they'd have the honor of kissing you goodnight."

"Is that what you'd do for your woman? Walk through fire to kiss her?"

"Damn right, I would. The day I find the woman I'm going to spend my life with, there's not a goddamn thing anyone could do to keep me from her."

"Then she'll be a lucky woman."

Staring down at Erin I realized the truth behind my words. I'd never seriously thought about finding a wife or settling down. Not while I had a dangerous job. But having Erin under me gave me pause. She felt right, the missing piece.

"Will you kiss me?" she whispered. Her voice was soft and unsure.

Maybe it was curiosity that had my mouth lowering to hers. Maybe I needed to know if the spark I'd felt the first time she'd kissed me was real, or if I only imagined how good she tasted. Her tongue brushed mine, and, in that split second, I had the confirmation I was after. I hadn't imagined anything, though I'd remembered incorrectly—she wasn't good, she was downright awe-inspiring. Erin's head lifted, eager to deepen the kiss, and I was too far gone from a simple swipe to stop her.

I held my body still, forcing every muscle not to grind into her like I wanted. She, however, wasn't motionless. Erin's hands roamed, bunching up my shirt so she could reach the bare skin on my back. The leg that wasn't pinned under me, wrapped around my waist, and she tried her best to rock into me. I was so enthralled with her kiss I'd forgotten all the reasons I'd thought it was a bad idea. The harder she pushed herself against me, the more friction there was on my cock. It was absurd the amount of willpower it was taking not to come in my pants.

"More," she panted. The word pulled me from my fog, just as it had done the first time. "Please don't pull away this time."

My cock begged me to take what she was offering, but decency and integrity won the internal fight. She, by some miracle, had somehow saved her virginity, and there was no way I was taking something so special in a flea-bag motel off the side of the highway. Erin deserved more.

"I can't. Not here. Not like this."

"Please, Colin."

There was no amount of pleading that would break my determination not to take her here.

"Sunshine."

"I'm ready. I'm begging you. Please don't stop."

Her hips lifted, and she moved her hands lower, shoving them under the material of my pants massaging my bare ass.

"Erin . . ." Now I was the one begging.

"Just touch me."

Sweet mother of God. I'd never been so tempted in my life. The sweet smell of her excitement, the silk in her voice, her soft hands on my body. But it was more than the physical temptations, it was the promise of her. The fragments of my solitary life all being drawn into her orbit. I didn't understand the pull and wasn't questioning it.

"No further."

"No further," she agreed. "But I want to touch you, too. Take these off."

"No. My pants stay on."

"Colin."

"No. My pants do not need to come off for *me* to make *you* feel good."

I rolled to my side and got on my knees. Fuck, she was beautiful. Too beautiful and too special to have to touch the nasty comforter with her bare skin. This was wrong, all wrong.

"What's the matter?"

"I can't Erin. Not here in this bed. The thought of your naked flesh touching anything in this room is repulsive. You're too good for this."

"I'm not—"

"You are. I swear there are very few things right now that could stop me from getting you off, but this is one of them."

Her face fell in defeat, and I hated it. Hated that it made me think of the first time she'd kissed me, and I'd lied to her, purposefully hurting her feelings.

I lay back down and gathered her into my arms, pulling her body mostly over mine.

"Remember the night of the charity event when you called me a coward?"

"Yes." Her body locked, and she started to pull away.

"Relax, sunshine." I waited until she went lax to continue. "I lied to you that night. You were right. I was there with you in that kiss, a hundred percent. I felt the connection."

"What stopped you?"

"Same thing that should be stopping me now. Your dad."

"Should be or is stopping you?"

"Should be. I told you the reason we stopped tonight."

Unable to resist touching her, I let my hand wander under the bottom of her shirt and trailed my fingertips along the curve of her waist. The skin under my touch pebbled into goose bumps, doing nothing to help my hard-on deflate.

"How is it possible you're still a virgin?"

Erin busting out laughing was not the answer I'd been expecting.

"Sorry." She tried to control her giggles. "I've never been asked that."

"How is it possible no one's ever asked you? You're almost twenty-five. It's practically unheard of nowadays."

"Sad, isn't it?" She laughed some more.

Sad? There was nothing sad about it. As much of an asshole it may've made me, the fact that no man had been inside of her, yet there she was asking me to be her first, turned me on more than it should've of. Erin was a goddamn marvel, I'd say she was the eighth wonder of the world. Erin was sexy and smart and when she let down her guard, she was funny. It truly didn't seem possible.

"Nothing sad about it, sunshine. I just can't wrap my head around the fact."

"It's a lot easier than you think. Once my dad started running for president, we all got protection during the campaign. Someone was with me twenty-four seven. After he won, it continued. I wasn't all that eager to give it up in high school anyway. But in college there were a few guys that had caught my attention, but as I said, the secret service were always there. Then, with the one serious boyfriend I had, I thought we were going in that direction but I overheard him talking to his dad about trying his hardest to get them an invite to meet my dad. I quickly ended things. After that, dating seemed like it was more trouble than it was worth. And sex was off the table."

"What an asshole."

"Then I met you. When I finally got up the courage to make the first move, you shut me down."

Fuck, that stung.

"I was trying to do the right thing. I didn't think I was

good enough for you. Then there was the fact that I was hired to—"

"Protect me. I know. But you also didn't like me much. You thought I was a spoiled bitch."

"I was wrong."

"About the spoiled part maybe. But I was being a bitch. By the time you came along and were placed on my detail, I was over being babysat. Over being told what to do, and where to be. Where I couldn't go. After everything that happened with Olivia, I was wrapped in cotton and suffocated. I didn't understand why, beyond the obvious, and no one would explain anything to me. I turned into someone I'm not proud of. You know what the worst part was?"

"What?"

"I was embarrassed. I felt like I was a child that needed watching over."

"You never had anything to be embarrassed about."

We both were silent for a long time. I was enjoying the weight of her body pressed onto mine, perfectly content to lay there all night with her in my arms.

"Thank you."

"For?"

"For thinking I'm something special."

She'd done the impossible—rendered me speechless. My stomach clenched, and my heart pounded in my chest. Something changed that night as I lay in the dark with Erin. Something deep and life altering. At the time I couldn't place the feelings her words had evoked, but as the days passed, the emotion became evident. I was falling in love.

CHAPTER 9

COLIN HADN'T BEEN EXAGGERATING when he'd said he wanted to get an early start. We left the motel before sunrise. Thankfully, no one had broken into the car while we'd slept. Though, as Colin said, it was a rental, and I didn't think he cared all that much. Walking out that morning, seeing the condition of the driver's side and the damage the bullets had done brought everything back into the forefront of my mind. There was no denying I was in serious danger. I couldn't pretend my situation away this time and go about my day like I'd done over the last seven years my dad had been president. I'd always viewed the guards around me as a nuisance instead of a necessity, like Colin had pointed out. Now I was seeing the error in my thinking. If Colin hadn't been there, I would've been dead or, worse, taken.

My biggest fear had always been being kidnapped. I knew what my friend Olivia had gone through, and she'd been extremely lucky. I doubted very much if someone got a hold of me the outcome would be the same. I was what the agents called a high value target. There wasn't a question about whether or not I would be tortured, it was a matter of how badly. And that was something I prayed I never found out.

WE'D BEEN ON THE ROAD FOR HOURS, AND I COULDN'T STOP stealing glances at Colin. His blond hair was shaved close on the sides, but the top was long enough to look sleep tussled.

"What are you looking at?"

He looked my way and smiled. With my feet up on the dash and the seat back reclined a little, I could almost pretend we were on a vacation road trip. The sun was fast rising behind us, painting the sky in purples and reds.

"You."

"Me?"

"Yep. Anyone ever tell you, you look like Brett Young?"

I couldn't believe I'd told him that. Maybe my lack of sleep was affecting my good sense.

"Don't know who that is, sunshine."

"What?" I was shocked. Everyone knew who Brett Young was. "The country singer."

"Still have no idea who that is."

"I don't know if we can be friends."

Colin's laugh filled the car, and my insides warmed. "We can't be friends because I don't listen to country music?"

"It depends. If you tell me you like boy bands, then no."

His chuckle continued. "Fuck no."

Well there was that. Maybe I could forgive him for not listening to country.

"What kind of music do you like?"

"Depends. I have hard rock playlists for working out. Some mellow shit when I'm driving. Heavy metal when I'm getting my gear ready before we go on an op."

"Screamo stuff?"

"No. Metallica, Linkin Park, Green Day. But I also like Phil Collins, Passenger, Imagine Dragons. You know, good music."

"Okay. I guess we can be friends. But I think we're gonna need to introduce you to some country."

"I'll listen to your country if you agree to go to dinner with me when we get back to D.C."

My breath caught, and my throat tightened. *Did he just ask me out on a date?*

"Dinner?" I asked tentatively.

"Yeah, you know, the meal that comes after lunch."

"I'll have to think about it," I teased. "I also need to check my schedule. See if I can pencil you in."

"You do that. And while you're thinking about it, I'll put on some Metallica."

"Oh, no, you don't." I covered his hand when he reached for the radio. "I like this station."

I actually wasn't sure what type of music was playing, I hadn't been paying attention. It could've been one of his heavy metal playlists for all I knew. I'd been too lost in my thoughts to listen to the music quietly coming through the speakers.

"Will there be a kiss after you take me to dinner?"

"Hell, yes."

His answer made my belly swoosh. I couldn't help remembering what he'd said last night about a man walking through fire for the honor of kissing me. When I'd asked him if that's what he'd do, he said if he ever found the woman he was going to spend his life with, nothing would keep him from her. I couldn't help wanting to be that woman. I didn't need him to walk through fire for me, last night he'd shown me all he needed to. As frustrated as I was, he wouldn't touch me, his reasons had solidified my feelings. Never had anyone thought I was special. Most men, would've taken what I was offering. But not Colin.

The rest of the ride was spent talking about inconsequential things. Likes. Dislikes. Favorites. Individually they didn't mean a whole lot, but put all the pieces together and I had a vivid portrait of who Colin was. His life was scary and exciting. He was a man with strong convictions, who truly believed in the work he did. Colin had a heart for service and it didn't matter how hard he tried to play down his sacrifices, he couldn't hide them. He was humble about his accomplishments but confident in his ability to carry out any mission he was given. The mix of the two was intoxicating.

COLIN PULLED INTO A LONG DIRT DRIVEWAY, AND I WAS IN AWE of my surroundings. It was beautiful, with tall evergreens lining both sides.

"Wow. This is really pretty."

"Wait until you see the cabin. Abe and his wife, Alabama, have done a great job fixing it up."

I didn't have to wait long; a gorgeous log cabin came into view, and, once again, I was awe-struck.

"I could live out here for the rest of my life and be happy."

"Really?"

"God, yes. After the last seven years, I'd be happy to live in peace and quiet. I've had enough people busy-bodying in my life. After my dad leaves office, I just want to fall back into obscurity and pray everyone forgets my name."

"Doubt that's gonna happen, sunshine."

Colin parked in front of the house, told me to wait, then came to my door. This time, as he scoped out our surroundings, I was grateful. He'd been hyper-vigilant the entire drive and just because we were in damn near seclusion, that hadn't changed. Once out of the car he quickly ushered me in, giving me no time to appreciate the huge, wrap-around porch we'd used to enter the cabin. I wondered if I'd be allowed to sit out there in the morning with a cup of coffee while enjoying the calmness the wooded area provided.

"What about our stuff?"

"I'll get it in a minute. Let me show you around."

He guided me through the open living area, a comfy looking couch sat in front of a fireplace, and I wondered if it was too warm for a fire. I could picture us cuddling on the couch watching the flames dance.

He led me into a surprisingly well-appointed kitchen. "Abe and his wife must come here often. There's fresh fruit on the counter."

"He knew we were coming and stocked the house with the essentials," Colin explained.

"That was nice of him."

"Abe's a nice guy. So are the rest of his team. But I doubt the guys did it. My guess is Alabama, Caroline, and the rest of the women heard we were coming and rallied together to make sure your stay was as comfortable as it can be."

"Me? Why do you think that?"

"Because if it were just me, Abe would've dropped off a case of MREs, a few bottles of water, and a brick of ammo. They're great guys but not so great they'd want me to have fresh fruit and . . ." Colin opened the refrigerator. "All this shit."

"All this shit" was milk, a bottle of wine, lunch meats, cheeses, blocks of butcher paper neatly stacked, an assortment of condiments, and other miscellaneous items. Whoever took the time to shop for us had gone all out.

"And I'm sure the shower is packed full of girly shit," he added.

I was in desperate need of a shower and was eager to find

out what "girly shit" they'd left. All of the stuff I'd brought with me was back in Killeen. Colin's idea of a go-bag and mine were two different things. I had a change of clothes, my passport, and my purse. He had guns, extra bullets, extra passports and identification for both of us in different names, and cash. Lots of cash, actually.

Without warning, Colin stepped in front of me and pulled his gun from his holster. I was getting ready to ask him what was happening when the front door opened.

"Yo!" a male voice bellowed.

"You almost got yourself shot," Colin said and lowered his weapon.

"You must be losing your touch. I wasn't exactly quiet when I got out of my car."

"Erin, this is Abe." Colin ignored the man's jab. "Abe, this is the First Daughter—"

"Just Erin. Please." I stopped Colin from making the formal introduction. "It's nice to meet you, Abe. Thank you for letting us use your cabin. It's beautiful."

It took all my energy not to shrink under Abe's scrutiny. He didn't hide the fact he was giving me a thorough inspection. But not in a creepy or lewd way. It was almost as if he could read my innermost thoughts and was analyzing them. When he relaxed a fraction, so did I.

"No problem. Glad you two made it. My wife and her friends stocked everything up for you, but I'm supposed to ask if there was anything else you need. Something about shampoo and shit."

Colin chuckled, and when I turned his way he said, "Told you so."

"I'm sure whatever they got is fine. After where we stayed last night, I wouldn't complain if I had to scrub down with laundry soap."

"Heard about your problems back in Killeen. Tex called

with an update. The asshole you ran off the road was taken into custody. He flipped quickly. Told the cops he and his buddy were each paid five grand to run you off the road. All they were supposed to do was box you in and keep you there until someone else came to get you."

"Did he say who paid him?"

"The usual. Some guy in a suit. Paid in cash. Met in a parking lot with no cameras. No make or model of the car the man was driving. Used a burner phone. No names. The only fuck up they made was Tex was able to trace the burner number purchase to a convenience store in D.C. They're going over the security footage, but without a general time frame of when the phone was purchased or a description of the person who bought it, it's most likely a dead end."

Abe set the duffle bag he'd been holding on the coffee table in the living room. "These are from Zane. New laptop and phones. He'd like for you to check in ASAP. The perimeter alarms are on and the live feeds are being watched by your team and Tex. All my guys will be alerted if the property is breached. If you don't want six angry SEALs storming the house, please send us a text if you leave."

"'Preciate all your help."

"Don't mention it." Abe smiled. "Hope your stay is low-key and pleasant. Erin, would you like to check what my wife left and make sure it's to your liking?"

"I'll be happy with whatever she left. Please tell her I said thank you. And you, too, thanks again for the use of your home."

"It's not a problem. It's what we do. We take care of our own. Zane and his team have had our backs a time or two, and we have theirs."

Boy, I'd love to hear some of those stories. Colin downplayed his military service and what he currently did, but I bet he was every bit the hero I thought he was.

"I'm gonna check in with Zane," Colin said, opening the bag and pulling out a phone. "I'll call you with an update in the morning."

"Sounds good. Welcome to California, Erin. Talk to you tomorrow."

After Colin walked Abe to the door, he closed it and set the locks and alarm.

"Do you mind if we hold off on dinner until after I talk to my team?"

I tried to remember if Colin had always been thoughtful or if that was something else that had changed, too. His attitude toward me in general had definitely transformed, which scared me. My infatuation had grown into something more. With each hour that passed, each new tidbit of information he gave me about himself, and each touch, I fell more and more. Everything was moving at warp speed, and when I tried to slow myself down, I'd remember how freaking short life was. How I'd overthought everything my whole life and for once I just wanted to let go. I wanted to throw caution to the wind and enjoy whatever crazy journey I was on.

"Not at all. I'd actually like to go up and take a shower."

"I'll go up with you."

I followed him upstairs and into the master bedroom. After he checked the closet and bathroom, I was given the all clear, and he started to leave the room.

"Colin?"

"Yeah?"

He stopped in the doorway and turned to face me. My breath caught in my throat and the words died on my tongue. He looked fierce. Gone was the man who'd held me all night long and back was the warrior, the protector. The caring side of Colin was a turn-on, but this side of him was downright hot.

"Nothing. Never mind."

"Okay. I'll be downstairs if you need anything."

With one last appraising sweep of his eyes, he walked out the door.

Why did my body warm from just one glance?

I stayed in the shower for a long time, wishing the warm water could wash away my troubles. I'd done a good job hiding my fears from Abe, however, I couldn't forget what he'd said, people had been hired to take Colin and me. They were supposed to run us off the road and keep us there until someone could come and retrieve us. Not only was I in more danger than I'd thought, but Colin was also.

How had my life come to this?

CHAPTER 10

"How the fuck did they find us?" I asked Zane.

As soon as I'd come back downstairs, I'd called in. I wasn't surprised when Zane answered and told me he was putting me on speaker so the rest of the team could talk to me as well. Even at the late hour they were all still at the office.

"That's unknown," he answered.

"What *do* we know?"

"We know the woman from the hotel is Alena Zoellick, and her partner, who rigged up Erin's apartment is Conrad Volle."

"How in the hell did he get in?"

"Maintenance. Erin put in a legit request with the building. Conrad waited and found an opening," Declan answered.

"Shit."

"That about covers it. They've been playing the long game. Conrad's been working at Erin's building for over six months. Though his employment application lists his name as Connor Vicks," Garrett added.

"Who are they working for?"

"Henry Shultz. Conrad was all too ready to give up his

boss once Zane and Leo applied some pressure." Declan chuckled.

I didn't doubt the other man caved under Zane's demands. I had first-hand experience what Zane's idea of pressure was. He would've rained hellfire down on the asshole until he was begging to spill his guts.

"Abe said the guys from Texas have been detained."

"They have. Each were paid five K to detain you. From the description of Shultz, it seems he's behind the attack and the surveillance on Erin."

"What the fuck? Why can't we find Shultz? And, again, who leaked our location?"

"Tex and Garrett are working on both," Zane assured me. "You sit tight and don't let anything happen to her."

It pissed me off Zane was treating me like I needed a directive to protect Erin.

"No shit, Sherlock."

"Or we could end this sooner rather than later, and you can bring her back to Maryland and we can—"

"I swear on all things holy, if you even suggest we leave her unattended and use her as bait, I'm gonna lose my mind." The team erupted in laughter, and I didn't find anything funny about what Zane had said. "You think I'm fucking joking? I'm five minutes from locking her ass in an underground bunker and going hunting myself. These fuckers were in her house. Violated her privacy. They crashed into us. They shot at her. But more than all that, they've scared the shit out of her. She's trying to be brave. But she's terrified. That ends for her. And it ends soon. So, either you and Tex shut this shit down, or I will. And when I'm done and have a warrant for my arrest, she'll be safe."

"Just checking," Zane weirdly said.

"Checking what?"

"That you're all in."

"I'm all in," I confirmed, realizing the meaning of my statement went beyond the mission.

"Good to know. We'll check in later. Garrett has eyes on the outside perimeter, but there are no cameras in the cabin. Someone will be watching the monitors twenty-four seven."

"Copy that."

"Colin?" Leo spoke up.

"Yeah."

"That master shower is big enough—"

"Fuck off," I cut him off. A fresh wave of laughter came from my team, and to my surprise I smiled. "Assholes. Got shit to do. I'll call in later."

"Yeah, like—" I disconnected before Jaxon could finish.

I pocketed my phone and took a moment to gather my thoughts. I could remember a time in the not so distant past when it was just Jasmin, Zane, Jaxon, Leo, Drew, Eric, and me. Then Drew retired and Linc replaced him. Thankfully, he and Jasmin sorted their shit and everyone could finally tell Jasmin the truth about what happened to her in Russia after she'd been captured. Lying to her had gone against everything in me, but it had been necessary.

Then Olivia had come along and brought Leo to his knees. I'd never seen a man fall for a woman so quickly. Not long after that, Violet barged into Jaxon's life, bringing her twin brother, Declan, with her. Then Eric died. A moment in time that will haunt me forever. He selflessly gave his life to save the team. I still missed him every fucking day. Now Zane had Ivy. And somehow, she'd done the impossible and rounded his jagged and sharp pieces. He was still a ruthless son of a bitch, but with her, he was a different man. He showed her a side of himself he'd never shown us.

Was it possible Erin could be that for me? The woman who could take all the broken and splintered fragments of my soul and puzzle them back together.

"That bad, huh?" Erin's voice pulled me from my thoughts.

I opened my eyes to find her sitting on the stairs with nothing but a towel wrapped around her body. Good Christ, she was beautiful. Even with the worry lines on her forehead and puffy, red eyes, she was prettier than any woman I'd ever seen. I hated that she'd obviously waited until she'd been alone to cry. I didn't want her to hide anything from me. Not anymore. I wanted her to seek me out when she needed comfort and reassurance. She'd been alone for far too long.

"I've been in worse situations."

"Someone really wants to kill me?"

Her whispered words gutted me. I was serious when I told Zane he only had a few days left. There were places I could stash her where no one would find her and I could go in search of this Shultz guy by myself. I didn't care what it took, or what happened to me as long as, in the end, she was safe.

"No, sunshine. There's nothing pointing to that."

"So, just take me then."

"What are you doing down here?" I asked, not wanting to answer.

"I don't have clean clothes. My bag's in the car."

"Damn. I'm sorry. Give me a second."

I jogged out to the car and retrieved both packs as quickly as I could. I took a few deep, cleansing breaths and tried to rein in my anger at the situation. I also needed the time to get my libido in check. We may've been in the middle of an uncomfortable conversation, but I was still a man. And she was a sexy woman, with only a towel wrapped around what I knew was a terrific body. I'd have to be dead for my cock not to jump and take notice.

When I got back into the house she was still sitting in the

same spot. "Come on. Let's get you dressed before you get cold."

She nodded but didn't speak when she stood and went up the stairs. I tried my hardest to keep my eyes off her ass, but it was damn near impossible. The sexy sway of her hips called to me. With each step the towel gathered, revealing more skin. Toned, tanned flesh I wished I could sink my teeth into.

"Thanks." I hated the fear I could hear.

I set the bags down on the bed and pulled her close. "I'm gonna keep you safe."

"I'd rather die than let them take me."

"What?"

"I know what they'd do to me. It'll make what happened to Olivia look like a walk in the park. If someone wants me it's so they can torture my father. I can't . . . I couldn't . . . I wouldn't survive that."

"I promise you, I'll do everything in my power to stop that from happening or die trying," I vowed.

"What did Zane say?"

"Can we get you dressed and fed first? Then I'll tell you what I know."

"Promise?"

"Promise."

She dipped her chin and gave me a nod before she dropped the towel and turned to open her bag. My hands shook with need, and I shoved them in my pockets before I could reach out to touch her. My feet were cemented in place as I watched her dress. When she finally pulled a shirt over her head, covering the last of her exposed skin, I reached a hand out and waited for her to take it.

"Let's go make something for dinner."

She let me lead her back downstairs and into the kitchen. With very little conversation we made dinner together. By the time we'd sat down to eat, and I'd filled her in on what the team had found, she'd pulled further into herself. When I suggested we call it a night, she agreed without argument. I didn't like her easy acquiescence, I fucking hated that she looked and sounded defeated. I wanted her full of snark and humor. Confident and at peace.

I helped Erin into bed and didn't bother to leave the room when I changed into a pair of sweats. She stared blankly at the ceiling, and I silently vowed to take out every person who was responsible for her retreat.

"Come here, Erin."

She rolled to her side and with tear filled eyes whispered, "Make love to me. Please make me forget."

"No, sunshine. But I'll hold you."

"But you said—"

"I know what I said. And I stand by my previous statement. However, the first time I make love to you, it will not be because you want an escape. It will be because you want me so badly, you're mindless."

"But I do want you. I've wanted you for months."

Once again, I was at war with myself. I knew what it felt like to want to escape from the thoughts racing through your head, even if for only a little while. However, I couldn't give her what she wanted, not fully. I wouldn't be a regret; someone she looked back on with remorse or worse—shame. But I could give her something.

"Kiss me, Erin."

She started to lower herself and I met her halfway, immediately taking over. My hands cupped her face and pulled her closer. All I needed was for her to take the first step and I'd lead her where I wanted her. The kiss was smoldering from the moment our lips touched and our tongues tangled. Damn, the woman could steal my breath. Erin broke the kiss, ripped her shirt over her head, tossing it aside, and I was dumbstruck for a moment; she was perfect. Not too big, not too small. The right amount of mouthful, with pink, puckered nipples I needed to taste.

I leaned up and sucked one into my mouth. Her moan filled the silence, and I watched her eyes flutter closed. I pulled off and moved to the other side. She was struggling to get her pants off and with an audible pop she freed her nipple from my mouth to accommodate her movement. And seconds later she was gloriously naked. Only this time, I could touch her.

"Are you sure?"

"Yes."

Her answer was certain and quick.

"Roll to your back."

She licked her lips, dropped to her back, and my cock jumped at the sight before me. So pretty. So innocent. I shouldn't have allowed things to go as far as they had, but I wasn't stopping. I wasn't going to deny either of us what we both wanted any longer.

I came up on my elbow and looked down at her. "Tell me if I'm hurting you or if you want me to stop."

A slow, sexy grin settled on her lips, and she answered, "I will."

The smile told me she thought she'd gotten her way. She hadn't. But she was soon going to learn, I didn't need to make love to her to make her forget. My fingers would be enough. And next time, and there would be a next time, she'd learn that my mouth was even better.

CHAPTER 11

I COULDN'T REMEMBER a time I'd been so nervous. Sure, I'd yanked off my clothes bold as brass but inside I was anxious. Just because I'd never inserted part A into part B didn't mean I'd never fooled around before. But this felt different. I hadn't asked but I assumed Colin was well and thoroughly experienced when it came to sex. I was so worried I wasn't even sure where to put my hands.

"Relax," he murmured in my ear before he placed a soft kiss on my neck. "We're gonna take this nice and slow." His tongue trailed down the side of my neck, over my collarbone, and down the slope of my boob. "I want to taste every inch of you."

Oh, Lord.

He continued his exploration, licking around one areola then the other. I jolted when his hand moved from my hip, his thumb traced the crease of my panty line, or what would have been, had I been wearing any.

"Easy, sunshine. We're goin' slow, remember?"

"Uh huh."

Colin's hand hadn't moved, but his mouth did. He sucked

and nibbled and licked all around my breasts and down to my stomach. When his tongue dipped into my bellybutton, I lifted my hips, causing his hand to slip farther between my thighs.

"Touch me."

"Not yet."

His torturous exploration of my body seemed to go on for hours. His hands and mouth seemed to touch me everywhere but where I wanted him to. I finally had enough and wrapped my hand around his wrist and tried to bring it to where I needed it.

"Spread your legs wider," he told me but didn't allow me to force his hand. "Put your leg over my hip, sunshine. I want you completely open."

I was way past being embarrassed and immediately put my leg over his hip, giving him full access to my most private parts.

As his hand slid closer to my core, he whispered, "Are you sure?"

"Yes."

"Kiss me, Erin." His throaty demand sent shivers down my arms.

I was so lost in the magic I felt when our lips connected, it took me a moment to register his finger was gliding up and down my slit until he circled my wetness and pushed in.

"Holy—"

He pulled the digit out and slid two back in. My grip around his wrist tightened and my nails dug in. I needed something to hold onto. Something to ground myself as he envoked a riot of sensations. I lifted my head until my mouth latched onto his neck. He tilted his head, giving me better access. I kissed every part I could reach as his fingers stroked faster.

"Oh, God," I moaned. "More." I lifted my ass off the bed, trying to get his fingers deeper.

He twisted his hand and rubbed along the top of my inner muscles and added his thumb to my clit. The added stimulation had me biting down on his neck.

"Christ," he groaned but made no move to make me stop abusing his skin.

I fought the urge to close my legs as the tingling began, and heat started to spread over my entire body.

"That's it, Erin. You're almost there."

"I can't."

I started to close my legs, trying to ward off the explosion that was building.

"You can, baby. You're there. I can feel it. Let go."

His thumb pressed down harder, and my hips bucked. It was too late, I couldn't stop it. I screwed my eyes closed and let the orgasm take over.

"Damn. So, so, pretty." He was slowing his movements, bringing me back to earth, and before I was ready his hand disappeared from between my legs and his fingers were in his mouth. "You taste just as good as I knew you would." I must've looked shocked he'd sucked my essence off his fingers, well, because I was, but his chuckle confirmed he'd seen my surprise.

"Kiss me, Colin."

"Kinky," he whispered and brushed his lips against mine. "Wanna taste yourself on my tongue, do ya?"

I didn't bother answering, instead, I took what I wanted and licked the seam of his lips until he opened. I would be perfectly happy lying in his arms kissing him for the rest of my life.

Whoa. Where did that come from? It was too soon to be thinking about the rest of my life. But there it was, niggling in the back of my mind. Colin was everything I'd hoped to find in the man I'd share my life with.

All too soon he broke away, kissing the corner of my mouth, then my forehead, and tucked me close to his side.

"It's been a long day, we should get some sleep."

"What about you?"

"What about me?"

"You didn't—"

"Sunshine, all I need is this. You in my arms, relaxed, and ready for a good night's sleep."

I cuddled in closer and willed my tears not to come. I'd never felt more safe and secure in all my life. Not even when I was a teenager living behind a tall metal gate with armed men standing guard.

CHAPTER 12

I WAS five minutes away from going thermonuclear. We'd been at the cabin for five days and had barely made any headway. Erin and I had just finished lunch when Zane had texted to tell me he needed to talk and would call in an hour. He wanted Erin present and was going to send some images for her to look at. I wanted her as far away from this as possible. She was still trying to put on a brave front, but each night when we got into bed, she begged me to hold her. Not that she had to ask, I wanted her tucked close. We'd only been sharing a bed for a little more than a week now, and I couldn't imagine her anywhere else but next to me.

Last night when she'd asked me to make love to her, I'd gotten her off using my fingers and mouth again. Much to my cock's dismay, I still hadn't allowed her to touch me. At first, it was because I didn't want to take advantage of her vulnerability. Now, it was because I wanted more. I had to know if it was me she wanted or if I was simply convenient. It would gut me if the only reason she wanted to be with me was because of some sort of hero worship. Not that I was a hero, but she did view me as the man that was keeping her alive.

She'd mentioned more than once, how she'd rather die than be kidnapped. I understood her fear, however, it killed me the choice was even on her radar. She should be out living her life, smiling, happy, carefree, and not thinking about lose-lose options.

"Ready?" I asked, sitting next to Erin on the couch.

"Yes," she answered in the affirmative, but her shaky voice told me she was anything but.

I answered the phone, but before Zane could start I asked him to wait and muted the phone.

"You don't have to do this," I told her.

"Yes, I do."

"You don't. But more than that, you don't have to pretend with me. I know you're scared. And, sunshine, that's okay. I hate watching you worry, but I really hate that you think you have to hide from me."

"I just want to get this over with."

"All right."

Knowing I wasn't going to get Erin to open up while I had Zane on hold and the images she needed to look at loomed over her head, I gave in.

"I'm back," I told Zane.

"You logged in?"

"I am."

Once I confirmed my computer was online and on Z Corps network, a picture of Erin and a man came onto the screen of my laptop.

"Do you know this man, Erin?" Zane asked.

"Yeah. That's Hal Simpson. He's a donor. I believe he's an investment banker."

"How long have you known him?"

Erin sat quietly for a moment, twisting her hands in her

lap. Her knee was shaking, and her discomfort came off in waves.

"Um, I'd say, about a year. Maybe a little less. I'm trying to remember what event I first met him at, but there have been so many it's hard to say."

"Has he ever expressed interest in you?"

My irritation spiked at Zane's inquiry, I didn't like where this line of questioning was going.

"In me personally? I don't think so. And if he was interested, he never did anything weird if that's what you're asking."

"That's exactly what I'm asking. Did he ever ask you out? Try and get you alone? Say or do something that made you uncomfortable? Ask too many questions about your dad?"

"No. He never asked me out. But now that you mention my dad, he never asked anything about him. Strange."

"Why is that strange?" I asked.

"Because everyone always asks. And I mean, everyone. Some are more invasive than others. But since he's become president there hasn't been a single person, other than Liv, that hasn't asked me something about him."

I could believe that. People were inherently nosey. They wouldn't be able to help themselves, they'd have to ask her something about her dad, even if it was small.

"It's actually not so strange." Garrett entered the conversation. The screen in front of us changed to a side-by-side picture. The right side was a professional portrait of Hal Simpson and the left was a cropped image of him from the charity event. "Hal Simpson is Henry Shultz, the man who is behind surveilling your apartment and the man who hired the men to kidnap you."

Erin's entire being shifted from unease to utter terror. I was happy the team couldn't see us, not that I gave a fuck. I pulled Erin onto my lap. Fucking Garrett had to bring up the fact someone wanted to take her—her biggest fear.

"However, his name is not Hal Simpson; it's actually Michael Greenwold. He works for the NSA."

"Why would someone from the National Security Agency pretend to be someone else? And why would they want to hurt me?"

"Christ," I muttered. "How far down the rabbit hole are we?" I asked the team.

"So far I'll be shocked if we'll ever find our way out. Greenwold is the head of an NSA counter-intelligence team. POTUS shut down the special collection service unit, code named Angel, when he found out a tech-specialist wrote a program to spy on the general population of US citizens. Millions of emails and phone calls were intercepted."

"Found out? How did he find out?" I inquired.

"Tom's not being forthcoming about how he received his intel. Nor he is telling us the full scope of the program. The only thing he's willing to provide is that it was presented as a data-dump and back-up system for all intelligence gathered overseas. He's aware there's a shadow team working, mostly in the black, but it was his understanding the team was concentrating on cyber counter-intel and system security. They employ some of the most effective hackers in the world."

"I take it Greenwold isn't happy his collection service was dismantled."

"You'd be correct. He's asked for, and was denied, several meetings with Tom. He also tried going around him to the vice president to ask him to speak to Anderson."

By the time Garrett had finished his brief my head was pounding. "The VP is a slimy prick. Did he talk to Tom?"

"Oh, yeah. VP Perkins tried several times to get the president to reinstate Angel, but he won't budge on this. We all know how he feels about spying on his own people. They know they're fighting a no-win situation. Unless—"

The vice president wasn't Zane's favorite person. Power had gone to Perkins's head and he'd made questionable decisions over the years.

"They get their hands on Erin," I provided.

"Correct. We have a team in place to bring in Greenwold. You have twenty-four hours until this is all over." Zane was quiet for a moment before he continued, "Red is going black, zero contact for at least forty-eight hours. Gold Team will be on standby, Declan's staying behind with them. Once we have Greenwold out of the country, Dec will be in contact."

I wasn't surprised Zane had given Declan Gold Team. He'll make one hell of a team leader. The time he'd spent as a deep-cover agent had taught him a lot. But Dec had something the military, CIA, or the NSA couldn't teach—good instincts. It sucked losing him as a member of the Red Team, however, he was restless, still beating back demons he didn't want to share. Maybe this is what he needed to find the salvation he was after.

"Copy that."

"Wolf's team has been briefed. They're ready if there's a need. Everything straight there?"

Knowing that Wolf and other SEALs in the area had our backs made me a little less apprehensive about my team being out of the country.

"Five by five."

"You two hold fast there and you'll be home soon."

"Roger."

"Erin?" Zane called out.

"Yeah?"

"Your dad wanted me to tell you he's proud of you. He also asked me to tell you he's sorry."

Erin bowed her head and closed her eyes, but not before a tear rolled down her cheek.

"Tell him I love him and I'm proud of him, too. He taught me to never give in to those who try and make you go against what you believe in. I'm proud my dad has stood by his convictions."

"Will do. You two stay safe. Out."

I closed the lid of the laptop and placed my cell phone on the table next to it before I settled back on the couch with Erin, still on my lap. I couldn't begin to put into words how impressed I was with how she was handling everything. Not to mention, how very wrong I'd been about her, she was not even close to being the spoiled princess I'd thought her to be. She was strong and capable. Her courage and composure were remarkable.

"It's almost over." Instead of smiling like I thought she would she frowned, and her eyebrows drew together. "What's wrong?"

"Nothing. Everything. I don't know."

"Break it down. One problem at a time."

"I'm scared. Really scared. And I'm afraid after this I always will be. Which makes me a total baby because Olivia was actually—"

"Don't compare yourself to her. An imminent threat can be just as damaging as the act. Does that make sense?" Erin shook her head. "Yes, Olivia was held hostage and some bad shit happened to her. But it happened quickly. She didn't know it was coming. You knowing someone is out there looking for you, waiting to grab you is almost worse. They're terrorizing you. There is nowhere you can go to get away from the knowledge. But I promise you, when this is over, you'll move on."

"What happens when all of this is over?"

"What do you mean?"

"With us?"

Thank fuck, she asked. I'd been waiting to have this conversation but didn't want to push her.

"We continue to take things slowly and figure out where we want this to go."

"I don't want slow."

I had to smile at the vehemence of her statement.

"We need slow. I *need* to know you're with me every step of the way. And you *need* time to make sure I'm who you really want. The real me, not the man hired to protect you."

"I already know you are."

"Then I need to know that."

"Why? I'm telling you you are."

I waited until she finished nervously shifting on my lap, and her eyes settled on mine. I'd learned a lot about Erin, most was a contradiction from what I'd thought in the beginning. I knew she was headstrong and smart. Independent and funny. All great qualities for a woman to have. But there was one thing that stood out the most. When the shit hit the fan, and we were in a life or death situation, she didn't cower and hide. Even though she was frightened, she stood next to me, ready to help. Erin was strong and brave and had my back. She was willing to do what it took to save our lives including shooting out tires if necessary. Couple that with everything else, I knew she was the woman I wanted in my life in a very permanent way.

"Because, I'm falling in love with you. And before I'm ass over tea kettle, I have to know you're with me."

"I'm with you," she whispered. "As a matter of fact, I'm a few steps ahead of you. But I'll wait until you catch up."

Sitting on the couch in Abe's cabin in the middle of an op wasn't the place I ever thought I'd admit to her I was falling in love. And it certainly wasn't the place I thought I'd utter those words to a woman for the first time—ever. But it was where we were, and the woman sitting in front of me was, indeed, the first woman I'd ever said the word love to. There was no more denying that's what I was feeling.

Some of her hair had fallen out of the clip she'd used. Reaching behind her, I released the rest of her hair, letting it cascade past her shoulders and down her back. I threw the plastic fastener onto the table and fisted a handful of her silky strands, pulling her lips to meet mine. Erin's hips rocked over my hard-on and after the last few nights it wouldn't take much to make me shoot off in my jeans. The friction was damn near painful as I tried to control the fast-building pressure.

"Erin."

"I want to touch you." She didn't wait for my answer. Her hands were at the bottom of my shirt, yanking at it. I sat up, allowing her the freedom to pull it over my head. "Damn."

Her hips stopped rubbing against me, but her hands roamed my chest and abs, giving me a small reprieve.

"Have I ever told you how sexy your chest is?"

I was no stranger to compliments on my body. Men and women alike had commented while I was at the gym. But hearing her say she liked what I looked like made my stomach tighten, and my heart constrict.

"Thanks, sunshine. Glad you approve."

"I'd approve more if you'd let me take off your pants."

Now, that made my cock twitch.

"I don't think that's a good idea."

"What if I keep mine on?"

"Are you trying to bargain with me?" The corners of her lips tipped up, and I returned her smile. "God, you're beautiful."

"I'm not only beautiful but an excellent negotiator," she teased.

"Is that so?"

"It is. I think it's my turn. You've had the pleasure of having me at your mercy, and I've yet to get into your pants. Seems a little unfair."

"My mercy, huh? Is that what you call me having you screaming in ecstasy?"

"It is."

"I would hate for you to think I'm being unfair."

"Well, that's what I'm thinking right now. And the only way to rectify the unfairness is if you let me take your pants off."

I couldn't stop myself from laughing at her playful banter. There had been no other time in my life where humor had been a part of foreplay. But with Erin, her wit was just as much of a turn-on as her body. For the first time, I knew what it was to be attracted to a woman's mind. She was the whole package.

"One condition," I told her.

"What's that?"

"That you understand just because I've given you multiple, fantastic, out of this world orgasms, doesn't mean I expect anything in return." I was trying to make light of the situation. But I wanted to be clear I wasn't joking. "I told you, having you in my arms is more than enough for me."

"Out of this world, huh?" She continued to smile. "Fantastic, you say?" she asked as her hands reached for the button of my jeans. "Why don't we see what adjectives you can come up with after I'm done with you."

She drew the zipper down, and my cock threatened to tear through the cotton of my boxer briefs. Her finger touched the wet spot on the fabric where pre-come had already seeped from my cock, climbed off my lap, and stood next to the couch.

"Take 'em off."

Shit. This was really happening. I lifted my ass, and when

my jeans and boxers were halfway down my legs she took over and impatiently ripped them the rest of the way off. I had no time to worry about my cock bobbing free when she stepped between my knees and lowered herself to the floor. I was going to protest, not wanting her kneeling on the hard wood when her hand wrapped around my cock and squeezed. The objection died now that I had bigger things to worry about, like how I was going to stop myself from coming in three seconds.

"Easy, baby," I begged.

She removed her hand and I was both grateful and dejected I'd lost her touch.

"Oh, no you don't." I tried to stop her before she pulled her shirt over her head. "Your clothes stay on." But it was too late, her bra came off next.

"I'll keep my pants on."

This was not a good idea. I wanted to go slowly. I didn't want to make love to her in the middle of an op while emotions were running high. Even if I knew how I felt about her, I wanted her to be sure. And, at this point, it wouldn't take much for me to be the one begging for her to let me fuck her. All it took was her small hand wrapping back around my cock and slowly gliding up and down to make me forget. I forgot everything: the op, all the reasons I wanted to wait, why I hadn't let her touch me. Everything flew out of my mind as I focused on the feel of her.

"Is this okay?"

"Yes," I croaked out.

Her hand sped up, and she paused on the tip to gather more of the liquid now freely leaking. My head fell back, and I was in a trance, with each stroke she brought me closer to the edge.

"So good, Erin. Faster."

Her pace quickened, and my balls drew up. I'd known this

was going to be the world's fastest hand job but I hadn't known it was going to be this quick.

"I'm there. Don't stop."

Her tongue swiped the head of my cock, and my eyes flew open in time to see her pull the tip into her mouth and suck while her hand worked my shaft.

"Holy fuck. I'm gonna come. Pull off now if you don't want me to blow in your mouth."

I cautioned her once, but there was no time for a second warning before the heat rose, and jets of come exploded from my cock into her warm, waiting mouth.

"Erin!" I shouted as the last of my orgasm waned.

Jesus Christ, I could barely hold my head up, it felt like every ounce of energy I'd had shot out of my cock, leaving me exhausted.

Erin pulled off and settled back on her knees and looked up at me with her big, brown eyes shining.

"Out of this world?" she asked, still slowing stroking my softening erection.

"Yes."

"Fantastic?"

"Fuck, yes."

"Wanna 'nother one?"

The playful smile of her face was a thing of beauty. A smile I wanted to see every day. A smile I wanted to be responsible for putting there for the rest of her life.

"I think it's your turn."

"I think you should teach me all about this sixty-nine position I've heard about."

My dick jerked and instantly started to harden again at the thought of eating her out while she sucked me off.

"Let's go."

But neither of us made the effort to move. Our eyes stayed locked in the stare, the look conveying more emotion than words could. Yes, I was falling fast and hard for Erin. I was in for a world of heartache if, after we got home, she decided she didn't feel the same way. I'd been lying to myself earlier when I'd told her I was falling in love. There was no more falling—I was already there.

CHAPTER 13

I WAS EXHAUSTED and thoroughly satisfied. I'd lost count of how many orgasms we'd given each other yesterday and well into the night. I hadn't thought it was possible, and every time I told Colin I couldn't, he proved me wrong, wringing another one out of my spent body. He was . . . actually, there were no words for what he was. Magnificent didn't begin to cover it. The man was skilled, that was for sure, but there was something else, too. I could feel the reverence in his touch. He still refused to have sex and I gave up begging him to. There would be no changing his mind, which went a long way in confirming he was the man I thought him to be. Honorable and true to his word.

"Anything from Zane?" I asked when Colin came into the kitchen.

"No. I don't expect anything from him for the next two days. Declan confirmed they have Greenwold."

"Where will they take him?"

"An undisclosed OCONUS location."

"What does that mean?"

I held up a coffee cup, and he nodded.

"Outside continental United States."

I poured his coffee and thought about how different things were. He'd yet to withhold any information from me since that first talk. I was sure there were some things he was sugar coating and I was okay with that. I didn't want the terrifying details, all I needed was to be told what was going on around me. And he'd more than shown me he trusted me with the information.

"What will happen to him?"

Colin accepted his cup and leaned against the counter. He was so freaking sexy I almost spilled the hot liquid down the front of my shirt. *Lesson learned, never stare at Colin while trying to sip morning coffee.*

"They'll place him in rendition. Zane and the team will try and extract as much intel as they can. Once the team feels they have everything they need, Greenwold will be left there and the guys will come home."

"How long will he stay there?"

"Indefinitely."

"Forever?"

"Yep."

Colin hadn't skipped a beat. His features hadn't changed, and he drank his coffee as if we were talking about the weather and not a man who was going to be locked away for the rest of his life.

"He has a wife and kids."

"He does."

"He'll never see them again."

"He won't."

"Colin!"

"What?"

"We're talking about a man's life. His wife and kids will never see him again. Don't you feel . . . I don't know . . . something?"

Colin set his cup down on the counter, took mine out of my hand and placed it next to his. He picked me up as if I weighed nothing, plopped me on the granite countertop, and stepped between my legs.

"The only thing I feel is relief."

"Relief?"

"Something you need to understand about me, Erin. I'm not a nice man. Not when it comes to the safety and well-being of those I love. I give zero fucks what happens to him. If it were up to me, he'd have a bullet in his forehead and no one would have to worry about feeding him for the rest of his miserable life. And if he cared about his wife and children, he would've thought twice about what he was planning. He knew what the repercussions were for plotting against the FDOUS. He still stalked you, terrified you, tried to kidnap you, and when that didn't work his cronies tried to kill you. So, sunshine, the only thing I wish was different is that it was me standing in front of him right now extracting information. Instead, my team gets the pleasure. Do not forget, Greenwold is a traitor."

"I don't know what to say."

And I didn't. I should've been afraid of the look on Colin's face and the fact he admitted he could easily kill a man. But I wasn't, I felt oddly safe.

"Nothing *to* say. But you're going to have to make a choice. This is my life. This is who I am and what I do. The government contracts me to take out the worst of the worst. The terrorists, traffickers, scumbags, and the horrible men and women our country doesn't want the good citizens to know about. This is me, Erin, a contract killer. You need to decide if that's something you can live with. I can't change who I am and what I've done."

"I don't want you to change."

"It's easy to say that standing here with me in front of

you. It will be something else entirely when I'm called out of your bed in the middle of the night and sent off to places unknown. There will be a lot I'll never be able to tell you. I may be gone a day, or a week, or a month. You'll never know the where, the who, or the why, but you can be sure when I return, I'll do so with blood on my hands."

"Your job is important. You protect people. I know you can't tell me the specifics of what you do. I've learned a lot in my seven years living in the White House. I understand operational security. And I would never ask you to compromise a mission. But you have to understand, I'm stronger than you think. For the record; you don't come home with blood on your hands. You come home a hero—"

"Don't make me out to be something I'm not."

I moved my hands from his shoulders up to his face and rested them on his cheeks, taking a moment to choose my next words carefully. "I know you don't think of yourself as a hero. Less than one percent of the US population has served in the military. Of that, less than thirty percent has seen combat. That makes you part of a very special group of men and women who have put themselves in harm's way for this country. Breaking that down further, I'd guess that of those thirty percent, only a handful purposefully and gladly would continue to do so, simply because they are needed. There is no glory in your job. No awards or accolades. It's thankless and dangerous, and you do it because someone has to. You answer a call not many are brave enough to. That is a hero. I won't lie to you, it scares me. I saw a very minute part of what you do in the car last week. I was so terrified when we were being shot at, I couldn't think straight, but not you. You handled it like it was no big deal, an easy day for you. So, I get it. There will be secrets between us. Time will separate us, and danger will be a part of our lives. But if, at the end of the day, that means I get you, I'm okay with it. All of it."

He didn't look like he believed me. His eyes bore into mine, searching for some discrepancy or indecisiveness. He wouldn't find any. There was no hesitation on my part. I could handle his job, all I needed was for him to give me a chance to prove it.

"If it gets to be too much, I need you to promise to tell me. I couldn't live with myself if what I do makes you unhappy or—"

"I promise. When have I ever kept my mouth shut?"

His cheeks moved under my hands, and I both felt and saw his smile.

"Okay. Are you hungry?"

"I'm not. But I'll make you something if you are."

"Nope. Keep your ass planted right where you are, and I'll make myself something."

And that's what I did. I stayed sitting on the counter and watched him move around the kitchen.

"How's Olivia doing?"

Colin's head whipped around, and his eyes widened. I guess I shouldn't have been surprised by the look of shock on his face. For months, I'd avoided any conversation that involved Olivia and had gone out of my way to not to see her.

"She's doing great. She and Leo are ecstatic the baby will be here soon."

"A girl, right?"

"Yep. I can't wait until she's a teenager. We already have a pool going on what age the kid will be when the first boy comes knocking on the door. We even have a side bet on whether Leo answers with a handgun or rifle. Right now, it's two to one, rifle."

"That's so bad." I laughed. "Poor Livie. She's going to have to sneak her daughter out of the house for her first date."

"There's a strong possibility that'll be the case. Leo is a

little crazy when it comes to Olivia. It wasn't pretty when we found her. Something clicked for him that day. He carried her out of that filthy room and has never wanted her anywhere but by his side since."

"I like that for her. She deserves it."

"Did you know he threatened to quit his job and take her on the run?"

"No."

"Grab your coffee and let's go sit on the porch. I'll tell you the story."

I hopped down and followed Colin out into the cool late morning air. Even after only being here less than a week I was positive I could be happy living in this house forever. The fresh pine smelled so good and the rustling of the trees was peaceful.

Colin brushed some leaves off of the chair and offered me the seat. Once we were both settled, he started eating and told me the story of Leo and Olivia between bites. How'd they'd driven across the country. How she came to know her biological father. And how, Pam, her mom, had caused quite the scene, forcing Leo to take some drastic measures to keep Pam from harming Olivia. I was so sad for Pam and Olivia. They'd been so close, I'm sure Olivia was heartbroken when her mom had been diagnosed with a brain tumor. My mom and Olivia's mom were close friends, and I'd been kept up to date on Pam's condition. Thankfully, she'd made a full recovery after an experimental surgery and was doing well.

"Why did Leo threaten to quit?"

"Zane told him we were going to use Olivia as bait to try and draw out the bad guys."

"What? Would he have really done that?"

"Fuck no. He wanted Leo to step up and admit his feelings for Olivia. We all saw it. When Leo ran out of the house with Olivia in his arms, and the house exploded behind him, he covered her with his body. There was no thought, he simply protected her. When we got in the helicopter, he held her in his lap like she was the most precious thing in the world. And when Pam tried to take her home, even though Olivia was still in danger, he went toe-to-toe with her and made it clear she was going with him."

"I like Leo. That time he came to D.C. with you for the Governor's Ball he was nice."

"I'll be sure to tell him you think he's *nice.*" Colin chuckled. "I don't think many people would call him that."

"I want to see her. Do you think . . . I mean . . . would she want to see me?"

"Yes."

"You're not just saying that to be nice, are you?"

"There's that word again. Sunshine, I am not a nice person. I don't blow rainbows and unicorns just to save someone's feelings. I'm too honest for that. Olivia wants to see you. She's asked many times."

"I need to explain to her why I pulled away."

"You do. She misses you and thinks you're mad at her."

"I know. I was wrong. Maybe when we get home, we can go to their house and see them." I was worried I'd said the wrong thing when the expression on Colin's face changed. I couldn't read the look but it was intense. "Did I say something wrong?"

"No, sunshine, you said everything right."

Now I was really confused but instead of asking him to clarify what he meant because, honestly, I was still worried, I changed the subject. "Tell me about the guys."

"Linc and Jasmin just had twins a few months ago. Two boys. Jaxon and Violet met on an op. She's an interesting woman who was put in a tough spot. It took a while for the team to come around and like her, but we all have. We understand why she had to do what she did. Violet actually met your dad in the basement of an old barn we used to have. He grilled her pretty hard, but, in the end, she won him over, too. Jax told me before we left for Texas they're expecting a baby but hadn't told the team yet.

"With Violet came her twin brother, Declan. He's a good guy. Zane and Ivy are happily ensconced in their penthouse, up high, away from everyone. If Zane had it his way they'd never leave, he likes his privacy, but Ivy has done wonders making him socialize with everyone. There was a time when he carried such a heavy burden you could see him starting to crumble. Ivy changed that, changed him. We're all thankful she's come into his life."

I wondered if he knew how his face lit when he talked about his friends. He was obviously very close to them. I'd say, closer to them than to his own family. That made me kind of sad.

We fell into a comfortable silence while Colin ate his breakfast. My eyes scanned the yard and fell on a soccer ball not far from an old wooden shed.

"Did you know I played soccer in high school? I was a mid-fielder."

"I can see that. Bet you were good."

I stood and walked down the two steps to get to the grass. I looked back over my shoulder at Colin. "I was very good. Wanna play a little one-on-one? Maybe place a little bet on who can score the first goal?"

His handsome face broke out into a wide smile and butterflies erupted in my belly. Maybe I could convince him tonight was the night. I was more than ready to have sex with him.

Before he could answer, his phone rang, and he fished it out of his pocket.

Yeah. Tonight, was definitely the night. I'd beg and plead if I had to. I wanted Colin so badly I could hardly stand it.

CHAPTER 14

My eyes followed Erin as I placed the phone to my ear, damn she was cute. Declan's words barely registered when I saw what she was going for. A soccer ball. A ball that hadn't been there yesterday.

"Stop!" I shouted.

At the same time Declan barked, "They're there! Go! Go! Go!"

I dropped the phone and hopped the railing. My body collided with Erin's, we hit the ground with a thud, and I rolled her under me. First the innocent looking soccer ball had detonated then the unmistakable whistling of a rocket-propelled grenade flew over us and hit Abe's cabin. The world around us exploded. We needed to get the fuck out of here.

"Stay behind me, we're going for the car." I yanked my Sig out of my holster and quickly pulled Erin to her feet. Our backs hit the driver's side door and I pushed her to her ass on the ground.

"Don't move."

I felt her hand around my ankle, and she pulled my backup Glock free.

"Where are they?" Erin's words barely registered over the ringing in my ears.

I scanned the area, not seeing anyone through the thick smoke bellowing from the cabin. The shrill of an RPG sounded before a second one hit the house.

"Jesus Christ!"

Abe's cabin was demolished. Debris flew, and the fire from the house was quickly spreading to the pine trees surrounding the property.

"What's that?" Erin looked up at the whooshing sound above us and pointed the gun in her hand toward the sound.

The smoke was too thick to see the exact location of the distinctive sound of helicopter rotor blades. However, I knew it was hovering above us.

"We're gonna have to make a run for it into the woods. You ready?"

I held my hand out and hoisted her up when she shook her head. "Are you sure this isn't your team?"

"Very. Sunshine, you need to shoot anyone that comes into view. Can you do that?"

"Yeah."

Her hand holding the Glock trembled, and I reached out to steady it. "Just like at the range. You can do it."

"Yeah. Just like at the range. I can do that."

"Damn proud of you. You go first. I'll be right behind you. Straight into the woods."

She took off in a full sprint to where I'd pointed just as the first boots hit the ground. Two men in all black with two more fast roping down from the still invisible helicopter. She pointed and shot, hitting the first man in the chest. He stumbled but recovered. I hadn't had time to tell her not to aim for the chest. Their body armor would stop the 9mm round with ease.

I sent a head shot to the second man, and he crumpled to the ground, leaving three advancing and more coming down the ropes.

"Just shoot!" I yelled to Erin as we continued to run.

There was no hope of us making it to the woods. There were too many of them and we were out gunned. I had one fifteen round magazine and would be out of ammo before this was over.

"Fuck!" I roared when I saw a black rifle pointed directly at Erin.

There was no time to think, no time to try and disarm the shooter or take him out. I did the only thing I could do I grabbed Erin halting her progress and threw us to the ground, covering her body the best I could. With no body armor any of the rounds fired in our direction would easily penetrate, going through me before hitting her.

"I'm—" My words were cut off by a searing pain. Erin wiggled under me freeing her hand holding the Glock and shot.

My vision blurred and the last thing I heard before my world went dark were Erin's screams.

Mission failed.

MY STOMACH ROILED, AND MY HEAD POUNDED. ERIN'S ANGRY voice and pleas for help echoed in the room as I slowly came to. How the fuck was I not dead? I'd felt the bullet hit my back and a second one to the side of my neck. I took stock of my wounds and realized they had to have used non-lethal rounds to subdue me. The way my stomach was revolting and my mind was still fuzzy there had to have been a tranquilizer used as well. Where the hell was I? But more importantly, where was Erin?

"Oh, good, you're awake. Just in time to join the party." I vaguely recognized the man's voice but in my current state I couldn't place it. "Erin here was about to ask daddy dearest for help."

I opened my eyes to find Erin sitting in a chair, her arms tied to the sides. But that wasn't what had my attention. The blood trickling down the side of her face had me seeing red.

"I will kill you for this," I spit out. "Each and every one of you will die."

"You always were a cocky son of a bitch. I think Zane teaches you all to be arrogant, self-righteous pricks. If you haven't noticed, you're not in the position to be making any kind of threats." The man laughed as did several of the other men in the room. None had removed their balaclavas, keeping their identities concealed.

"If you know Zane, then you know this is not going to end well for you or your band of pussies. He will rain hellfire down on you. There will be no place you'll be able to hide. Your only option is to let us go."

The man lifted his chin to the men standing next to me and with no way to protect myself from the onslaught of blows, my head snapped to the side as one man punched me in the face and a second used my ribs as a punching bag. Goddamn, that hurt. I gritted my teeth against the pain that spread over my body.

"Fuck you!" one of the men shouted in my ear.

"Enough!" The men stepped away, and the man who seemed to be in charge spoke again. "I've heard that speech before. I believe your boss has already used that threat. But you know, the funny thing is, I'm still breathing. I believe her daddy even threatened rendition. Yet, here I am." He stretched his arms out wide and turned to Erin. "Remember what you're going to say?"

"I'm not saying anything," Erin said in defiance. I would've been proud of her for being so brave if the slap the man had delivered hadn't rang out loudly, followed by her scream.

"This will go so much easier for you if you just cooperate. All you have to do is tell your dad to sign one simple document. That's all, Erin, and you go home."

"And Colin?" she asked.

"He's as good as dead. I have unsettled business with him. But you can save yourself and walk out of here in a few hours. As soon as your dad signs the papers, you leave."

I was getting ready to tell her to save herself and ask her dad to sign the papers. It wouldn't take Zane long to put the pieces together and undo what it was this man wanted. However, she spoke too soon.

"No deal. You'll have to kill me, too."

"Erin!" I shouted.

"Shut him up," the man said.

I closed my lips tightly as one man tried to insert a piece of fabric into my mouth. The second man's punch to my solar plexus had me involuntarily gasping for air. I was fucked. My hands were chained above my head, and there were four men in the room. If Erin wasn't in there with me, I'd have a better chance, but as soon as I made a move they'd use Erin against me. She had no way of protecting herself tied to a chair, sitting in front of a table with an open laptop pointed at her.

"Suit yourself. Don't ask. Your dad will sign those documents one way or another. The easy way or the hard way."

"Fuck you!" she yelled. "He won't sign them. You know he won't. He doesn't give into men like you. Not even for me. So kill me now. Get it over with."

Fuck. I knew what she was doing. Her biggest fear had become her reality. We'd been taken. She'd told me more than once she'd rather be killed than held against her will. She was so frightened of being tortured she was goading them into killing her right there, right then. I had no way to tell her to stop.

The only saving grace was the man holding us was not stupid. He was far from it. He wouldn't kill her. It had taken me a few minutes to place the man, but I knew exactly who he was and why he wanted me dead.

"Oh, no, princess, you have some work to do first."

The former CIA director, Charles Warren, stepped aside, allowing one of his men to take over. Smart. If the president or anyone else heard the man's voice, they'd immediately know who he was. I was surprised it had taken me as long as it had to figure it out. But when Warren mentioned Zane and the threats he'd made, it was easy to put two and two together.

We had an issue with Warren. He'd withheld information about the kidnapping of the deputy director of the CIA. His extreme dislike of Zane Lewis had put our mission in jeopardy and had caused my teammate Lincoln Parker to be held hostage longer than he should've been. The president had been outraged at Warren's stupidity. He'd indeed threatened to place him in rendition until he'd cooperate. In the end, he'd caved and given us the intel we needed but still landed himself in a world of shit and Tom had fired him as Director of the CIA.

A red light flashed on the small camera connected to the top of the computer screen, and I could see the angle showed both her and me.

Fuckers!

The image on the screen was replaced by Tom Anderson's angry face.

"Jesus Christ, Erin! Are you okay?" His voice was unusually gruff.

"I'm fine." I couldn't see her face but I knew she was choking back tears. "Don't do anything they say, Daddy. Don't—"

"You have twenty-four hours to reinstate Angel or you'll never see your daughter again." The man to Erin's side yanked her head back and she yelped in pain. "The sooner you sign, the less your daughter suffers."

What the fuck? There was that goddamn program again. What the hell was so important about Angel that the men in this room were willing to die to have it up and running? And how in the fuck did the disgraced ex-director of the CIA get involved in an NSA counter-intelligence program?

"Don't do it, Dad. They're going to kill us either way."

"Erin. Listen to me, sweetheart. You're going to be okay. I'm going to get you out of there soon."

"Just kill me!" Erin screamed and spit at the man next to her. "Do it. Dad, don't sign anything. I'm not walking out of here without Colin."

I jerked the chains and tried to spit the cloth they'd shoved in my mouth out. She needed to stop antagonizing them. They were not secret service agents she could push around and who would eventually give in. These men would slit her throat without thought or remorse. She was nothing to them, a means to an end. Nothing more.

"You'll have my signature in less than twenty-four hours. There better not be one more mark on my daughter or so help me God I will burn down this country looking for you." There was no mistaking the look of rage on the president's face.

The feed disconnected, and Warren closed the lid to the laptop.

"There. That wasn't too difficult, was it?"

"Fuck off!"

"Such a filthy mouth. What would your mother think?"

"My mother would be proud. She taught me not to ever give in to bullies."

Warren untied her hands and yanked her up, face to face with him. "Is that what you think I am, a bully? Princess, I'm your worst fucking nightmare. And if you don't start behaving, I will slice you up bit by bit while Colin over there is forced to watch. Is that what you want? The last thing he sees before he dies will be the woman he swore to protect mutilated. Because I can arrange that. He knows he failed. He knows he's going to die. But most of all, he hopes you get out of this alive so there will be some honor in his death."

Erin's gaze swung to mine, and she flinched at the sight of me. I pleaded with every fiber of my soul for her to stop taunting them. All I needed was time to figure out how to get us out of this mess. Time I wouldn't have if she continued to push.

"Fine."

Thank God!

"Let's go, princess. Time to get you settled."

Warren dragged Erin away, her eyes not leaving mine until she disappeared from the room. I wasn't happy she was out of my sight but pleased she wouldn't witness the beating I knew was coming. It didn't take but a second after the door clicked shut behind her for the wailing to start. I swallowed my agony, not wanting her to hear. She was scared enough as it was. Anything I could do to save her anymore fear, I would. I could take anything for her.

CHAPTER 15

IT HAD BEEN a long time since I'd been shoved into the room and told to sit down and keep my mouth shut. The only reason I'd done what I was told was because I couldn't miss the look on Colin's face. I didn't need to hear his words to know he wanted me to follow directions. It took everything in me not to provoke the men further; I would rather they kill me now. I was trying to be strong, but panic was setting in. This was my worst nightmare come true. My biggest fear. Not only that, I was afraid they were going to kill Colin. I believed the man when he told me he'd slice me up in front of Colin before they killed him. I couldn't do that to him.

I was sitting on the concrete floor, praying for a quick death when the door was swung open and two men dragged a badly beaten Colin inside. I started to stand but stopped when one of the men told me not to move.

"Here." A third man set down a bucket and dropped some rags on the floor.

Once Colin's handcuffs were secured to another chain, the men exited the room, and I crawled over to his prone body.

"Colin? Can you hear me?" I whispered.

I was so thankful when a faint grunt hit my ears.

"I'm so sorry." I didn't know what I was apologizing for but I didn't know what else to say.

I dipped a rag in the bucket of water and started to clean some of the blood off his face. There was so much of it I had to clean the cloth after every pass. It took several attempts to wash away all the red liquid before I could find the source of the flow. I put pressure on the largest gash, trying to stop the bleeding. His moans cut me to the quick. I was having a hard time even looking at his battered face. I was afraid to lift his shirt and see what wounds there needed care. The sight would be more than I could handle.

I felt his hand on mine, and his eyes opened into tiny slivers. "You're doing great."

"No, I'm not."

"You are. I know this is hard. I'm proud of you."

"Shhh. Don't try and talk. You need to rest."

His eyes closed, and I went back to rinsing out the blood-soaked rag. This was bad. Really bad. With Colin hurt, I didn't stand a chance. After a long bout of silence, during which I'd thought Colin had either gone to sleep or had passed out, he started to speak again. I nearly jumped out of my skin.

"I need you to promise me something."

"What?"

"No matter what happens to me, you stay quiet."

"I can't—"

"You can. Someone *will* come and get you, and I need you to be in one piece when they do."

"I'm not going to let them do this to you again."

"You don't worry about me. I need you to promise. Right now Warren and his guys have no idea what you mean to me, if they did, they'd exploit it. We need them to think I'm nothing more to you than a bodyguard. If I have a chance and I think I can keep you safe, I'll make my move. But when I do, I need you to make yourself as small as possible. Stay out of the way. And, Erin, no heroics. Do not try to help. If your dad sends in a team to get you, get down and let them do their job. No helping."

I understood what he was saying but I couldn't stay quiet if they started hurting him in front of me. I couldn't. I wouldn't. I knew myself too well. I was already on the verge of breaking. If I saw Colin being beaten to death, I'd try and stop them. But I didn't tell him that. Instead, I gave him what he needed to hear, my acceptance.

"Okay."

"I'm serious. I have to know you're walking out of here even if I don't. My dying wish, Erin. You alive and in one piece."

Dying wish. I wanted to scream at the unfairness, cry at the desperation of our situation. He couldn't die. Not when we'd finally found each other.

"Okay. But, Colin, you're not going to die."

"That's the plan, sunshine. The next time they take us out of this room, you stay quiet and let me figure out a way to get us out."

That part I could do.

"Okay." I lowered my head to his ear and whispered, "I love you."

"You, too, Erin. So fucking much."

I pulled his shirt up the best I could, angry red welts dotted his torso.

"I'm sure it looks worse than it is." I doubted that very much but kept my thoughts to myself. "Did you see how we got here? Where we are?"

"No. You passed out, and when you were pulled off me, one of the guys stuck me with a needle. When I woke up, I was tied to the chair in the other room and you were chained up. That guy immediately started telling me all I needed to do was tell my dad to sign some documents and I'd be free to go. Do you know who he is?"

"Yeah. The former director of the CIA. Your dad fired him about a year ago. But he and Zane have had issues for many years. The man is a lying scumbag, but I never thought he'd go this far. I can't figure out how he came to work with the NSA. There's no way your dad would've allowed that."

"What if my dad didn't know?"

"Your dad knows everything. And I mean everything."

"Could he be working as an independent contractor? Would my dad know then?"

I didn't know all the ins and outs of government contract work, but a friend from college had gone to work for a computer company that had been awarded many contracts.

"I'm not sure. But I know the man who brought you into this room is Charles Warren."

"Does he hate Zane enough to really want to kill you?"

"Fuck yes." His answer made me flinch, and I was rethinking this forthright version of Colin. Maybe he'd been right all along, and it would've been better to be kept in the dark. The truth scared me even more. "The good news is, Zane Lewis makes Warren look like a fluffy kitten."

"Not sure that's making me feel better."

"It should. It means no one is going to let us rot away in here."

"Okay."

"Thank you for taking care of me, sunshine."

"I'm sorry you're hurt so badly."

My apology sounded stupid even to me, but I wasn't sure what to say. The fear from being captured was threatening to take over. I wanted to be the brave, strong person Colin thought I was. I wanted to prove to him he had a reason to be proud of me. But it was hard and getting harder by the second. Seeing him bloodied and broken scared me more than the men outside the door. If they could do that to a big, strong warrior like Colin, I hated to think what they could do to me.

"This is a walk in the park. Trust me, I've had worse."

"That's really not making me feel any better," I grouched.

"Lean down here and give me a kiss."

"I don't want to hurt you."

"Kiss me!"

"Okay."

I leaned down and, as gently as I could, placed a soft peck on his cut lips. I didn't care I could taste blood, I needed the connection. His love was the only thing that was going to get me through this.

"You taste like sunshine and a fresh summer breeze."

"Is that why you call me sunshine?"

I could never figure out the silly nickname but never wanted to ask.

"No. I call you that because you're the sun in my otherwise dark life."

Now was not the place, but when we got out of there, I was going to ask why he thought his life was so dark. I didn't think it was. He was a good man with a big heart.

"What happens now?"

"We wait."

"Okay."

Waiting was the last thing I wanted to do but it seemed we had no choice.

THE DOOR BANGED AGAINST THE DRYWALL AS IT FLEW OPEN, and I jerked awake. I couldn't believe I'd fallen asleep.

"Time's up, princess. Let's see if daddy signed the papers."

"Time's up? It's been twenty-four hours?"

Colin twitched his arm, reminding me to be quiet.

"Nope. I knew it would only take a few hours. He won't hand the documents off to the courier until he sees your precious face one more time. Up you go."

Shit! I didn't want to go anywhere without Colin but I didn't want to draw attention to him.

"All right." I stood on wobbly legs and tried to get my bearings.

"You, too, asshole. This is gonna be fun."

Colin groaned but made no attempt to move. He was hurt but he'd been able to talk just fine before I'd fallen asleep.

"Get him up," the man I believed was Warren said to the two men behind him.

Yes, this had to be Warren. He not so nicely grabbed me by my bicep and tightened his grip until I came up on my toes. "You're going to be a good girl, right? Sit in front of the camera and smile big for daddy. I'm warning you, one wrong word and Colin will watch you bleed."

"Yes. I'll be quiet." Those were the words I'd spoken, but in my mind I was telling him to screw off and die a slow, painful death. The spineless bastard still hadn't taken his black mask off.

The two men hauled Colin to his feet. They'd unchained him from the wall, but he was still cuffed. Now that we were in the brightly lit room with the computer and chair again, I could see the bruising on Colin's face. I pinched my lips together and did my best to stop the tears from falling. He was right, if they knew how much I loved him, they'd go harder on him. I had to stay quiet, for him.

I wasn't tied to the chair this time. Warren simply shoved me down to sit and opened the laptop. I looked over my shoulder in time to see Colin's hands being chained above his head. His eyes were mostly closed, and he was being extremely compliant. Was it possible he was hurt more than I'd thought? I tried to think of different ways I could negotiate Colin's release, but I'd promised not to give away our secret. Anything I said would only make things worse. I remembered the man holding us had been the director of the CIA, he wasn't a stupid man. So instead of begging for the man I loved to be spared, I remained silent, sitting and staring at a blank screen like a coward, doing nothing to save myself or Colin. I didn't know how much more I could take. How much further they could push me before I broke and begged them not to hurt Colin any more than they already had.

"You don't have to say a word. Just sit here and keep your mouth shut. Once your dad hands the documents off, you'll be free to go," Warren told me.

I nodded my false agreement, saying nothing, hating him with all my being, and wishing he'd rot in hell. I'd never thought I was capable of taking a life. But right here, right now, I knew I was. If I had the chance, I'd kill the man in front of me. The disgust I felt for him far outweighed any sense of morality I'd once had. Within the span of a few seconds, I understood how and why Colin did the job he did. How easy it would be to kill a man as vile as Warren and feel no remorse.

Warren stepped away, and another man dressed in all black hit a few keys on the computer. Once the camera was turned on, he stood by my side.

My father's angry face filled the monitor, and I was taken aback. I'd seen my dad mad before, or I thought I had, but I'd never seen look this angry. I felt like I hadn't seen him in years instead of weeks. I desperately wanted to tell him how sorry I was for the way I'd acted over the last year. All the arguments we'd gotten into over what I thought was him being overprotective. It seemed he'd had a good reason to worry.

"Where's the reinstatement?" the man asked from beside me.

My dad held up a slip of paper, the presidential seal easy to see and my father's scrolling signature at the bottom, but I couldn't make out what the body of the document said. My father hadn't taken his eyes off me. They didn't drift over my shoulder where I knew Colin was chained up. He didn't look around the room at the two other men dressed in black. He simply gazed at me, his features were hard, and his expression was cold. A look I'd never seen on the man who'd tucked me in at night and read me stories. The gentle dad who'd taught me to ride a bike and hugged me tightly when I fell. I didn't know the man staring back at me.

"Erin, I want you to get on your knees and pray God forgives me for what I've done."

What? My dad was not a religious man. He believed in a higher power and was spiritual but he'd never requested prayer before.

"Okay, Daddy." The tears I'd been holding back fell, and I couldn't help but to speak even though I'd been instructed not to. "I'm so sorry."

"Nothing to be sorry for, sweetheart. You just do as I say and kneel in prayer."

"Enough already with the praying bullshit!" the man beside me shouted. "We get it. There's a stain on your sanctimonious soul. We'll call you in an hour and tell you where you can retrieve your daughter."

He slammed the lid on the laptop closed and then picked it up, smashing it on the cement floor. Shards of computer parts scattered across the room. "How long until it's up and running?" the man asked Warren.

"Everything's in place. Should be just a matter of minutes

once the SAP order reaches the NSA. Angel will be back online immediately."

"Good. My team will take the girl to the drop and leave you here to take care of your business. We're even now, Warren, no more favors."

"Favor? Is that what you call this? I did what your boss was too much of a pansy-assed coward to do. Tom Anderson has two weaknesses. His wife and his pretty little daughter. He was never going to cave with stupid pictures and hand-written threats being sent to him. Do you know how many threats come in daily? Hundreds. No one takes them seriously. There are thousands and thousands of pictures of both Erin and Clarissa Anderson floating around the FBI. Every crazy person with a cell phone takes a picture of one of them and threatens any manner of the most psychotic shit you could imagine. This was no favor. Your boss owes me for this. Me taking out one of Zane's operatives is a bonus. One less asshole to hunt you down. I'll be in touch, and I fully expect to be compensated."

I hoped Colin was conscious and paying attention to what Warren was saying. Maybe there was something valuable in what he said. My mind had spiraled as soon as he'd mentioned there were thousands of threats against me and my mom. No one had told me that. I mean, I knew people threatened politicians and their families, I wasn't that stupid. But no one explained that people took pictures of me and threatened me every day. Did my mom know? Did my dad? Or was this one of the things his *people* took care of so he could concentrate on running the country? What the hell?

Warren and the other man continued to bicker back and forth when Colin's movement caught my eye. He'd reached up and was holding onto the chain holding his arms above his head. I was pretty sure earlier he'd let his hands dangle loosely. His eyes were also opened a little wider, and he was watching the three men in the room carefully. Warren and one man stood next to me, and the third was still by his side.

The room suddenly shook so violently ceiling tiles started to fall. Fight, flight, or freeze. I'd heard the saying before, however, never had I experienced it. I froze in place and watched with fascination as Colin swung his legs and brought them around the man's neck. With a jerk of his thighs, the man's neck snapped with an audible crack. The other two men rushed Colin, and I remembered my dad's plea, *get on your knees and pray*, suddenly his words made sense. He knew help was here.

I crawled under the table and waited, but when no one immediately came through the door and Colin's grunts got louder, I couldn't stay there. I looked on the floor for anything I could use as a weapon. A shard of the laptop's case was within reach. I picked it up and, without thinking, ran full speed at the man who now had a gun pointed at Colin. The man turned but before he could do anything, I thrust the plastic spike as hard as I could into the side of his neck. He stumbled, and we both fell to the floor. My head smacked the concrete so hard it bounced and we rolled. I needed to get up and get the gun but I couldn't move I was so dizzy.

With a roar that rivaled the sound of the explosion back at Abe's cabin, Colin had the chain free from the hook that was holding him hostage and had it wrapped around Warren's neck.

"I told you I'd kill you, motherfucker!" he yelled.

Warren fought and kicked at Colin, trying to get free, but the chain was too tight around his throat for him to do much.

"See you in hell."

Colin lurched back, and Warren's feet came off the floor. With a sickening snap, Warren went limp, and Colin dropped him unceremoniously on the floor. The door slammed open and two loud bangs rang out. I turned to see the man I'd stabbed drop the gun that he'd been pointing in my direction.

With his hands still cuffed and dragging a chain, Colin stalked toward me.

"Clear!" someone yelled from inside the room.

Colin didn't seem all that worried about the new arrivals, so I remained on the floor, still too dizzy to move, and now with the added ringing in my ears it made standing damn near impossible. He stopped at my side and held his hands out.

"Get these fucking things off me," Colin growled his orders to one of the men dressed in black.

Black gloved hands worked the lock on Colin's handcuffs. Once his hands were freed, he knelt next to me and picked me up. Standing didn't seem to be a problem for him. He lifted me as if he hadn't received two severe beatings in the last few hours.

He looked down at me, and our eyes locked. "Is it over?"

"Yeah, sunshine, it's over."

My body quaked in relief, and I buried my face in his chest and sobbed, too overcome with emotion to say or do anything else. He was alive. We'd both made it.

It was over.

CHAPTER 16

"Six tangos down," Brooks said, coming into the room. "How many did you count?"

"Only saw four. Warren and three others," I returned.

"Warren? Charles-motherfucking-Warren? Piece of shit extraordinaire?" Declan asked.

"One in the same."

I held a shaking Erin in my arms and watched Declan yank the masks off the men in the room. I didn't recognize the one Erin had taken down but the other man I knew. We'd worked a CIA contract with him years ago. He'd left the agency and word was he was doing contract and mercenary work. Seems Warren had kept in contact with his old operative. Not good.

"All clear," Max announced, joining us in the room. "The team is waiting. The helicopter is here."

"Where the fuck are we?"

"Joshua Tree National Park. About a hundred and sixty miles northeast of San Diego."

"Erin needs a medic."

"We're headed to Twentynine Palms. Z and the rest of the

guys are waiting for us there. ETA ten minutes," Dec informed me.

I didn't bother sparing Charles Warren's corpse a second glance. My woman needed medical attention. I'd died a thousand deaths watching Erin stab the dirtbag in the neck. His gun had been pointed directly at her chest; she was mere seconds away from being shot. By some miracle she'd gotten the drop on him, and they'd fallen to the floor. But the sound her head made hitting the concrete made me think she'd cracked her skull open. Thank God, it hadn't, but there was no question she had a concussion. I wasn't sure if she was the world's bravest woman or the stupidest one. She could've been killed. For all intents and purposes she should be dead, the asshole had a clear, point-blank shot. I wasn't going to look a gift horse in the mouth, but we'd be having a conversation about her following directions and never putting herself in harm's way again.

I followed Declan out of the maze of hallways and squinted when the harsh sunlight hit my face.

"Close your eyes, Erin."

"I think I'm going to throw up."

"It's okay."

"What is?" she mumbled, her face still pressed against my chest.

"To throw up."

"I'm not going to throw up on you."

"I'm not setting you down. So if you need to throw up, do it."

With every step I took, my ribs screamed in protest. Her body jostling against the broken bones. Thad turned to say something and saw me wince. "Want me to take her?"

"No."

"If you puncture a lung from carrying her—"

"Then the doc can patch me up. She's not going anywhere."

"Copy that."

He jogged ahead of us and climbed into the helicopter. Declan and Max helped hoist me into the cabin. Once we were in, I damn near collapsed in the seat.

Every goddamn bone in my upper body felt like it was either cracked or bruised. Pain radiated everywhere. I tried to cover my grunts with a cough but even that hurt.

"Let me up."

"No, sunshine."

"I'm hurting you."

"No."

"But—"

"Erin, right now, no matter how much pain it may cause me, I need you in my arms. I need to feel you breathing. I need you close so I can reassure myself you're alive. Please, just give me this."

The pain was nothing compared to the relief I felt.

"Okay." She burrowed back in and tightened her arms around me.

"You know," Kyle started. "We had a bet going whether when we got to you it was going to be a rescue mission or a cleanup. Just want it known, I said cleanup. Good to see you, brother."

"Fuck, you too, man. I thought we'd have a few more hours before you got to us."

Now that all the guys had taken off their masks, I could see the concern etched in their faces. I hadn't worked an op with Thad, Max, Kyle, or Brooks, but we'd trained with the Gold Team. They were a good group of guys. It looked like Declan fit right in.

"We were already in San Diego on standby. Something felt off. Greenwold went down too easy," Declan told me. I was anxious to hear more about what he was talking about but right now with, every part of me hurting, I couldn't concentrate on his words. I just wanted to hold Erin.

Thank God, she was alive.

MUCH TO MY EXTREME IRRITATION, ERIN AND I WERE separated the moment we landed at Marine Corps Air Ground Combat Center Twentynine Palms. The Marines of the 7th Marine Regiment didn't fuck around. They'd welcomed us on the rooftop of the Robert E. Bush Naval Hospital with automatic weapons drawn at the ready and escorted us into the building. Declan promised he and his team wouldn't leave Erin's side as she was wheeled away from me on a stretcher.

I was hell-bent on walking into the exam room on my own and threatened to shove the wheelchair up the male nurse's ass if he tried to get me to sit in it one more time. I wasn't trying to be a tough guy, but it hurt like a mother-fucker to sit, not that I'd admit it. I just wanted my ribs wrapped so I could get back to Erin's side.

"Jesus, man. She's not going anywhere," Leo said as we waited for the doctor to come into the room. "Stop pacing."

My team had all been there, waiting for us to arrive. Zane was pissed, and I was a little worried about what he'd do when I told him who was behind the kidnapping.

"Really? Is that why when Olivia was in the basement of the barn and was being examined after you rescued her you stood watch over her like a caged beast waiting to kill anyone who dared get near her?" I reminded him.

"So, it's like that, is it?" The asshole chuckled.

"Exactly like that. I just want a fucking ace wrap so I can

see for myself she's all right. Is that too much to fucking ask around this goddamned place?"

Before I'd finished my sentence, the door opened and in walked Tom Anderson with a murderous look on his face.

"Tell me you took care of the bastard that hit my daughter."

"I did," I confirmed.

"I want a full AAR in my hands in the next hour."

"Sorry, sir, but the after-action report is going to have to wait."

"Come again?"

"The AAR is going to have to wait. All due respect, sir, after the fucking doctor gets me patched up, I'm going to Erin. I couldn't give two fucks about any reports anyone wants. All everybody needs to know right now is Warren's dead and my woman is scared out of her mind and needs me. Everything else is bullshit and can wait."

"Your woman?" he asked.

"Mr. President." His growl reminded me he hated the formality when we were in private. "Sir. Tom. I know this is a shit time to tell you this, but I'm gonna marry your daughter."

Not the best way to tell a father you were going to marry his daughter. But I didn't have the time nor the inclination to fuck around.

"Is that so?" He laughed. "Leo, mind giving us a minute alone?"

With a shake of his head and a smile, he left the room.

"Is that your version of asking for my permission to marry my daughter?"

"No, sir, it's me telling you I love your daughter and I will do everything in my power to take care of her for the rest of my life. I'm going to make her my wife. Sooner, rather than later."

The president's head tipped back, and the room filled with raucous laughter.

"I see. Zane told me things had changed between you and Erin. Not that I was surprised. I saw it back in D.C. the first time you worked her detail. And I knew I was right, when you looked like a man beaten down when she was giving you trouble. No man I'd rather have by her side. If she'll say yes, you have our blessing."

I stared at Tom in shock. I hadn't realized how badly I'd wanted his approval.

"Thank you," I choked out.

"No. Thank *you* for keeping her safe."

"She did that all on her own. No offense, but your daughter cannot follow directions. She didn't stay hidden like we both asked. Instead, she risked her life and ran like a wild animal at a man with a gun pointed at her and incapacitated him faster than I've seen trained men do."

"Sounds about right."

"I love her," I blurted out unnecessarily.

"Nothing more a father can ask for."

The door opened and in walked a young doctor who looked fresh out of the academy. He took one look at the President of the United States and started stumbling over his words, like a star-struck groupie.

Christ Almighty, can't a man get timely medical attention in this place?

CHAPTER 17

"WHAT DID THE DOCTOR SAY?" Colin asked from beside my hospital bed.

It had almost been an hour since I'd seen him, and, from his still wet hair and new clothes, I'd say he'd had a shower. Now that all the blood had been washed away, it was easy to see the green and purple marks on his face.

"I have a concussion."

I was hoping he wouldn't press and ask the severity but Colin being Colin wanted all the facts.

"How bad?"

"A bad one. Tell me about your ribs."

"They're broken." He didn't elaborate further; instead, he wanted to know more about me. "How bad, Erin? Did they do a CT scan? An MRI?"

"Yes, I had a CT scan. I need to stay here overnight. I'll have an MRI in the morning."

"Where's the doctor? I want to talk to him."

"Colin, wait." I stopped him before he could go for the door. "I'm fine."

"The goose egg on your forehead, the cut over your eye, and the concussion say otherwise."

"And . . . how are you?"

"I'm fine." He waved away my concern.

"Right. So the broken ribs and black eyes *you* have make *you* fine. But a bump on my head makes me not?"

"It's not a bump, Erin. I heard your head bounce off the floor. *Heard* it. You were so dazed you couldn't move. Baby, that's not a bump, that's a fucking brain injury. And let's not forget everything that happened before that."

"Believe me, Colin, I can't forget—any of it. Not the house exploding, the gunfire, men jumping out of helicopters, watching you get shot, then beat to a bloody pulp. I remember it all. Crystal clear."

I hadn't meant to snap at him, but I wasn't stupid. The last thing I wanted to do was die here in the hospital of a TBI after all we'd survived.

"Erin—" His tone softened, and he cupped my cheek with his hand. "I'm sorry."

"No, I'm sorry. I shouldn't have said that. I don't want to talk about my head right now. I just need *you*."

The scrape of the chair on the linoleum floor made me wince and as much as I'd hoped Colin missed it, he hadn't. He picked it up and carried it the rest of the way to the side of my bed. With his lips pinched together in a hard line, he sat but didn't mention it.

"I'm not going anywhere." His hands were warm when he picked up mine and inspected the bandage. "What happened here?"

"I guess the piece of plastic cut my palm when I used it to . . . you know." He brought my gauze-covered hand to his mouth and gently kissed it. "I didn't need stiches. A band-aid probably would've sufficed."

"Do you want to talk about it?"

"Kinda. I mean, I don't, but I do. Shit, I don't know what I'm saying. I think I just want to get it over with. Does that make sense?"

"It does. We can talk about anything you want. For however long you want to."

I sat, trying to gather my thoughts. But the longer I remained quiet, the harder it was to get the words out. I wanted to spew everything out at once and never have to think about it again. It felt like I had a demon in my belly, and the longer it sat in there, the more venom seeped into my soul. I needed to exorcise it but I didn't know how. I didn't know if talking about it would make it better or worse.

Colin didn't seem to be as tongue-tied. "I was so fucking terrified when the first explosion went off. All I could think about was we were out there all alone with no backup. If something happened to me, you'd be on your own." His gaze zeroed in on mine. "That by itself gutted me. But knowing how scared you'd be if you were taken was worse. When I was hit, and darkness was pulling me under, all I could think about was how I'd failed the one person I wanted more than anything to protect."

"You didn't fail me. You jumped on top of me and covered my body with yours. You were willing to die for me. And I thought you were . . . I thought you were dead." I almost choked on my words. When his body had gone limp, I thought for sure he was gone. I laid there under his heavy weight and wished I could follow. I didn't want to live the rest of my life knowing Colin had died because of me. "Then I woke up in that room and you were chained up. I thought they'd hung you."

"Did they hurt you while I was passed out?"

"No. I tried to fight, but one of them injected me with

something and it was lights out. I'm not sure how I got the cut on my forehead, but I don't think they hit me."

"I'm so fucking sorry, Erin." My chest tightened at the rawness in his voice.

"How did they find us?"

"I haven't talked to my team yet. I waited for fucking ever for the doctor to come in. After the fresh out of med school kid looked me over, I took a shower and waited for the nurse to wrap my ribs and came straight here. Everything else can wait, you couldn't."

"Thank you. I saw my dad."

"I did, too. How was he when he saw you?"

I'd been doing so well not crying but remembering the look on my dad's face I lost it.

"He looked horrible. I've never seen him so angry and sad and horrified in my life. It hurt to see him stare at me with such anguish. He barely spoke."

"You know he's not mad at you, right?"

"He looked disappointed."

"He is. In himself. In me. In the men who thought he could trust. He's fucking angry at the world. At the men who dared to touch you. At every single person who was behind you being hurt. But the one person he is not mad at or disappointed in is you."

"But—"

"No buts. He's a man whose daughter was taken, threatened, and hurt. Someone will pay for what they've done. And they shouldn't be afraid of Zane or me even. When your father finds the men responsible, hellfire will rain down on them like this world has never seen."

"I thought they were dead, the men who took us. That Warren guy—"

"Hey. You're safe." Colin stood and sat on the bed next to

me, forcing me to move over. He gathered both of my shaking hands in his and held on tightly.

"But if there are more—"

"Erin. I promise you, you're safe."

I didn't believe him. Not when this wasn't over. I'd thought it was, but it wasn't. And, suddenly, I was more frightened than I'd been when I was locked in the room with a bloody Colin.

"Sorry to interrupt, but Tex is calling in. We need you," Zane said from the doorway.

"Then you can come in here," Colin answered.

"It's not secure."

"Then you don't need me. I'm not leaving Erin. And before you ask, yes, it's like that. And, no, nothing will make me leave this room. My woman is scared out of her head and there's not a goddamn person that is going to drag me out of here."

"Christ. Can't any of you keep your—"

"Careful, Z."

"I was going to say, emotions in check." Zane cracked a smile, showing off his dimples, and I knew he was lying. He would have said something crass if Colin hadn't stopped him. "And here I thought Jaxon and Leo were crazy. But you? You had to go and fall for the untouchable. Please tell me you've spoken to her father. The last thing I need is to lose one of my best operatives."

"I did. I have his blessing."

"Well, fuck me running."

"What? You talked to my dad about what?"

I was getting whiplash trying to follow Zane and Colin's conversation.

"I did."

"You told him? About us?"

"If by *us* you mean I told him I was going to marry you, then, yes, I spoke to him about us."

"Marry me?" I nearly inhaled all the oxygen in the room and didn't exhale until I started getting dizzy.

"Can you give us a minute?" he asked Zane. When the door shut behind him, Colin turned back to me and took my unbandaged left hand in his and toyed with my bare ring finger. "Yes, sunshine, marry you. This is not how I'd envisioned this going, but I can't wait. One day soon, when I can get down on my knee without feeling like a rib is going to puncture a lung, I'll do this again. I want you to be my wife. I want you by my side. I *need* you by my side. When I thought I was going to die, you were the last thought I had. The only regret I had before my eyes closed was that I'd never gotten to tell you how much I loved you. How I wanted more time, more days, more minutes, hell, even more seconds with you. You made me believe in love, the kind that burrows deep and courses through your veins. The kind that never ends. I'm not the easiest man to get along with, but, sunshine, I promise you, I'll do everything in my power to make you happy for the rest of your life. I'll support you every way I can. I'll cheer you on. I'll pick you up. I'll celebrate and mourn with you. Anything you want. All I need is you."

The giggles that bubbled up were not what he'd expected. But once they started, I couldn't stop them, not even when he looked at me like I'd grown three heads. Thankfully, they finally subsided, but tears took over, still preventing me from answering. If I didn't get myself under control soon, I was afraid he'd take back his proposal.

"Yes," I finally sobbed. "Sorry. I don't know if I want to cry from joy or laugh because I'm ridiculously happy, which seems like it should be impossible after everything that has happened. I don't know what I should be doing, but my answer is yes. Yes! I want to be your wife. Yes, I want you by my side for all of those things. A hundred yeses. But, I get to be all of those things to you, too. I love you, Colin. I think I've loved you from the first time your bossy ass stepped into the White House residence and told me you were taking over as my personal detail."

"Bossy ass, huh?" Colin smiled.

"Well, you did admit you're hard to get along with."

"I love you, sunshine."

"I love you, Colin. What did my dad say?"

"He told me I had his blessing. He's not a stupid man, Erin. Thinking back to the last conversation I had with him, he knew what he was doing."

"And what was he doing?"

"He could've sent you anywhere in the world, hid you anyplace, but it was his call sending us to Texas together. My guess, he knew the more I was around you, the easier it would be for you to wear me down."

"Wear you down?"

"Yeah, you know, get me to give into your wiles," he teased.

"Colin!"

"I'm kidding, sunshine. I suppose I hadn't hidden my feelings as well as I thought I had."

I didn't know what to say, so I stayed silent and thought about how over the top happy I was. The knock on the door broke the spell and Zane, my dad, and the rest of Colin's team walked in.

I didn't want to admit it, but I was thankful Colin wouldn't leave the room. I wasn't ready to be alone yet.

CHAPTER 18

"Hacked?" I asked Tex as I glared at the cell phone on the roller table at Erin's bedside.

The room was filled to capacity. Zane, Leo, Jaxon, Linc, the president, and Declan all crammed into the small space.

"Yes," he ground out. "I've warned the others to discard all tracking devices."

"So that's how they found us. Through Erin's jewelry," I surmised. "Motherfucker! How is that even possible?"

"I'm good—goddamn great, actually," Tex started. "The person who got into my system did not get through the layers of protection I have. They cracked my passcodes. Do you have any idea how difficult that is? Damn near impossible. Whoever got into my computer isn't better than me, they had help."

"Like the NSA," Jaxon surmised.

"Correct." I don't think I'd ever heard Tex so angry in all the years I'd known him.

"Are you secure now?" Zane inquired. "What about Beth?"

"Beth seems to be unaffected. She's under radar. Me? Not so much. If by secure you mean, have I changed passcodes, rerouted, and added more protection, then yes. If you're asking if it can't be done again, no."

"Well, isn't that fucking special." Zane looked to the ceiling and spoke again. "How the fuck could this happen?"

"Angel," the president spoke for the first time.

"Are you ready to explain exactly what this program is and why the hell the NSA is so hell-bent on it being up and running? Not to mention, we still need to figure out how that fuckstick Warren is tied in." Only Zane Lewis could get away with taking that kind of tone with the President of the United States.

"Not here I'm not."

"Why is that?" Zane continued to press.

"Because they're listening."

"How in the fuck is that possible?"

"Do you have a cell phone in the room?"

"You know damn well we do. We're talking to Tex on one."

"That's how."

Every man in the room went silent. It wasn't that we bought into government conspiracy theories, but we all knew how easy it was to use a cellular device as a listening device. Albeit illegal, we'd done it a time or two ourselves. The NSA and CIA weren't the only ones with the capability. However, they weren't supposed to abuse the capability without a warrant.

"Well, there you have it." Zane shook his head in disgust. "Wheels up in thirty, and we'll continue this conversation when the fuckwits at the NSA can't eavesdrop. Just to add since you're listening, I'm coming for you, all of you. Your boy Warren paid for his lesson with his life. No one crosses my team and lives to tell about it. Tex, we'll be in touch when we can."

"Copy that. Good luck."

Zane angrily stabbed the disconnect button on his phone and left it on the roller table.

"I'll see you all tomorrow," I told Zane. When he narrowed his eyes in confusion, I continued, "Erin has a concussion and is scheduled for an MRI in the morning."

"I'll be fine, Colin. You need to go with them."

"Not a chance."

Was she crazy? There was no way I was leaving her in California with a severe head injury.

"But—"

"No buts, sunshine. I told you I'm not leaving your side and I'm not."

"I'm sure Gerard would stay with me," she continued.

I sat on the edge of the bed, careful not to jostle her, and my eyes zeroed in on the cut on her face. Thank God, she was okay. I would've taken a thousand beatings if it meant she remained untouched. She had to be the craziest, senseless, bravest, toughest woman I'd ever met. I was still in utter shock her ill-advised plan to rescue me worked. It was the riskiest attack I'd ever witnessed and that was saying something.

"I see you're still not understanding me. In the span of twenty-four hours, we went from lazing around a cabin to a full-blown military-style attack. An assault team took you, drugged you, tied me up, and you nearly killed a man. When all that sinks in, I'm going to be here. When someone needs to wake you up through the night because you have a concussion, it'll be me. When you go for your MRI, I'll be there with you. Nothing is more important. Nothing is going to change so drastically in the next day. Everything will wait."

"But what if it does, Colin? What if something else happens? My dad signed those—"

"Sunshine, that was for show. And if something else

happens, then someone else will handle it. Because I will be . . . right . . . here."

"He's right, Erin. I wasn't thinking when I suggested we leave now. If it were Ivy in a hospital bed, nothing would make me leave her. A nuke could take out the eastern seaboard, and I'd still stay with her. We'll leave tomorrow after your MRI, providing your doctor clears you to fly."

"Don't cry, sunshine. Everything is going to be fine." I wiped away a tear as it slid down her cheek and reveled in how warm and soft her skin was. We'd gotten lucky.

"I feel like I'm holding everyone up."

"You're not." Tom's booming voice carried over the quiet conversation Zane was having with the rest of the team. "May I have a moment alone with my daughter?"

I looked back at Erin and waited for her to give me a sign she was okay with me leaving the room. If she wasn't, I'd have no problem going toe-to-toe with Tom. He may be the president but right then, in that room, he was simply her father. And if my woman wanted me, I wasn't leaving.

When she smiled and gave me a nod, I leaned down to kiss her forehead, careful not to irritate the gash.

"I'll be right outside," I told her.

I stood but before I could get more than a few steps, Tom's hand landed on my shoulder, halting me.

"Thank you."

"No need to thank me."

"One day, when you're a father, you'll understand. There is a need. I want you to know I appreciate everything, and I mean, everything you've done for my daughter."

"You're welcome."

The six of us made our way into the hall in silence.

"Ma'am, do you mind if we leave these here with you?" Zane held out his cell phone to the nurse behind a large, curved desk.

"Sure."

All of us set our phones in a pile and followed Zane to the end of the corridor. Not too far from Erin's room.

"What the fuck?" he barked. "Run me through what the hell happened."

I gave Zane and the others a minute by minute rundown on what had taken place at Abe's cabin through when the Gold Team had come in for the rescue.

"She did what?" Declan asked.

"Brother, it was like watching a movie in slow motion. I caught her out of the corner of my eye as Warren and one of his men were wailing on me. I told her to stay out of sight and, no matter what, not to do or say anything to draw attention to herself. She fucking promised." It would be a long time before the visions of her putting her life in danger left the forefront of my mind. "He could've killed her. And he would've if you and your team hadn't come in when you did." While I'd been taking care of Warren, the man next to Erin had grabbed the gun she'd knocked out of his hand and was pointing it at her head. The barrel of the pistol was a mere foot from her. He wouldn't have missed, and she wouldn't have survived. "I don't know which one of them took the shot, but I'm indebted to them for the rest of my life."

As I'd expected, Declan didn't say a word. I knew he'd never tell me which man on his team was responsible for taking the shot that saved Erin's life. I also knew, whoever it was didn't want the credit or my thanks.

"Did Warren say anything?" Leo asked.

"Not about how he was involved, just that the plan was his to take Erin to force Tom to sign the reinstatement of Angel. He was too caught up in his normal 'I hate Zane Lewis' bullshit to make any sense."

"Jesus Christ!" Zane muttered and scrubbed his hand over his face.

"All of this comes back to this Angel program."

"We're dead in the water without Garrett or Tex. As soon as Garrett heard what happened to Tex, he literally starting unplugging every machine in the building. Jasmin said she'd gone into the office with the twins to catch up on paperwork and Garrett was yelling at everyone to disconnect the landlines. It's absolute chaos over there," Linc informed us.

"We're not dead, just beat up. Kinda like Colin's face. It might not look pretty but it still didn't stop him from asking the girl to marry him." Zane chuckled even though what he said barely made any sense. "I take it she said yes."

"She did."

"That's love right there, friend. Cause I gotta tell you, you look like someone used your face for CQC practice," Leo threw in.

"Not so much of a pain in the ass anymore, eh?" Zane loved to use your prior words against you whenever he could.

"Oh, she's still a pain in the ass."

"Right. But none of us could ever fall in love with a delicate flower. We need spice and vinegar to go with our sweet," Jaxon commented.

He wasn't wrong. Not with our overbearing personalities.

"Speak for yourselves," Declan, the only single one in the group, told us. "I think you're all crazy. One day I'll find a sweet wallflower."

"And you'll be bored out of your skull," I informed him. "Men like us, we don't do boring. We need a soft place to fall after a tough mission but a woman who can still put us on our ass when we go too far. Take Leo for example, Olivia entertains his over the top craziness only so far. Then she has no problem telling him to back off."

"That she does." Jaxon chuckled.

"Yeah, laugh it up, Jax. I've seen Violet tell you where to

shove it. And let's not forget she pulled the same shit Erin just pulled by not following directions." Leo crossed his arms across his large frame and smirked good-naturedly.

"He's kinda right. Miss Loose Lips willingly gave herself up," Zane added.

"To save my wife and babies' lives," Linc reminded Zane.

"I didn't say she didn't have good reason. Only that she and Erin both put their lives in danger for our sorry asses."

"And what, Ivy's a walk in the park? The woman puts up with no bullshit ever." Jax had Zane there. Ivy was easy going until she wasn't. And when she wasn't, it was world war three.

"Fuck no, she's not. That's what makes her the perfect woman. I know where I stand with her. And in case I missed it the first time she tells me I'm being an asshole, she kindly reminds me a second time, only louder. But when shit goes sideways, she never complains. When I pull inside of myself and the guilt starts to jerk me under, she's there. Not a day has gone by I haven't thought about how lucky I am. How lucky we all are."

"Y'all enjoy your domestication. For years my ass was stuck deep undercover with the filth of the world. Now that you all are off the market, that means there's more available tail for me. And I plan on enjoying it." Declan winked.

He wasn't fooling any of us. He thought he was, but we'd all been there. Loneliness was a given for men like us.

"Whatever you say, Dec," Lincoln started. "There was a time I thought the same thing. We were living the good life. Shootin' guns, killin' bad guys, high on the adrenaline rush. Then walked in a five-foot-nothing hellcat and knocked my world off its axis. Jasmin changed everything. One day, when the woman you're meant to spend the rest of your life with barges into your life and ties you in knots, you'll gladly allow it. Unless you're Colin. Then you fight it and pretend you don't see what's right in front of your face."

I kindly flipped Lincoln the middle finger.

A look of sadness passed over Declan's face before he quickly masked it.

"Still can't believe you asked her, man. Congratulations. Maybe now you can bring her around and see my wife. Olivia has been worried about her."

"We already talked about it. She feels bad about what happened this last year and wants to make it right."

"Nothing to make right. As long as she's in Olivia's life, that's all that matters."

"Agreed."

The door to Erin's room opened, and her father stepped out. As much as I enjoyed bantering with my team, I'd rather be with my woman.

"She's all yours. Take care of her," Tom said.

I was struck by the truthfulness of his words. She was all mine. In every way. For all time.

CHAPTER 19

"Are you sure you're up for this?" Colin asked for the fourth time since we'd left his house.

I'd done nothing but sleep, or I should say, tried to sleep, for the last two days. After my MRI showed no swelling or bleeding in my brain, I was given the all clear to fly home. We landed at Andrews and went straight to Colin's house in Annapolis. True to his word, he hadn't left my side. As a matter of fact, he was following the doctor's orders to wake me up once an hour—down to the second. I didn't know how he was functioning. He had to be exhausted.

Zane had called yesterday and asked if Colin would come into the office today, and the only way he'd agreed was if I went with him. So that was where we were headed. And if I was going to spend the day lollygagging around his office, I thought I should ask if Olivia could meet me there since Leo would be at the meeting as well. At the time I'd thought it was a good idea, however the closer we got to the downtown office the more nervous I became.

"Sunshine?"

"Sorry. Yeah, I feel fine."

"You sure? You were out of it there for a minute."

"Just thinking about Olivia. What if she doesn't forgive me?"

"You've got nothing to worry about. I talked to Leo and she's thrilled you texted her."

"But what if—"

"The sky falls? A bus pulls in front of us? The world explodes?" he joked.

"Stop. I'm being serious."

"I know you are. You're working yourself up for nothing. I'm more worried about you taking it easy than anything. The doctor said—"

"Yes, I know what he said. Relax. No exercise or strenuous activity. I'll be sitting in your office talking, not PT'ing."

"He also said no stress."

"Last night I offered you a perfectly reasonable stress-relief option, but you turned me down."

"Reasonable? Sweetheart, me giving you orgasms while you have a concussion isn't going to happen."

"Why not? All I have to do is lie there."

"Right. You don't just lie there. Your head thrashes, your hips buck, you scream in excitement. No part of that is relaxing."

"Fine," I huffed.

"I think I've created a monster." He chuckled. "Besides, right now, all I want to do is hold you. I want to feel your breath on my neck and your heartbeat against mine as you cuddle into me."

Okay, so I wanted to have sex, and I wanted to pout I couldn't have it but when he said things like that to me, it was hard to stay disappointed.

"I don't think you understand how hard it is to sleep next you while you're practically naked and not want to jump your bones."

Colin pulled into a parking garage, found an empty spot, put the car in park, undid his seat belt, and turned to me. "Jump my bones?" I could easily hear the humor in his voice and even in the semi-darkness of the parking structure, I could see his eyes dance with mirth.

"Something wrong with the way I talk?" He shook his head and grinned. "I would think someone with your sexual prowess and experience would understand how your nakedness could have a tingling effect on a woman."

It took a long time for Colin's amusement to die down. And when the laughter finally faded, I had to squeeze my thighs together to quell the ache his stare was causing.

"Sunshine, I'm dying to see you squirm again while I eat you out and go to sleep with the taste of you on my tongue. I'm counting down the days until I get to finally slide inside of you and make you mine, fully and completely. But I will never put you in danger, and, right now, you need to heal."

"I love all of that except maybe the not brushing your teeth after you go down on me part. Just saying."

His head hit the back of the headrest and once again he roared with laughter. "Goddamn, I love you, woman. Duly noted, brush teeth after pussy licking." He reached across the center console and picked up my hand, toying with the ring he'd placed on my finger. I loved when he did that. "You ready?"

So, that happened. Yesterday, a courier came by Colin's house and delivered a small package. He disappeared into his home office and when he reappeared, he lowered himself to his knee and asked me to marry him for a second time. With blue eyes gazing up at me, I said yes—again. He slipped a familiar diamond ring on my finger. And I was speechless as I studied the sparkling family heirloom. He explained my parents had sent it over with a note, while he wouldn't tell me exactly what it said, he did tell me my mother had given her blessing as well. Considering I now had my grandmother's ring on my finger, the very engagement ring my dad had given my mother, I'd assumed she shared my dad's sentiments.

"Yep," I finally answered.

"Whenever you're ready to go, tell me. I don't want you overdoing it."

"I won't. Promise."

"Right. Just like the last time you promised—"

"Do we have to go over this again? They were going to kill you, Colin. I wasn't going to sit there and watch the man I love get beaten to a bloody pulp."

"I know. I'm sorry, I shouldn't joke about it."

I waited in the car for him to come to my side and open the door. A habit from all the years of having personal bodyguards. "Sorry. I guess I can open my own door and get out. I'm just used to having to wait until someone comes around."

"And you should. I'll always open the door for you."

I looked around the parking garage and thought it was strange I hadn't seen any secret service. "Are there agents here?"

"Sure are," he answered.

"Huh. I hadn't noticed them."

"I told them they were to stay back. I didn't want you to feel like you were under lock and key. Besides, for now, you won't be anywhere I'm not."

"Thank you."

"Don't mention it."

Colin beeped the locks and placed his arm around my shoulders, drawing me close as we walked toward Z Corps headquarters.

"Hey, what happened to the rental?"

In all the excitement, I'd forgotten all about driving from Texas to California.

"Totaled just like Abe's cabin."

"Shit. How pissed is Abe?"

I felt horrible about destroying Abe's home. Not that we did it on purpose, but it was because of us the property had been infiltrated and the cabin had been on fire after two rockets, or bombs, or whatever the explosive devices were called had hit the house.

"He's not. They don't keep anything personal there, and he knows it will be rebuilt by Zane."

"I feel really bad about it."

"You shouldn't. It comes with the territory."

"Seriously?"

"Did I tell you why Fletch sold his house?"

"The one you bought?"

"Yep."

"I don't think so."

"It all started when, Sadie, the niece of a hotshot PI out of Dallas was being guarded by her now husband. Everyone was gathered at Fletch and Emily's having a wonderful evening until . . ."

Colin continued his story as we walked through the lobby of Z Corps. Only stopping to enter in a numeric code and place his hand on a scanner to get through the secure door that led to a long hallway.

"An RPG?" I gasped when he got to the part about the house exploding.

"Not one, but two." He stopped again, placing his forehead against the plastic shield of the retinal scanner. "It was a bad night."

The elevator door opened, and he motioned for me to precede him. "I'll say. Was anyone hurt?"

"Yeah. Fletch was pretty banged up and so was Chase Jackson."

"Damn. But they're both okay now, right?"

"Yeah, sunshine, they're both fine. But after what happened, even after the house was rebuilt, Fletch and Emily decided to sell."

"It's a beautiful house. Will we get to go back?"

"Anytime you want."

"I want to go back soon."

"Okay."

He leaned down and kissed the top of my head as the doors slowly opened. Thankfully, Colin still had his arm around me because the squeal coming from a hugely pregnant Olivia nearly gave me a heart attack.

Once my heart rate settled, and I took a good look at my best friend who I'd turned my back on, my heart broke. I'd been such a bitch. I buried my face into Colin's side and couldn't stop the tears from flowing. Olivia was pregnant, very pregnant, and I'd missed it. Almost all of it. For what? Why hadn't I'd seen her after she'd been rescued? Why hadn't I gone to see her after she'd married Leo? Why had I been so stupid to let so much time pass? Now there was a chasm I needed to bridge.

"Baby, what's wrong?" Colin was trying to get me to look up at him, but I wasn't ready.

"Erin?" Olivia called out. "Get your ass out of the elevator and let's go eat. I'm freaking starving. And I've waited for my one soda a day Mr. Bossy allows me to drink until you got here. I want my Dr. Pepper and I'm not going to stand here and wait for you all day."

"Um?" I could hear the uncertainty in Colin's response. He must have thought I'd lost my mind. "Are you laughing?"

I nodded.

Yes, I'd gone from bawling my eyes out to cracking up. Olivia, being Olivia, had pulled me from my self-pity that quickly.

"You look like you've eaten a beach ball, Livie. You sure you have room in there for food?"

I slowly pulled away from Colin and looked at my beautiful friend. She was glowing. Marriage and motherhood looked great on her.

"I know, right? It's all the food Leo's mom force feeds me. I swear they think I'm growing a linebacker."

"I've seen your husband. That's a strong possibility."

Olivia's face broke out in a smile and she held out her hand. "Damn, I've missed you. Missed this. Life has been . . . incomplete without you. Now let's go get me a soda before Leo comes out here."

"I heard that, *tesorino*."

Olivia rolled her eyes even though her husband could see her. "There was no doubt you wouldn't."

"You have two more weeks."

"I'm well aware." Olivia rubbed her belly. "All ten pounds of her is currently sitting on my bladder."

"Ten pounds?" I gasped. "Is that possible?"

"I'm joking. At least, I hope I am."

"Sweet Jesus, I was going to pray for your vagina if that were the case."

"Um. Not sure what I just walked in on." Jaxon chuckled when he joined the group. "Violet, Ivy, and Jas are up in Zane's office. I've been sent to tell you that they're going to eat without you."

"Damn. You people are serious about your food."

Liv grabbed my left hand and stared at my ring. "I was getting ready to tell you to hurry up so we could tell you the latest gossip, but it looks like you have some explaining to do, missy."

"I'll be in the conference room if you need me," Colin told me.

"Okay. Love you."

"You, too, sunshine. Please be careful."

"I'll keep an eye on her." Leo and Colin both groaned. Liv twisted her lips trying to hold back her smile. "What? It's not like we can get into any trouble in here. This place is like Fort Knox."

Liv and I left the men standing near the elevator, both of them chuckling and shaking their heads. And just like that, we picked up where we'd left off. Like no time had passed. True friendship can weather time, hurt feelings, and words unsaid. I knew Liv loved me, and she knew I loved her. At the end of the day she was my best friend—my sister. No matter what.

"What took you so long? Ivy wouldn't tell us her secret until you got back." A beautiful brunette said.

"Keep your pants on. Vi, Ivy, this is my best friend in the entire world, Erin Anderson, soon-to-be Mrs. Colin Doyle. Erin, this is Ivy, Zane's woman, and Violet's man is Jaxon." Liv pointed to each woman in turn.

That was one of the many things I loved about Olivia. I was simply me, not the first daughter. She never introduced me as anything but Erin.

"And my cousin returns," Jasmin said from the couch where she sat with the twins on her lap.

She looked damn good for having two babies not too long ago. I hadn't grown up with Jasmin. As a matter of fact, I hadn't known she existed until recently. Before her parents, my Aunt Erin and Uncle Robert died, they'd drawn up their will and asked my dad to let their close friend, Noah, raise Jasmin in case anything happened to them. My dad had already begun his political career, and ironically, they didn't want Jasmin to grow up the way I had. Stuck with guards and living behind a fence. He'd reluctantly agreed and had kept his promise to his sister and hadn't contacted Jasmin. I never knew Erin and Robert had any children and Jasmin hadn't known anything about her parents. Now that the secret was out, she and Lincoln had been to the White House a lot. My dad was thrilled she was in our lives, and so was I.

"Hey, Jas. How are my baby cousins?" I smiled at her, then turned to Violet and Ivy. "Hi. Nice to meet you."

"Getting big. Come take one." Jasmin held out one not so tiny bundle.

I took the baby and looked down at his face, and his father, Linc's, green eyes stared back at me, and I felt a pang of jealously. I wanted this. I always had. Even when I was in college and my friends were talking about grad school, politics, and careers, I'd thought about wanting a family. I didn't need a huge salary or letters after my name to make me feel important. Motherhood was what I'd always dreamed of. I knew in today's world it wasn't the most popular aspiration, but it was what I wanted.

"Which one is this?"

"Asher," Jas told me. "So. You and Colin, huh? Last time I saw the two of you together he was shaking his head and you were calling him an ass." The big smile on her face took the sting out of her words.

"Yeah, well, he turned out to be a loveable ass."

"Glad you're back. Linc said it was a shit show. Sorry I missed it. I'm still not cleared for duty for another month. Also heard my cousin is quite the badass."

"Colin's not too happy. He thinks I should've stayed in the corner, out of sight."

"Ha! That's what they all think. It's part of their DNA—me man, you woman. I protect, you look pretty." Jasmin chuckled. "Fuck that noise. I can kick some ass and still look good doing it. I'm proud of you and I know Colin is, too. You handled yourself well."

"Thanks."

"My team is dropping like flies. Now all we have to do is marry off Dec, and the family will be complete."

"I wouldn't bet on my brother settling down anytime soon. I think he's making up for lost time," Violet said. "Yes, congratulations. I adore Colin."

"That's right. Declan is your brother."

I remembered Colin telling me about Declan and the rest of team while we were sitting on the porch before . . . I shook my head trying to dislodge the memories of that day. I was here to enjoy my day with Livie and the rest of the women, not think about being kidnapped. Thankfully, Violet spoke before the recollection could take over.

"Yeah, my twin." Something that looked a lot like sadness passed over her face, and I decided not to ask any further questions. "Our parents died when we were young, and we were separated. I didn't see him for a really long time."

"That . . ." I didn't know what word I was trying to find.

"Sucks?" she helpfully supplied. "It sure did. But we found each other. It all worked out."

"What's the big secret?" Jasmin asked, changing the subject.

All eyes zeroed in on Ivy. "So . . . Zane and I did something." She smiled so big I couldn't help but to smile with her. "We, um, got married."

"What?" the other three women said in unison.

"When?" Liv asked.

"Yesterday at the courthouse. But we'll still have a big wedding. In about nine or ten months depending on how soon I can fit into a dress."

"Holy shit!" Jasmin laughed. "Are you telling us there's going to be a mini Zane Lewis running around?"

Ivy nodded.

"You're pregnant?" Violet asked.

"Yeah. Only nine weeks. It's still early, and I know you're

not supposed to tell people until after twelve weeks, but you're not *people*, you're all family."

Violet started to giggle and soon the others were laughing at her as she waved a hand in front of her face trying to stop herself. "I . . . I . . . I am, too." She laughed.

"Wait, what? Did you just say you are, too?" Ivy asked.

"Yes. Ten weeks."

I stood to the side, rocking Asher in my arms, and watched the three standing women hug each other. I was super happy for them but felt a little out of place.

"Holy shit. I can't believe you two are going to be pregnant at the same time. This is gonna be so awesome to watch Jaxon and Zane. Now all we need is to get Erin knocked up and it'll be even better."

"Yeah. That's not happening anytime soon."

"Why's that? Colin put a ring on your finger in like two-point-five seconds. And don't think I don't want to hear about how that happened," Liv said. "Does he not want kids?"

"He does. I think his mom is expecting him to provide her with like ten of them."

"Girl . . ." Jasmin laughed. "You better get on that soon. I've met Colin's mom, she's not kidding."

"What's wrong?" Violet's happy face fell.

"Nothing." I quickly waved her off. "Congratulations to both of you. That's really exciting. All four of you are gonna have little ones at the same time."

"Erin . . ." Liv started. "What's wrong?"

"Nothing. Maybe it's my concussion."

Jasmin barked a laugh. "You're a shitty liar. Something's wrong. Spit it out already, before Olivia gets whiny."

"I don't get whiny." Olivia crossed her arms over her enormous chest.

"You do, Liv. And be careful you're getting ready to lose a boob out of your V-neck," I told her.

"Jesus, I'll be happy when these things go down."

"Um. Don't they fill with milk? Hate to tell you, friend, but they'll get bigger." I motioned toward her boobs.

"Don't remind me. Leo says . . . hey . . . stop trying to change the subject by talking about my boobs."

Shit. I almost had her. She was so easily distracted, I could normally steer her away from a topic I didn't want to talk about.

Four sets of eyes pinned me in place. Using all of my tele-pathic abilities, I silently pleaded with Olivia to change the subject. I even raised an eyebrow, but she didn't get it. She tapped her foot impatiently and waited me out.

"We haven't . . . we don't . . . there hasn't been a place . . . ah, fuck it, I'm still a virgin. We haven't had sex yet."

Four jaws dropped, and it was so quiet in the room you could hear a pin drop.

"How in the actual fuck is that possible?" my cousin asked.

"Um, hello, president's daughter here. Secret Service. Personal bodyguards. Kinda hard to have sex when there is, literally, a man dressed in a black suit, armed to the teeth, standing next to you at all times."

"I just assumed you and Colin had. I mean, that he'd taken . . . you still haven't?" Liv stuttered.

"No! First, we were in a shitty motel room, and he refused to do anything with me there because he said I was too special to have my first time in a thirty dollar a night motel. Then we got to the cabin, and he took his sweet ass time doing really great stuff to me. Then he said he didn't want to go all the way until we got home, and I had time to think without the fear of being kidnapped on my mind. He said he didn't want me to regret it. It didn't matter what I said to him, he wouldn't budge. Then the fucking house exploded, he was shot, I was drugged, he was beaten nearly to death, I was scared, I stabbed someone, have a concussion, and now he says I have to wait until my head is healed." I finally took a breath after my rant and realized all the women were staring at me with a weird look on their faces. Well, everyone but my cousin, Jasmin was smirking. "What?"

"He said you were too special for your first time to be in a shitty motel?" Liv asked.

"Yes."

"He wanted to wait so you had time to think?" Violet asked.

"Yep."

"Really great stuff, huh?" Ivy giggled.

I nodded.

"Who the fuck knew Colin was such a romantic fool?" Jasmin added.

"Did anyone hear me? I'm in my mid-twenties and a virgin. I don't want to be a virgin. I've tried to not be one. But I can't get him to have sex with me. I think I'm like a golden unicorn or something, no one still has their V card at my age."

Liv broke out in a fit of laughter, and the rest followed. I didn't see what was so funny about my current predicament, but they sure found it hilarious.

When the laughter started to die down it was Ivy who finally spoke.

"Never in all my life, growing up the way I did, did I ever think I would be in a room with the President of the United States' niece and daughter laughing. Never did I think I would find a man like Zane and friends like all of you. Never, ever, did I think I would become a mother. I'm grateful for everything I have, but all of you, your friendship is the cherry on top of my really awesome sundae. And, Erin, that includes you. Welcome to our crazy family."

My eyes met Liv's and I forgot all about sex or the lack

there of and realized the only real friendship I'd ever had was with Olivia. Her circle had grown, and now mine had, too.

The five of us spent the afternoon getting to know each other. We ate, we laughed, we poked fun at one another. We talked about babies, and marriage. Nothing all that important or earth shattering, but deep down I knew with every word spoken, everlasting friendships were being built.

CHAPTER 20

THERE WAS SO much pent up aggression in the room it was sizzling. Leo, Jax, Linc, and Dec all looked murderous as we waited for Zane and the president to come into the room.

"Anyone else think this smells like shit?" Jax asked.

"Damn right it does. Once again, we're smack in the middle of a bunch of political fucks jockeying for position," Leo answered. "We all know how this works, extortion, secrets, and black ops, but what I want to know is why in the fuck the Angel program is so damn important to the NSA. This is not the first wiretap program, what makes this one different?"

"Because it's the ultimate spy program," Tom said as he and Zane entered the room. "All electronics were left outside of this room, correct?"

We all answered in the affirmative. Not that it would matter if we hadn't. The room was not only bulletproof and soundproof, but there were jammers as well. No electronic transmissions could pass in or out. The blackout shades had also been lowered over the thick polycarbonate, ballistic windows. Every precaution had been taken so the outside world couldn't intrude.

"I'll cut right to it," he started, and Zane dropped a stack of file folders on the table. Each of us reached to grab one. "Angel was originally designed by an NSA programmer as data backup for intelligence gathered overseas. I signed off on the program as it was presented as a way to facilitate a communication bridge between agencies. The intelligence community would have a centralized database they could all use."

"Let me guess, they found a way to misuse it?" Jaxon interrupted.

"That would be an understatement. It was almost immediately implemented to spy on the American people. As soon as I got word, I shut it down."

"Spy how? The normal telecommunication marker word taps?" Leo asked.

Most people in the US knew that if you were speaking on the phone and used certain words or word phrases, the government would record and analyze your call.

"No." The president looked like he was tired. "Total intrusion. Angel can access your cell phone camera and mic. Same with tablets and computers. An everyday American could be innocently walking into the grocery store and could be geo-tracked and, without their knowledge, any conversations they had could be recorded, analyzed, and stored."

"Nothing new," Linc muttered.

"I need to explain the gravity of the NSA's abuse of power. Imagine the unsuspecting population, sitting in the privacy of their own homes, having a conversation, and not knowing that those popular smart devices and virtual assistants had been recording their every word. While you think asking it to turn on your favorite music, order your laundry detergent, or tell you the latest news is convenient, being reconnoitered by a fucking speaker is probably not what people thought they were getting. People have refrigerators that are now chipped as a listening device."

"Other than the obvious infringement, what does the NSA have to gain? Targeting individuals on terror watchlists, I can understand. Everyday people? What's the play?" I asked.

"Power. There're infinite possibilities on how to use the intel gathered. Election fraud, warrantless surveillance, control, forecasting crimes, and illegal detainment. And let's not forget greed. Private corporations have their hands out as well. Not only do they fund the program but they have their own programmers involved. Independent contractors such as Warren are working side by side with the NSA, buying their way into a goldmine of intel."

"The golden age of surveillance. Even our goddamn tele-visions come with a warning not to talk about sensitive information because you're being recorded," Declan growled. "Utter bullshit. We willingly keep tracking devices on our person: watches, cell phones, and nanny-cams in our homes, everything is exploited."

"How did you find out?" I inquired.

"A Good Samaritan, who strongly believes in the consti-tution and fourth amendment, came forward. He saw what was going on and felt it was his moral duty to stop it. After I received the information, I waited a few weeks and contacted Greenwold. I made a surprise visit to an NSA black site and told him to shut the program down."

"Yet, you didn't dismiss Greenwold," Zane stated.

"Not until I knew how deep this went. Who else in my administration knew? Did my National Security Advisor know? Did the vice president? Someone in a congressional oversight committee had to know where millions of dollars were going. They always fucking do. Who received the kick-back for turning a blind-eye?"

"What now?" I asked.

"Now we watch them," Zane answered.

"And we do that how?"

"Tex." Zane smiled, both of his dimples showing.

Nothing good ever came from Zane Lewis being giddy. It meant he had a plan, one that no doubt would end with scumbags being six feet under.

"He's fucked. How can he help when his system was breeched?" Linc questioned.

"Tex is at the White House now. I sent Garrett and the Gold Team to PA to watch over Melody and the kids while he's here."

"You got Tex to the White House?" Leo whistled. "He must be pissed."

There were very few things that would make Tex leave his wife and kids behind in Pennsylvania, not to mention his plethora of machines. He didn't need to leave the house to implement a hostile takeover of the world. The man was that good.

"Pissed doesn't begin to cover how angry he is. Every single woman he's outfitted with tracking devices were potentially put in harm's way. The wives of his closest friends, abuse victims on the run that he helps, paramilitary contractors are now in jeopardy, and then there's what happened to Colin and Erin. He's not mad; he's positively, certifiably insane. I thought I had a short fuse and a bad temper, but Tex passed DEFCON about a mile back. I was a little afraid of him when we set him up at the White House," Zane told the room.

"I've given Tex everything he needs to shut this shit down." The president's tone was icy, but it was his stare that had my attention. It was cool and calculating and an impassive gaze he'd no doubt learned during his years as a UDT. The man was not to be trifled with. "I have every confidence

Tex will have the information he needs in a few days. Once his investigation is done, you'll be given the go-ahead to move in. Zane, I've never been one to tell you how to command your team or do your job but I will offer you these two words—extreme prejudice."

"Loud and clear," Zane returned.

"I'm headed back to Washington now and have a scheduled meeting at Camp David in five days. I hope this can be resolved by then." He turned to me and asked, "How's Erin?"

"As expected. She had a nightmare last night, but had no recollection of it when she woke up. She hasn't had any issues with her concussion and she'll go back to the doctor tomorrow for another CT scan."

"So you'll be in D.C. tomorrow?"

"Correct."

"I'd like to see you both after her appointment if you can spare the time."

I didn't like the ominous tone and readily agreed. I'd never witnessed him being anything but confident, but before I could place the emotion crossing his face he'd closed down.

Zane left to walk the president to the rooftop helipad, leaving the rest of us to go over the SITREP he'd provided.

"This shit is jacked," Linc commented.

"Anyone else pick up on Tom's demeanor?" I asked.

Something was screaming at me that the situation was about to go FUBAR. I'd learned a long time ago to trust my gut and it was telling me something was wrong.

"It was hard to miss. Think he knows something he's not sharing?" Jax asked.

"No. I think he laid it out for us. Though, he's not stupid. He must know there's more at play than the NSA spying," Leo added.

"The question is *what*." I continued to scan the papers in

front of me with a sinking feeling we were missing something.

"The *what* will present itself. It always does." Linc was correct, I only hoped it wasn't too late when we figured it out.

"Greenwold give you anything?" I asked.

"Not a goddamn thing that's useful. We didn't have as much time with him as we wanted. All he said was they're always watching. Not sure if he meant the NSA or someone else."

"I don't think he meant the NSA. I think this is bigger than Tom wants to admit."

"I think you're right," Linc agreed.

This was one instance I wished I was wrong. Bigger was not always better.

CHAPTER 21

"How did your meeting go?" I asked when we were in the car on the way back to Colin's house.

"Fine. The normal upcoming scheduling and payroll shit. Nothing exciting."

"I thought my—"

"How do you feel about grilling some steaks tonight?" He shook his head and put his finger to his lips.

All righty, it didn't take a rocket scientist to figure out he didn't want to talk about his meeting. He'd been so forthcoming lately, something new must've happened, and the swift change worried me.

"That sounds good."

"How did it go with Olivia?"

"Good. I tried to talk to her about why I'd been so distant, but she dismissed me and said it wasn't a big deal and she understood."

"I told you she wasn't mad."

"Yeah, well, I was still nervous. Ivy and Violet are really great. It's still so strange to see my cousin with kids. She's changed a lot."

"How so?"

I tried to think about how to explain the change in Jasmin. My cousin was hard as nails and just as tough as the men on her team. I suppose that came from her time in the Army. The only time I'd ever seen her break was when Linc had been presumed dead. She was at the White House monitoring a mission the guys were going on and she'd watched the house Linc was supposed to be in blow up. She'd lost it. My mom spent hours with her, trying to calm her down. Thankfully, Linc had escaped and he'd been rescued. But Jasmin had been a mess.

"I can't say she's gone soft, because that's not exactly it, but she only said fuck about fifty-two times instead of her normal five hundred. And when she found out Ivy and Violet were both pregnant, she didn't roll her eyes. She smiled and congratulated them."

"Wait. What? Ivy's pregnant, too?"

Shit. I hadn't meant to tell him that.

"Um, forget I said that."

"No shit. That's great."

"I'm already breaking the girl code and telling you secrets. Please don't tell Zane I spilled. I don't want Ivy mad at me. We had a really great time, and I want to be invited out with them again."

"Sunshine, neither would be mad. You're going to learn there are no such things as secrets in this group. But I wouldn't say anything. I'll wait for Zane to make the announcement."

"Really? I know a secret, and it's a really big one."

"Zane and Ivy got married yesterday at the courthouse?" he asked.

"Dammit. How'd you know?"

Colin reached over and placed his hand on my thigh. It was amazing how comforting his touch was.

"I know all." He chuckled.

"Come on. Really? How'd you know?"

"You know my job isn't exactly safe."

"I know."

"So, we have contingency plans in the event we don't come home from an op." That was a nice way of saying in case they died. I wasn't sure I liked where this conversation was headed or if I wanted to know the information he was about to tell me. "One is the company will financially take care of our spouse and children. Zane added Ivy to the policy yesterday and today the rest of us had to sign the paperwork. Each team has their own policy and Zane is covered by my teams'."

"Is it like life insurance?"

"Kinda. But better. We all have death benefits. This fund is for the extras. A little peace of mind knowing our families won't go without."

"How many teams are there?"

"Three. Blue, Gold, and us."

"Which one came to . . . get us?"

I couldn't get myself to say rescue. Get us sounded like they'd leisurely stopped by someplace Colin and I were visiting and offered us a ride home. I liked that explanation much better than the real version.

"Gold. Brooks, Max, Thad, and Kyle. Declan is taking over as team leader. They are our ghost team. They've been mainly deployed to the middle east. They specialize in stopping piracy and smuggling, both on land and in the Arabian Gulf. The major trade routes there are inundated with stolen antiquities and human commerce. It requires constant monitoring, so they stay there most of the time."

"What about Blue?"

"Blue comes and goes, but they've been gone more than

they've been home the last few years. They specialize in maritime piracy. They mostly stay on big freight ships."

"And your team? What do you specialize in?"

"Everything."

"I knew you were gonna say that."

We pulled into the driveway of Colin's house, and for the first time I really looked at the surrounding area.

"You kinda live in the middle of nowhere."

"How do you figure that, sunshine? Downtown Annapolis is fifteen minutes away and the mall is like twenty."

"Okay, fine, but you have no neighbors out here."

"You don't like it?"

My heart constricted at the concern in his voice.

"No, I do, it's peaceful out here. Just making an observation. I hadn't paid that much attention when we first came here."

"Because if you don't—"

"Colin, I said I did. I agree it's nice not living right next to someone. Remember when we were at Abe's and I told you I'd be happy living out there. Your place is perfect." He turned the car off but before he could open the door I added, "Besides, this way we can have private time in the hot tub on your deck and no one will see."

I loved the hungry look he got whenever I mentioned us being intimate. Now, if I could just get him to act on the emotion, I'd be golden.

"Our deck."

"What?"

"It's our house, Erin. And if you'd prefer to live somewhere else, we can sell this place and move. If you want to stay in D.C. I'll make the commute to Annapolis for work. Though I'd like for you to be close to Olivia and the other women. It'll make things easier on you when I leave on a work trip. But I understand if you don't want to give up your life in Washington."

In all the craziness I hadn't thought much about where we'd live or what would happen when he eventually had to go on a mission.

"There's nothing for me in D.C. I mean my parents are there for the next year, but when my dad's term is over they'll go back to Texas. That was the deal my parents made. My mom wants to retire there."

"We have the house in Killeen. Anytime you want to go there and visit them, we will."

"I love you, Colin. Thank you."

"You, too, sunshine. Let's get in the house."

Weirdly, he held his cell phone out and raised his eyebrows. I fished mine out of my bag and showed it to him. He nodded and opened the glove box, placing his in there and motioned for me to do the same. I had no idea what was going on, but I trusted Colin, and if he wanted my phone left in the car, I wasn't going to question him.

When I opened my own door and stepped out of the car before Colin could come around, he lifted a brow in reprimand.

"Seriously? We're in the garage, and the door is closed. Surely I can get out by myself."

"Not the point, Erin. The gentlemanly thing to do is to open your door."

"Are you telling me you're a gentleman?"

He was a lot of things, rough and ready, badass, lethal, sexy, smart, and kind. But I wouldn't classify Colin as a gentleman.

"With some things I am." The side of his mouth pulled up into a suggestive grin.

"And what things might those be?"

He tugged my good hand and pulled me into him. I loved

how much bigger he was than me. How, when he held me close, I was fully enveloped in his embrace. It was warm and safe, and I wanted to stay in his arms forever.

His head lowered, and he huskily whispered, "I'll always open doors for you. I'll always make sure you have the best seat when we're out. If you're chilly I'll always offer you my coat. If there's a puddle, I'll carry you over it. And, sunshine, I promise, you'll always take your pleasure before I do."

The tingling I'd grown accustomed to started, and I wanted to yell at him for turning me on when I knew there was nothing he'd do to help with the ache.

"You play dirty."

"I do. Dirty is fun."

"Ugh. Colin. Stop."

Standing in the garage he kissed me. Tongues tangled, and moans mingled. By the time he pulled back I was dazed.

"Come on, sunshine, let's get you inside."

I wordlessly followed, surprised when he passed the kitchen and led me to the master bedroom. He left me standing next to the unmade bed and went into the bathroom. I heard the water turn on and he reappeared shirtless. It took him no time to have me fully undressed. His pants and boxer briefs were the last to be tossed in the pile. This was not my first time seeing Colin nude, but it might as well have been the way my eyes roamed over his chiseled form. His chest was devoid of any hair, giving me an unobstructed view of his pecs. His well-defined six-pack was so damn hot I wanted to lick every individual valley. Below his bellybutton was a trail of light hair leading to a patch of trimmed pubic hair.

"Are you done?" Colin chuckled.

"Not yet. I haven't gotten to the good part yet. My eyes got stuck on your six-pack."

The laughter that filled the room was magical. I loved

hearing him happy, liked it even more when I was the source. His muscles jumped and twitched, and I found it fascinating to watch.

He led me into the shower, testing the water before he had me step in before him.

Colin held me close as the warm water sluiced around us. "You're so beautiful, Erin."

"Thank you."

We stood in companionable silence for a time, simply enjoying the feel of each other. When he stepped back to adjust the water, I picked up a bar of soap and lathered my hands before placing them on his chest.

"Do these still hurt?" I roamed over the bruises on his chest and lower to his stomach, avoiding his ribs.

"No. I'm sorry you have to see them. They'll be gone soon."

"I don't like that you were hurt, but I know you received every one of these marks protecting me. I will forever be grateful."

He lifted his hand and traced the tiny cut on my forehead. There was barely a bruise. Not like Colin, his face still looked like he'd gone twenty rounds in a boxing ring. It was a miracle he hadn't been hurt worse.

"I should've—" he started.

"Done exactly what you did. It's over. That's what you said. We can't go back and change anything. We're both here and alive. At the end of the day, that's all that matters, right?"

"Right."

He was humoring me by agreeing, but I'd take it. I needed all the reassurances he'd offer. I knew there was something else going on, and it scared me, but if Colin said I was safe, I'd believe him. I had to, his protection was the only thing keeping me sane. I couldn't fall apart, not when we weren't out of the woods yet. And if I thought about everything that had happened or looked too long at the marks on his face, or allowed the what-ifs to creep in, I'd lose it.

"You're thinking too hard." He kissed my temple. "Stop that and wash me, woman."

"Is this how our marriage is going to be? We shower, and you stand like a king while the lowly peasant girl bathes his royal highness?"

"Hmm, I like the way you think. Role play could be fun."

"Then I want you to be a medieval warrior and I'll be the fair maiden waiting for you to come home after a mighty battle. I can tend to your aching muscles before you ravish me." I could feel his body shaking under my palms as he tried to hold in his amusement. "Oh, wait, I know. You'll be the Spartan King Leonidas and I'll be Queen Gorgo, waiting for you to return with your shield and sword . . ." Colin's body stiffened, and he tilted his head. "What's wrong?"

"Queen Gorgo?"

"Surely you know who that is. The wife of Leonidas, the fiercest woman in Sparta's history."

"Yes, sunshine, I am well aware of who she is. I'm just surprised you do."

I loved history and once upon a time I wanted to be a history teacher, ancient Egypt and Greece were my favorites. My fondness of the subject fizzed once the 1800s came about.

"I studied ancient and medieval history in college."

He turned around, showing me his back. He had several tattoos. One was his family name across his shoulder blades and another was a shield, above it was the word "IF." I'd already seen them, so I wasn't sure why he was showing me now.

"Do you know what that means?"

I could only assume he meant the word "IF," his last name being obvious. "Of course. The word, "IF" is one of the single most important words in Spartan history. King Philip was invading Greece and he sent a letter to the Spartans saying 'If I win this war, you'll be slaves forever' the Spartans sent back a single word, 'IF.'"

He slowly turned back around and stared down at me. "You have no idea how much it turns me on that you know the meaning of my tattoo."

"You're weird."

"And you, sunshine, are my Spartan Queen."

"Does that mean I can only give you sons, since Spartan women are said to have been the only women of their time that produce real men?"

"Goddamn, it's so sexy you know that. Boys, girls, I don't care. As long as there are little ones running around our house the gender doesn't matter to me."

I locked eyes with my future husband and as crazy as it was he thought knowing random facts about history was sexy, I was happy he did. Though I was concentrating more on his statement about children. He wanted them, and I wanted to give them to him. Suddenly his mom's request for a million grandchildren didn't seem so silly.

CHAPTER 22

"How many kids do you want?" Erin asked.

"As many as you'll give me."

There'd been a reason I'd brought her into the shower, but the moment I pulled her naked body against mine all thoughts about today's meeting and what she needed to know flew out the window.

"What if I want to be like those people on TV and have nineteen and homeschool them all in a Texas compound?"

"Good thing you're young then. That's a lot of baby making."

Her small hands moved over my stomach, the soap had long washed away but her palms still glided easily over my wet skin. Before I could stop her, she gripped my dick with one hand, giving it a firm tug.

"I want to start the baby making tonight."

"Not until the doctor gives you the all clear."

"It's already been two days."

"It's *only* been two days."

I could hear the frustration in her voice, and I felt it, too. We'd gone to bed each night wrapped in each other's arms, limbs tangled together, and my throbbing cock trapped between us. However I'd rather cut my own arm off than hurt her. There was no way we were making love until she received a clean bill of health.

"Colin, I'm dying. I want you so badly."

"Turn around. Put your hands on the wall."

Her eyes flared in excitement. There wasn't a chance I was going to fuck her, and her first time certainly wouldn't be in a shower bent over but I could give her some relief. I molded my body to hers and let my hands roam the way they'd been dying to over the last few days. Starting with her full breasts and down her soft belly. My mouth latched onto her shoulder blade and nipped and licked while one hand made its way between her legs.

"Spread 'em," I murmured against her skin.

I circled her slit with two fingers, toying with the opening before I pushed them in.

"Goddamn, you're wet."

Erin's hips bucked, causing my cock to slide over her ass. The friction was enough to make me pause and try to stop my need to come. Why was it that every time we touched, I was on the verge of coming?

"Stay still, sunshine."

"That's not going to be possible."

I pinched her nipple and rolled it between my fingers before I told her, "You're gonna have to try. Let me do all the work. All you need to do is let go."

With two fingers moving deep inside of her, I lowered my other hand to her clit and trapped her against me. In a coordinated assault, I worked Erin into a frenzy.

"That's it, sunshine. You're so slick and tight I can't wait to make love to you." My hips moved in time with my fingers. With my cock trapped between us, gliding over her slippery backside, my own orgasm built.

"Colin!"

"Come on, let go."

Her head hung forward, and her body locked, and her pussy clamped around my fingers as she moaned long and loud. Just the sound of her chanting my name as she came around my fingers was enough to detonate my orgasm. Come shot out of the head of my cock, and I hoped I could keep us upright. Every encounter with Erin was the same —explosive.

When her orgasm waned, she sagged in my arms, I steadied her on her feet before I turned her back to the spray.

"You okay?" She nodded and smiled. "Your head?"

"Fine."

"Lean back."

She did as I asked, wetting her long, brown hair. I picked up a bottle of shampoo and squirted some in my hand. I'd never washed a woman's hair before, I'd never had the desire to. Actually, I'd never showered with a woman period. The act was more intimate than I'd allowed in the past. And showering now, with Erin, I knew I'd been right. There was something oddly personal about bathing with her I felt vulnerable and exposed. I was comfortable in my nudity, but standing before her, caring for her, and she for me, made me feel cherished. Which was an emotion I'd never felt and never believed I would ever feel. However, as we stood under the spray, taking turns washing each other, that was exactly what I felt.

"All done," I announced when I finished rinsing the last of the conditioner out of her hair.

"Thank you, that was wonderful."

"I like taking care of you."

She opened her eyes, and I quickly wiped the leftover suds off her brow before they could drip any lower.

"I like taking care of you, too. Thank you for letting me."

"Why are you thanking me, sunshine? It is no hardship having you touch me."

"Touching and taking care of are two different things. You're the type of man who takes care of others. But I don't think you allow anyone to take care of you."

It was amazing how well she could read me. There were plenty of things we'd never talked about, my desire to feel needed being one of them. Lots of little things I was looking forward to discovering and sharing. Tidbits of information we'd spend years weeding through. I couldn't remember a time in my life I'd ever been excited to see what the future held.

"You'd be correct." I leaned forward for a quick peck to her lips. "Before we get out, there's something we need to discuss."

"And it needs to take place in the shower?"

"Yep. Earlier you asked about my meeting." Erin's smile faded, and she was instantly on alert. I hated worrying her, but she needed to know the facts. "I'm sorry I blew you off in the car, but it wasn't safe to talk about it there. Your dad further explained what the Angel program is and what it's being used for. There's a lot I can't tell you. Not because I don't trust you or want you to know, but because I'm sworn not to tell *anyone*. All you need to know and understand is nothing of importance is to be discussed anywhere but here in the shower, and never with any electronic device nearby. Expect any email or telephone conversations you have to be monitored."

"Holy shit. That bad?"

"Worse than I'd thought. We need to be careful. As a matter of fact, let's not even talk about your dad at all, or anything that has happened. Don't mention Fletch and his team or Tex. For the next little while let's pretend we are Mr.

and Mrs. Jones. You are not the president's daughter, and I'm not a mercenary."

"So we pretend to be normal?"

I was grateful her smile was back. I was fast learning that Erin's moods could and would change with the second hand on a clock. But, mostly, I'd figured out she doesn't like the unknown. Once she has the facts and feels secure, she could handle anything. Just like the Spartan Queen we were talking about earlier.

"I thought you wanted normal?" I reminded her.

"But so soon into our relationship? I mean who wants normal this early? I'd always heard that once a groom says I do, it really means I do *not* take my wife on dates or woo her anymore but who knew it could happen before the nuptials."

"I believe the saying goes when a wife says I do, it really means I do *not* give blow jobs anymore."

"Huh? That would be a shame, personally, I quite enjoy you in my mouth."

Erin's face lit, and I laughed at her quick comeback. All those months with her, how had I missed how witty and funny she was? I wanted to go back in time and kick my own ass for being so blind.

CHAPTER 23

"Mom, I'm fine. I swear. The MRI even proved it. Clear bill of health. I may resume all activities except those that could cause a head injury. Lucky for us, I have no plans to learn how to box, so I'm fine."

I was sitting next to my mom in the private residence. On the very couch I'd cuddled to her side and bawled my eyes out after Lisa Howell told me no one was going to ask me to my senior prom because everyone thought I had a stick up my ass. The same couch I used to lay on when I had the flu, and my mom would sit beside me on the chair next to the sofa and watch me sleep. I would have known if she'd left the room, because sometimes I wasn't asleep. I'd close my eyes and pretend, just to see if she'd stay—she always did.

"What about another MRI? When is your follow-up appointment?"

"There are no more. Today was the follow-up."

I was done talking about my concussion. Colin had already grilled the poor doctor at Walter Reed this morning. We'd stayed almost a full hour in the man's office after the results came back, discussing every possible scenario. I was so over people talking about my head. I felt fine and hadn't even had any headaches or dizziness after the initial impact.

"I owe you an apology, Mom."

"Why on earth would you owe me an apology?"

"For starters, I've been a pain in the ass to you and Dad over the last year." I smiled when my mother's lips flattened. A lady doesn't curse, after all.

"Erin, sweetheart—"

"Mom, you know it's true. I just want you to know I'm embarrassed over how I behaved. I also need to acknowledge I've been rather selfish."

"Selfish? There is not a selfish bone in your body, dear. You give of yourself more than anyone I know. We are very proud of you."

"No, Mama. Selfish in the way I felt about you and Dad and the time you both spent working."

My mother's face fell, and she looked at her lap. Damn this was not going the way I'd hoped.

"What I mean to say is, you and Dad have set an example that I could not be more grateful for. Mama, please look at me." She lifted her tear-filled eyes to mine. "I'm blessed to have a mother who has taught me the importance of family, community, working hard, and service to others. Through your actions you've taught me all I need to know about being a wife and mom one day. How to be a strong person. I am so proud to call you my mama. I'm proud of you, for all you've accomplished. But most of all, I'm honored to have you as a friend. I won't squander our time together ever again."

My mother carefully patted her cheeks, brushing away her tears. I couldn't help but to giggle. Always the lady, even in private. There would be no streaks on my mother's face—ever.

"Maybe I should have—"

"Done nothing differently. This is on me, Mom. Me behaving like a spoiled brat."

"Sweetheart, every daughter needs her mama."

"And, thankfully, I had you. You were there for me every time I needed you. Any time it mattered. You have a tough job, tougher than Dad does. You're the one that holds this family together. You support Dad in every way and give him the strength he needs to run this country. You're a wife, a mom, and a Halloween costume designer." I smiled, remembering all the dress-up clothes she'd made for me. "You're a cook, a party planner, and a homework checker. I can't even list all your jobs. And I haven't even touched on your duties as the first lady."

"Thank you for saying that."

"It's the truth." She opened her arms, and I gladly leaned into her embrace—Clarissa Anderson gave the best hugs. They were warm and heartfelt. She'd never withheld her affection. Not from me or my father. They were demonstrative when we were in private. There was no doubt my parents loved each other deeply, and me as well.

"I love you to the moon, little rabbit," my mom whispered and kissed my head.

I sighed at the old, familiar nickname and cuddled in closer. My parents had called me, little rabbit until I'd become an obnoxious teenager and deemed myself too old for the name. I think my dad started it after I asked him to read me *Guess How Much I Love You* for the five hundredth time.

"And all the way back," I finished.

There was a knock on the door, and my mom slowly pulled back, straightening her skirt before she turned in the direction of the sound.

"Yes?"

"Excuse me, ma'am. Miss Anderson," the secret service

agent started. "Mrs. Parker, Mrs. Cain, Mrs. Lewis, and Mrs. Gillonardo are here to see you. They were not on your schedule but they are on your approved list. Would you like me to send them up?"

"Yes, of course. And would you please ask Betty to send up some refreshments. Oh, and make sure there is a can of Dr. Pepper included."

"Yes, ma'am."

"Dr. Pepper?" I laughed. "You don't drink soda."

"No, but I know poor Olivia would like one. You know when I was pregnant with you, I still drank coffee and had iced tea everyday. I don't buy into this whole no caffeine thing. Look at you, you came out perfect."

"Thanks, Mom. What else did you do? Smoke a pack a day?"

"Erin! I've never smoked a day in my life. Though I did try one of my daddy's cigars once. My girlfriends and I snuck into Daddy's study and got into his bourbon." My mom chuckled, and her slow Texan twang came out. "We were drunker than Cooter Brown. Molly Hayworth thought we should smoke a cigar. We were sophisticated ladies, you know."

"How old were you?" I couldn't help but laugh at my mom.

"We were sixteen and tying one on for sure. Anyway, we finally got it lit, and I was getting lightheaded from trying to inhale. We were a mess."

"What happened?"

"Daddy came home early and caught us. He was madder than a wet hen." My mom was grinning ear to ear. "Not because we were in his study smokin' his cigar, but we'd drank his expensive, sixteen-year-old bourbon." My mom stopped to laugh some more. "Daddy was yelling the house down about how a bunch of girls had wasted a bottle of twenty-four-hundred-dollar whiskey. He wasn't wrong, the whole bottle was gone, and we spent the rest of the night taking turns in the bathroom upchucking."

We were both laughing at my mom's retelling of her wild years when the girls walked in.

"Sorry to interrupt," Liv said.

"Nonsense. Come in." My mom waved them into the living room.

"What's so funny?" Jasmin asked, pushing a stroller.

"My mom was just telling about her drinking her—"

"Erin Lynn Anderson. Hush up now." Boy, it was easy to ruffle my mom. "Bring those babies over here and let me see them."

Jasmin pushed the huge contraption in my mom's direction. "Do you have any idea how hard it was to get this up here? I was worried, Asher and Robby were going to need a full cavity inspection. Sheesh."

"She's not joking. Everyone is a little uptight today. Everything okay?" Violet asked.

"Yes. Yes. You know how it is. Now, what did you bring?" My mom pointed to the box in Olivia's arms.

"Wedding magazines." She smiled.

"And I picked up a planning book, just in case Colin gives you time to plan. Though Zane said Colin said he wanted to marry you, like, yesterday." Ivy pulled a spiral organizer out of her bag.

"And Leo told me last night that Colin said he would marry you today if you'd agree," Liv threw in. "Oh, and he does want kids. Like, a lot."

"Today?" The four women standing in front of me all nodded. "That's crazy."

"Let's all sit down," my mom offered. "What kind of wedding do you want, Erin?" She cut straight to the chase.

"I don't know."

With everything that had been going on, I hadn't begun to think about planning a wedding.

"Big? Small?" Violet asked.

"Small. Just us. I don't want any publicity. No reporters or gossip rags. I don't want anyone outside of this room even knowing. Except Colin's family, of course. The media has made my life hell, I won't let them ruin this."

"Small then. Would you like a long engagement?" my mom inquired.

"No. I want to marry Colin as soon as possible."

"Your dad and I would like that very much. We discussed it last night. Of course, you can have any size wedding, and at any venue you'd both like, but we knew you'd want a small gathering. We were thinking the Blue Room would be nice—"

"No. Not the Blue Room. I want to get married here, in this room."

"Here? In the living room? But there are so many places—"

"Here is perfect. Here in this room where you are simply my mom, and dad is just dad. Here, where we're a normal, everyday family. This is where I want to do it. I'll talk to Colin tonight."

"You don't have to, he says yes," Jasmin said as she rocked one of the babies.

"No, he doesn't. I have to ask."

"No. You don't. Zane said Colin said he'd marry you any time, any place. So, he says yes to getting married here."

"There sure is a lot of he said, he said going around the office for a bunch of badass commandos." I laughed.

"Please. They gossip more than any women I know. There are no secrets with them." Ivy shook her head. "So, now that we know the where. Let's plan. You need a dress, flowers, a cake . . ."

Ivy prattled on, but I no longer heard what she was saying. Not because I didn't care, but because it was like I was living in a dream world. A world I never thought I'd have. I had friends. Real friends who liked me for me. A handsome, strong, smart man who loved me despite our rocky start. And my mom. She looked so happy I couldn't stop staring at her. If I end up living my life half as well as her it will have been a life worth living.

CHAPTER 24

"Whaт's with all the extra security?" Zane asked when he entered the situation room where the president and I were waiting. "How'd Erin's appointment go?"

"Good. She's all clear."

"That's good news, Olivia's been worried," Leo said.

"Yeah. Thanks."

Once everyone was in the room and the door was closed, Tom tapped a brown folder in front of him. "This is why."

He slid the folder in my direction. I opened it and cringed. It was an eight by ten image of a man lying dead from a gunshot wound to the back of the head.

"Who is this?" I pushed the picture toward Zane.

"My informant, Brent Benzo. A man I've told no one about. Not even the five of you knew who'd given me the information on the Angel program. Not a single soul knew."

"When did this happen?" Zane asked, shuffling through the pictures.

"This morning. He was entering an NSA black site. The building is in Richmond, Virginia."

"What's the note say?" I asked, scrutinizing the image closer. There looked to be a piece of paper in Brent's hand.

Tom shuffled through the file until he pulled out the pictures he wanted.

"Any place. Any time," Zane read the message. "Tex any closer?"

"Yes, he's putting together the pieces. He's happier than a pig in shit down in the basement. Gerard delivers his meals personally and keeps him watered. No one else in the White House but the two of us know he's down there, and I don't think he's slept," Tom told the group.

"He's hunting." I chuckled. "Men don't sleep when they hunt."

"I've moved my meeting up. I leave for Camp David tomorrow. Gerard will stay here, as far as the rest of my detail will know, he has a stomach bug and can't fly. I'll be back by dinner."

"Do you think that's wise?" Zane asked before I could.

"When have I ever given into a threat? Do you think some fuckwit is going to stop me from running this country?"

Tom Anderson was a lot of things, one who backs down wasn't one of them. Even if it meant putting himself in danger. I guess I knew where Erin got it from.

"All I'm saying is, someone with extreme capabilities took out your man. They've taken Erin. Maybe postponing your trip is the smart thing to do," Zane tried to appeal to his sensible side.

"All the more reason for me to go. Right now, someone thinks they have me by the balls. But they're about to find out mine are made of brass, and I will never give in."

Zane let out a sigh. "I figured you say that. Let's go over what we know."

"This is Tex's latest SITREP."

Tom handed the situation report to Zane. While he was

going over the latest intel, I studied the picture of the crime scene.

"I see two surveillance cameras on the building." I pointed to the picture. "Where's the footage?"

"Tex is working on that now. He's also checking traffic and security feeds from the surrounding buildings," the president answered.

"Listen up," Zane started. "Tex found the connection between Warren and the NSA. Get your note cards ready because this shit is layers deep. Warren has been employed by Camio-Telecomm for the last year. They were running in the red until Warren came aboard and Camio was awarded an 889-million-dollar DOD contract. The North America Industry Standard code shows the scope of work awarded as telemarketing and product services in the amount of 660 million."

"We know the NAICS codes for the contract are bullshit. What's the real contract for?" Linc inquired.

"Information gathering," Zane continued. "After the contract was awarded, Camio acquired a small media outlet for an overinflated price. It was a bad move on Camio's part, but with the government money coming in they could afford it. Once Tom nixed Angel, the contract was terminated."

"So, Camio is behind Erin's abduction and the threats against Tom," Jaxon stated.

"What was the information being collected used for?" I asked. "I'm not tracking how spying on the American people would help telemarking."

"But it would help the news outlet Camio purchased," Leo deduced.

"Bingo." Zane tossed the SITREP on the table. "Once Camio knows how the general population feels on any given topic they can control the narrative. Either in support of the topic or against. How easy will it be for them to put out false information and influence public perception one way or another. Interference, meddling, and manipulation."

"Warren wasn't after influencing anyone," I told the room. "His sole purpose was revenge. He wanted me dead to rub Zane's face in it. He didn't care about anything else."

"I agree." Zane's voice hardened. "Two birds, Colin. He got to line his pockets and piss on me. That is until he underestimated you."

Just thinking about Warren had my blood boiling. He'd set all of this in motion because Zane had exposed his lying ass for the coward he was. He'd stalked Erin, scared her, kidnapped her, and tried to kill me.

"Smart bastard," I said.

"What?" Declan turned to look at me.

"He knew. He didn't give the first fuck about Angel. He fucking knew Tom would never actually cave and reinstate the program, even if he took Erin. As soon as Tom had her back, he'd shut that shit down. Hell, he'd dismantle the whole cyber division if he had to. But Warren knew, once there was a threat against Erin, he'd hire us to protect her. He never cared who was with her, only that Camio took her and her guard alive."

Not a word was spoken, but every man in the room knew I was right. It could've been any one of us hanging in that room, and Warren would've been satisfied. His only objective was to torture Zane Lewis.

But there were still too many loose ends. We were missing something.

"Where does Greenwold fit into this? He's the asshole that's behind the cameras in Erin's apartment and hiring those guys to run us off the road. I'm assuming Tex has figured out the cyber, counter-intelligence department is behind his system breech?"

"He's still working on it, but that is the assumption, yes," Tom answered.

"And the other 229 million from the contract? Where did that go?" Zane asked.

I'd completely missed the extra money. It was a damn good thing Zane had the ability to keep his emotions in check, because right then, I was too angry remembering the look on Erin's face when Warren told her he was going to kill me. How she'd endangered herself to come to my rescue while the pussy needed me chained up in order to beat me. But more than all that, I was concerned Erin had watched me kill him. I hadn't brought it up or asked her how she felt about it. I was too afraid. The last thing I wanted was to draw attention to what she'd witnessed but I needed to.

"Hasn't been found," Tom told him.

"Are you sure you don't want to wait and stay—"

"No. Business as usual." Tom remained firm in his response.

Damn stubborn man.

"Change of topic," the president announced. "I hear the women are upstairs planning your upcoming wedding."

My five teammates chuckled. I had to admit I was happy I wasn't involved with the planning. I didn't care where or when. As far as I was concerned, the sooner the better.

"I'm happy to hear that."

"Any requests?"

"Twenty-four hours' notice so I can get my parents here."

"And your sister?"

"Deployed with her ship. I doubt her command will fly her home for a wedding. We know the drill."

"More than most," the president agreed.

My parents did understand more than most. With two children who served they had no choice but to learn to go with the flow. Sometimes leave was scheduled and then was taken back. Deployments came to end, until they were extended. The assholes in the world didn't care about things like holidays, birthdays, weddings, or babies being born. Bad people didn't take a vacation just because the calendar said so. Keira would be sad she missed my wedding, but she'd do what she always did while she was deployed—her job. She was a great sailor, and even if she wasn't there physically, she'd send her love. She always did.

CHAPTER 25

"LET ME GUESS, this is why you bought this house," I said to Colin as we walked through the wooded area of his property.

"It is. We have fifteen acres back here."

There it was again—we. He now did it with everything. *We* have a house in Texas. *Our* car, *our* hot tub, *our* life. Each and every time he said it, I wanted to pinch myself to make sure I wasn't back in my D.C. apartment dreaming all of this up.

"As much as I love it here, and spending time with you, I know you brought me back here for a reason. What's wrong?"

He stopped walking but didn't let go of my hand. Not only had I had an MRI today, but the doctor had taken off the stupid bandage on my right hand. The cut I had on my palm was healing nicely and didn't hurt. I wouldn't be swinging across monkey bars on it anytime soon, but everyday activity didn't bother it.

"You didn't ask about my meeting today." Before I could remind him, he'd told me not to talk about anything important he went on. "But I know you're interested and I told you I'd tell you what I could."

His blue eyes bore into mine, and he looked extremely uneasy.

"What happened? Is everything all right?"

"We're getting closer to puzzling everything out. Remember the man Warren, the one I . . ." His words trailed off.

"Yeah, of course I do." Colin winced, and I wondered why he'd flinch thinking about a dead man who'd tried to kill him.

"We were the reason you were taken. My team and I. Warren was obsessed with Zane and was hell-bent on some sort of sick revenge. He knew if someone threatened you, your dad would hire Z Corps to protect you. He used the people he was working for, convinced them to take you and, in the process, me, too."

"That seems like a lot of work to get revenge. Wouldn't it have been easier to hire someone to just kill you?" Shit. That came out wrong. "I didn't mean—"

"I know how you meant it, sunshine. Do you know what the going rate for a hit is?"

"Hmm, that would be a no. I've never tried to hire a hit man."

"You're talking about half a million for a good one. Now triple that for a man like me."

I was afraid to ask what that meant. I could guess, but I didn't want confirmation.

"That's a lot of money."

"Money Warren didn't have. So he went through the trouble."

"But he's dead. So you're safe now, right?"

"Yes, *we* are safe now." Colin tightened his grip on my

hand. "I want to talk to you about what happened. What you saw."

"I know never to tell anyone," I rushed out.

"Sunshine, I'm not worried about anyone knowing what I did. I'm worried about what you saw."

"What about it?"

I was confused and thought back to that day and tried to remember the details. Which was odd, because I'd been striving to forget them. But if there was something I'd missed or forgotten that could help them put the last puzzle pieces together, I'd try.

"You saw me kill a man. I think we need to talk about that."

"No, you didn't."

"Baby, I did." His voice had lowered, and his tone turned cajoling.

"No. You. Didn't."

"A man is dead because of me, Erin."

"You didn't *kill* him. You were protecting yourself and me. You didn't just walk up to someone and take their life."

"You're right. But it doesn't change the fact he died by my hand."

"Does that bother you? I didn't think about how it might have affected you, I was just grateful we were alive."

"Fuck no, it doesn't bother me."

"Then why are we talking about this?"

"I need to know if it bothers *you*. I didn't think about it that day. And after, I was more concerned about your concussion. Then making sure you weren't having nightmares about being taken from Abe's cabin."

I contemplated everything he'd said and came to the same conclusion I did every time I thought about all that Colin had done for me. I always came first. Nowhere in his statement had he mentioned himself, or the injuries he'd sustained. Or the lives he'd taken. It was all about me, all the time. I wasn't sure if it made me selfish or not but that was one of the many things I loved about him.

"You killed two men in front of me," I corrected. "Two men that had beaten you. Two men that had kidnapped me. Two men that had threatened to kill you in front of me. You did what you had to do to protect us. You walked through fire, for me, for us. How could I feel anything but gratitude for that?"

"Through fire?" His face softened.

"You said—"

"I know what I said. I'm just surprised you remembered."

"It's what kept me sane. Those words helped me stay strong. I knew you'd find a way out. You told me that when you found the woman you loved there wasn't anything you wouldn't do for her. You'd walk through fire. And you did. I won't ever forget what you did for us."

"Damn, I love you. Are you sure you're okay with it?"

"I said I was."

"Okay. So tell me about this wedding you're planning."

I welcomed the change of subject. On our walk back to the house I told him about everything we'd arranged. My mom had a women's luncheon this weekend, which she'd offered to cancel, but I told her not to. Both, Colin and I wanted to get married as soon as possible but this weekend was seriously pushing it. We decided to do it in three weeks. That gave everyone enough time.

"You're sure you're all right with a small wedding and it being in the residence?" I asked as we approached the back deck.

"Absolutely. It's perfect."

"I was thinking, if they can, I'd like your parents to come before the wedding. I'd like all of us to meet and get to know each other before we walk down the aisle."

"They'd like that. My mom's already tried to get on a plane multiple times."

"She has? Why didn't she come?"

"I wanted you to get settled first. My mom can be, overwhelming."

He was protecting me again. Just like he always did.

"Don't be silly. Tell her to come. She can go with us to pick out my dress. Though, it's going to be like a covert CIA operation trying to keep the media vultures from finding out."

"Are you sure?" Colin's face brightened.

I stepped closer and put my arms around his waist, careful not to hurt him. "I'm positive. I'm nervous, I want them to like me. And I'm bummed Keira can't come. But we'll send her the pictures. Hey! Maybe we can live stream it to her. Would she be able to watch from the ship?"

He didn't say anything for a long while. But when he did, my heart was full. "Thank you for wanting to include my parents. My mom is going to love you, and I know it will mean a lot to her to go with you to find a dress. My dad is an old Irish man who is a sucker for a pretty lass. He'll be wrapped around your finger in two seconds."

"Does he have an accent? Will he call me lass?"

"He doesn't have one, unless he's trying to sweet-talk my mom. Growing up, we knew to leave the room when Dad broke out the Gaelic."

"That's sweet."

"Sure, if they're not your parents."

"Tell me more about them," I requested.

"I'd rather tell you about other stuff."

I liked the sparkle in Colin's eyes.

"Other stuff? What kind of other stuff?"

"The kind of stuff I can only whisper in your ear when I have you naked in bed."

My core twitched, and I really hoped this was going where I thought it was.

"Hmm, I didn't know there were such things one could whisper only while naked. Guess I need to get to the room and undress so I can hear them."

I heard Colin's chuckle behind me as I sprinted for the door. I liked the playful side of him. I also like the strong, protector side, too. And I hated to admit it, but even the brooding, irritated side of Colin—it was hot, too.

I was yanking my shirt over my head when I caught sight of Colin standing in the entrance of our bedroom. I tossed the bunched up fabric in his direction, but it fell short.

"Are you going to join me?"

"In a minute."

"What are you waiting for?" I asked as I pulled off my slacks.

"Nothing."

"Then why aren't you undressing?"

"I'm enjoying watching you."

"Well, *I'd* be enjoying myself if you'd at least take your shirt off."

I was a little surprised when he pulled it over his head and smiled. I thought I'd have to ask him more than once. "Better?"

"Hmm. Not yet. I think the pants need to come off to make it even." I motioned over my mostly undressed body. "I'm only in my underwear."

His pants came off, but he remained where he was. I reached around and unclasped my bra, letting the straps fall down my arms. I reached for the elastic of my panties, and Colin finally moved. I involuntarily shivered when his hungry gaze met mine.

"I get the pleasure of removing those."

I stood frozen in place, suddenly unsure what I was

supposed to do next. He scooped me up and started toward the bed.

"Your ribs," I admonished.

"Are fine."

He gently laid me down, pushing my legs apart as he climbed between them. We were touching from hip to chest, Colin's face rested in the crook of my neck, kissing the sensitive skin there.

"Are you sure about this?"

"Yes."

"You don't want to wait until after we're married? It's only three more weeks," he teased, or at least I hoped he was teasing.

"Seriously?"

"Are you on birth control?" he continued to speak into my neck.

"No." I tilted my head to the side giving him more room.

Crap. I hadn't thought of birth control. I hadn't been having sex so there'd never been a need.

He lifted his head, we were almost nose-to-nose, and I had to blink a few times to focus as he was so close.

"The choice is yours. We can use a condom if you want. I get tested for everything regularly through—"

"Shhh." I placed a finger over his mouth. "I trust you. I don't want anything between us."

Colin's lips twitched before he placed his mouth near my ear and blazed a wet path down the side of my neck, to my throat, and lower still, stopping at my breasts, kneading and massaging them before he sucked a nipple into his mouth.

"God that feels so good," I moaned and arched into his touch.

He went to the other side, lavishing the other nipple with the same attention, before continuing his downward movement, nipping and kissing my stomach before stopping at the juncture of my thighs. He looked up at me and smiled.

"Hold on, sunshine, this is gonna be quick."

"What is?" I asked through the lust induced fog.

"You coming in my mouth."

With a long, slow swipe, he licked from my ass to my clit. I would've come off the bed if he hadn't had one arm over my belly, anchoring me in place. His tongue swirled, sucked, and stabbed into my wet center. He was an absolute expert when it came to my body. He knew exactly what to do to drive me to the brink of insanity. The craziest part was, he could have me on the verge of orgasm quickly or draw it out and make me beg. He was in full control, I had no say in my body's reaction to him.

"So good, Colin," I groaned, not sure if I wanted to shove him away or plead with him to never move. My legs trembled, and the pressure built to nearly painful. The press of his tongue on my clit was all I needed to topple over.

"Oh, God!" I couldn't stop the scream as pleasure tore through me.

Colin continued to play as my orgasm slowly faded, when he hummed with his lips still on my clit, my ass shot off the bed. "No more."

Chuckling, he lifted his head from between my legs and the sexiest, wickedest smile I'd ever seen played on his wet lips.

"Damn, you taste good." His tongue darted out, and he licked his bottom lip. Good God, that was hot.

He moved up my body, taking one of my legs with him. Settling in the cradle of my hips, he wrapped the leg around his back and fell forward on his elbow.

Face-to-face.

My world narrowed to only Colin. I swear my breath caught in my lungs and my mouth went dry.

"Sunshine," he whispered, his voice thick with emotion.

The head of his dick nudged my opening, and my eyes fluttered closed. A few moments later when he still hadn't moved, I peeked at him through heavy lids.

"Colin. What are you waiting for?"

"You to look at me." The pad of his thumb traced along my jaw to my ear and back. The touch so feather light, making it even harder to open my eyes. "I need to see you."

I opened my eyes and swallowed past the lump in my throat when he slowly pressed inside of me. My back arched, and my heels dug into his lower back.

"Promise you'll never leave me."

"Promise," I rushed out.

"Never, Erin. I need you. I can't ever go back, now that I know you exist, that a love like ours is real, and I've finally found you. I won't survive if you leave me."

I was having a hard time forming a response as he gently glided in and out of me. His thickness stretching me to the max. "I'll love you every day, like we don't have tomorrow. I promise."

His hand on my cheek hadn't stopped moving, and his eyes were still glued to mine. It was in that moment, while Colin made love to me, we became one. Bodies, hearts, and souls. I didn't know where he finished and I started. I didn't want to know. I wanted to be lost in him forever.

"Please don't stop," I begged.

He stopped talking but not moving; his unhurried strokes caught my body on fire. In and out, leisurely, deliberately driving me to the brink of insanity.

"Faster, Colin."

"We have all night, there's no rush."

He continued with his slow pace, the only sounds in the room were his breath mingled with my moans. I couldn't take it anymore. I needed more.

"Harder," I begged. "Please."

"Hitch your leg up higher." He didn't wait for me to comply. His hand moved from my face and his fingers dug into the back of my thigh as he thrust into me hard.

"Oh, God."

"You are so beautiful. Wrap your arms around me."

"Holy—" My words were cut off, and my back arched. His hand moved from my leg to under my ass and he lifted.

"That's it, baby, move your hips, grind into me."

Colin's words no longer made sense, my mind was mush, and instinct took over. I squeezed my leg around his waist, allowing me to move with him. He pounded away, and all I could do was try and keep up.

"Fuck. You feel so good."

His mouth crashed to mine, and if I'd thought he'd dominated our kisses before, I'd been wrong. *This* was dominance, raw, carnal, pure. Everything felt right. My nails clawed his back and when he wrenched his lips from mine and threw his head back on a loud moan, my pussy fluttered. It was like the dam had broken, allowing all the pent-up passion we had for each other to unleash. Our world had narrowed to the clashing of teeth, groans, grunts, and the slapping of our bodies as we came together.

"Don't let go, Erin. Don't ever let go."

"I won't."

I held onto him tighter, hoping he'd understand I needed him just as much as he needed me.

"I love you, baby." His words were soft and gentle and in direct contradiction to his punishing thrusts.

"I love you." I tilted my hips more, and my orgasm slammed into me. "I'll never let you forget how much."

"Erin. Look at me."

When the daze started to fade, and his face came back into focus, I was mesmerized by his gaze. His eyes had gone soft, but all the muscles in his neck had tightened. His body shook, and with one last thrust he planted deep, and, finally, his head fell forward as he groaned his pleasure.

I waited until Colin lifted his head before I whispered, "Only you."

His eyes drifted closed, and I knew he felt my words, just as much as I had when I'd said them.

CHAPTER 26

"I'm happy your mom is coming early. What time does her flight get in today?" Erin asked from the passenger seat.

"Her flight arrives at BWI at noon," I reminded her.

"And you arranged a car to pick her up? She's not offended we can't get her ourselves?"

"Relax, sunshine. Everything is taken care of. And, no, she isn't upset."

"All right. I'm just nervous."

Last night after we'd made love and before we made dinner, I called my parents. My mom was thrilled Erin wanted to include her. Ten minutes into the conversation, she asked to speak to Erin and the two of them spent nearly an hour on the phone while I cooked. By the time I got the phone back, my mom was in tears declaring Erin was perfect. I hadn't heard most of what was said, but Erin must've agreed to give my mother the twenty million grand-children she desired. My dad wasn't coming for another two weeks. After he'd retired it took less than a year of him being home with my mom all day for him to decide sitting still wasn't for him. He's a volunteer fireman. He needed to give the station notice to take him off rotation.

"I don't see how that's possible. You and my mom talked forever. She already loves you."

"But what if she gets here and sees what a pain in the ass I really am?"

"What's that supposed to mean?" I asked, pulling into the parking garage.

"Come on, Colin. It's not like I live a normal life. Between the paparazzi always around doing their best to catch me doing or saying something stupid or the secret service hovering, what if your mom gets annoyed or thinks I'm too much trouble?"

Once I had the car stopped, I took my seat belt off and turned to face Erin. "Look at me, sunshine." Her worried eyes came to mine. "She's not going to get annoyed, not with you. My mom is a pint-sized momma bear. The only thing we should be concerned about is her giving some intrusive photographer a piece of her mind."

"Okay."

I knew she didn't believe me, but this was one of those times no amount of talking was going to convince her I was right. She needed to see it for herself. I knew my mom would welcome her into the family with open arms.

"I'm sorry we had to come into the office today. I wanted nothing more than to laze in bed with you all day."

Memories of last night flooded my mind when her cheeks pinkened. The first time we made love will forever be seared onto my heart. Knowing what she gave me, that I was the only man who would ever have her was insanely gratifying. Watching her fall apart under me was something I'll never forget. But it was the second time, after dinner, when she pushed me onto the bed and had her way with me. *That* was a thing of beauty. She was confident and vocal. Just like everything else in Erin's life, when she wanted something, nothing stopped her. She took and took, and I was willingly at her mercy.

"I wish we never had to leave the house. We could stay in a bubble and forget the outside world. But I actually have a lot of work to do. And I should start looking for a job."

"You have a job."

"You realize I don't draw a salary from the charity, right? I donate it back monthly."

"Do you enjoy the work?"

"You know I do. I love it."

"Then why would you stop?"

"Because I need to make money."

I took a moment to choose my words carefully. But the longer it took to think of a nice way to say what needed to be said, the more I realized there was no such way.

"I'm just gonna say this, and it may make me sound like an asshole, but I am who I am, and there's no use hiding it. I don't need you to contribute financially. Even if you had the means and made more money than me, I still wouldn't take it. This is not an 'I'm a man, you're a woman' thing. This is me, I provide, I protect, I do anything and everything to give you what you want. That's my job."

"And what's mine, Colin?"

"To love me and support me."

"That's not a job. Those things are easy, they're a given. You're my husband. Of course, I'll love and support you."

"It won't be as easy as you think. I'm bossy and—"

"I know who you are, Colin. But I'd like to feel like I bring some sort of value to our marriage."

"I want you to listen to me very carefully, sunshine. You depositing money into an account doesn't mean jackshit to me. Me coming home to you after a shit day, means something. You giving me a soft place to fall when a mission has gone to hell, means something. Knowing you're by my side, means something. Us being a team, and you loving me, means the world to me. There is no dollar amount on the value you bring to my life or our marriage. If you want to continue to work at the charity, do it. If you want to go back to school, do it. If you want to be the CEO of a fortune 500, I'll stand by you. If you want to stay home and learn to paint, sunshine, I'll hang every masterpiece you create on the walls. Whatever decision you make, needs to be because it's what makes you happy and not based on money."

"If you change your mind and need me to work, you'll tell me?"

"I won't."

"Promise me you'll tell me."

I didn't like how uneasy she looked sitting next to me worrying her bottom lip. I had money, plenty of it, but if the day came we needed more I'd work five jobs before she'd ever have to take a job she didn't want.

"I promise."

"Thank you." She smiled. "You ready to go in?"

"No. Not until you lean over here and give me a kiss."

Erin's smile grew, and my heart jumped. Damn, but I loved seeing her happy and knowing I made her face shine like it was now, even better.

"Is this a fax?" I asked Zane, chuckling as I read the old school cover sheet. "I haven't seen one of these in years."

I'd spent the last two hours going over the SITREPS Tex had put together. Yesterday, my gut told me we were missing something big. Today, after going over everything again, it was screaming at me. Warren was a douchebag, thankfully, a dead one. His role and motivation were clear. I could even understand Camio Telecomm's interest in the Angel program being reinstated. They needed the information it gathered. Partly for the news outlet they'd purchased, but mostly for the contract money to stay in business. I've seen men do some fucked up shit for less.

What I couldn't figure out was the connection between Greenwold and Warren, beyond the obvious. Warren had to have had something big to hold over the man to make him flip and go along with terrorizing Erin. There was nothing during his time with the NSA that would suggest he'd turn. His record was spotless, not even a hint or rumor of impropriety. Michael Greenwold was well liked and respected. What the hell had changed?

"Tex sent it. I forgot we even had a fax machine until Ivy brought the report to me," Zane answered.

Declan and I stopped going over the reports we had spread over the conference room table and waited for Zane to go over the document.

"Christ Almighty. Either of you familiar with Omni?"

"Yeah. It's a cross between the Freemasons and Skull and Bones," Declan answered.

"Only the most powerful players get invited to join. Most people think Skull and Bones are the ones behind the CIA, but Omni is a few more rungs up the ladder," I interjected. "Why?"

"Greenwold is a member," Zane informed us.

"How the fuck did Tex find that out? No one has ever been able to confirm the club's members."

"Seriously? I don't question how Tex finds anything out. You know who else is a member?"

"Warren?" I asked.

"Fuck no! That rat didn't have the clout to play with the big boys. Stephan Perkins."

"Vice President Perkins?" Declan inquired.

None of us were fond of the vice president. He was a yes man. Why Tom ever chose him as a running mate I'd never understand. They were opposites—polar opposites to be exact. Perkins is interested in power, Tom is not. With his second term coming to an end, and the oval office up for grabs, Perkins was running. He was pushing his own agenda hard, even going against some of Tom's policies. Seems Perkins was pulling out all the stops on his bid for the Oval Office.

"One more reason not to like the man," I announced. "But it's not all that surprising."

"No, but what it is, is Perkins, Greenwold, and eight other men all belonging to Omni, own shares in Militrix, parent company to several smaller companies. One being—"

"Camio-Telecomm," I interrupted Zane.

"That's illegal," Declan added.

"Sure as fuck is, but considering Tex had to dig to find the intel, I'd say no one else knows."

"Shit," I muttered. "And the other 229 million? Where's that?"

"Earmarked for a transoceanic cabling in the Gulf of Bahrain. The scope of work follows the King Fahd Causeway."

"Sea mines?" Declan surmised.

"Don't know. Don't fucking care at the moment. I'm more concerned with Perkins and Greenwold's ties to the Omni and how they fit into the Angel program. I don't think Tom knows how deep this runs."

"What time is he due back?" I checked my watch. Tom should be landing at Camp David any minute now.

"He said his meeting should run about three hours."

"He's gonna go thermonuclear when he finds out."

"That's a goddamn understatement."

Zane's phone rang, and his brows pulled together as he studied the number.

"Goddamn telemarketers and their unknown numbers." He moved to reject the call but at the last minute answered. "What?"

There was a pause before Zane's body went rigid, and his face went white. Declan must've seen the look as well because he jumped out of his seat and ran to the door. After a sharp whistle and a hand gesture, he ran back into the room.

"Repeat that?" Zane requested and placed the phone on speaker.

"I repeat," Tex's voice boomed throughout the room, "we've lost contact with the pilot."

"Where?"

"I sent the coordinates to your phone. Wolf and his team are on the tarmac. ETA five hours. Rocco and his team are in Virginia training and en route. Ghost and the rest of the guys are in the air, they'll be here in three hours."

"Who else knows?"

"Gerard. President's orders are no one else is to be notified."

"Orders? He fucking knew?"

"He had his suspicions and left instructions regarding who was to be called in. Just you four teams, he doesn't trust anyone else."

"Fuck! Goddamn it!" Zane stopped and looked at the ceiling before grabbing a pen and paper off the table. "Codes and mission specifics?"

"Color of the day, white. Password, sparrow. Counter-sign, red. Mission name, marriage. They've got ten minutes on you, Zane. Stay dangerous."

Tex disconnected, and the room was silent.

"Wheels up in five." Zane jogged out of the room, and the

rest of us took a moment to allow the gravity of the situation to settle over us.

The President of the United States was MIA.

I didn't know which I was more concerned about, the search and rescue or how Erin was going to react.

Goddamn clusterfuck!

CHAPTER 27

I COULDN'T GET the last words Colin had said to me out of my head.

I promise we'll find him.

Find him.

My dad was missing.

I couldn't stop pacing. Jasmin, Olivia, Violet, and Ivy had all come into the office to stay with me while their husbands had gone out to find my dad.

The door to the conference room opened, and Jasmin had her pistol out of the holster on her hip and pointed in that direction before I could blink.

"Jasmin." My mother's smooth voice carried. "I don't believe that's a proper greeting for your auntie, is it?"

My mother's brow raised, and Jasmin lowered her weapon. "You can never be too careful."

Gerard was standing behind my mom, looking angry. Angrier than I'd ever seen him before. And that was saying something because I'd pushed the man to his limits with all my sneaking off.

"Come here, little rabbit." My mother opened her arms,

and I lost it. Her arms tightened around me, and she let me cry on her shoulder. After a few moments, she murmured, "That's enough, Erin."

"What?" I raised my head so I could look into my mother's face.

"Dry your eyes. That's enough crying."

How could she say that? My dad was out there somewhere with a target on his back. If something happened to him, I didn't think I'd ever be able to stop crying.

"Dad is missing," I said unnecessarily.

"Your father is the strongest man I know. And he's smart. He's also surrounded himself with men who will stop at nothing to find him. Right now, our job is to not fall apart. He needs us to be positive."

"But what if—"

"What if, nothing. Dry your eyes, sweet girl, your dad will be fine."

"How can you be so sure?"

"Because the man I married is a tough son of a bitch. A UDT. A sailor who fought and won in the most horrific of conditions. He will not break. He will not give in. The man I married will hold his own until the Calvary comes for him. And, this time, the Calvary is your future husband. Don't you have faith in the man you're going to marry? Don't you trust in his ability to bring your father home safely?"

I'd never heard my mom speak so strongly or with such conviction. Her confidence in my dad made me feel a fraction better about the situation.

"Of course, I do."

I was affronted my mom would suggest I didn't believe in Colin. I knew he was more than capable. I'd seen it with my very own eyes how deadly he could be.

"Good. Then you hold onto that trust. Don't allow anything else to creep into your mind. There is no other possible outcome. Your father and his men will be home safe and sound before the day is out. You can bet on it."

My mother stood tall, with her chin tilted in defiance. She believed what she'd said, believed in my dad. I needed to follow her lead and believe in Colin and the rest of the team to do their jobs.

"You're right, Mama."

"Damn straight, I am." I cracked a smile, not used to hearing my mother curse. "This isn't my first rodeo, little rabbit. Back when your dad was sent overseas to the war, we didn't have the luxuries the wives have now. There was no email, no cell phone, no skype, or messaging. We had letters, and very few of those actually made their way to the battlefield. There were months and months I was left to wonder how your dad was. I couldn't allow a sliver of doubt into my heart. I always knew he was coming home to me. Just like I know he's coming home this time."

I looked around the room, and all the other women had the same strength behind their stare as my mom did. She was right, I had to be the strongest I'd ever been. Not only for my dad and Colin, but for my friends. We were a team, these women and I, we had to stand together in a united front.

"So what now?" I asked.

"Now we wait. We keep ourselves busy and our minds occupied."

"Miss Erin, there's a Mrs. Doyle here to see you," Gerard said from the doorway.

Shit. Colin's mom. How in the world could I have forgotten her?

"Um. Can I go down and get her? Will someone bring her up? I don't know how to get through the security." My mom placed her hand on my shoulder and gently patted.

"Gerard. Would you please go down and get Mrs. Doyle?

And if it isn't too much to ask, would you please see if there is something in the kitchen? Water? Anything."

"Of course, ma'am."

When Gerard disappeared, I whispered, "That's Colin's mom, and I look like a total mess."

"You look stunning. Everything will be fine."

"I'm so happy you're here."

"There is nowhere else I would be. We'll get through this together. As a family. Right, ladies?"

My mom glanced around the room, smiling at each of my friends. Three yeses echoed and one goddamn right we will. One guess who uttered that wonderful statement just as Colin's mother happened through the door.

Thankfully, the beautiful woman smiled at Jasmin. "It's always a pleasure to see you, Jasmin."

"Mrs. D. Excuse my outburst. The guys keep telling me I need to stop cursing so much or the boys' first words will be shit and damn."

My mom groaned from beside me, and Jasmin shrugged her shoulders.

Mrs. Doyle's gaze landed on me, and her smile faded. She looked me over from top to toe before her eyes met mine once more. Oh, no, this was not how I thought my first meeting with Colin's mother would go. I tried not to fidget but I was shrinking under her scrutiny. What if after her examination she found me lacking? Would Colin change his mind?

"You're even more beautiful than your pictures. I can see why my Colin is so taken with you."

"Thank you, Mrs. Doyle." The other woman cleared her throat and shook her head, reminding me she'd requested I call her by her first name. "Alice. Thank you, Alice. This is my mother, Clarissa Anderson."

"Nice to meet you, Mrs. Anderson." Alice stepped forward to shake my mother's hand.

"Please call me Rissa." The two older women clasped hands. "I was just telling the girls here, that we are all family. There's no need for formalities." Before my mom let go of Alice's hand she spoke again. "I want to tell you, you and your husband have raised an exceptional man. We adore him, and he's one of my husband's most trusted men."

Alice blushed before tears pooled. "Thank you for that. We worry about him."

"We always worry about our children, don't we? It doesn't matter how old they are. Let's sit. We have a lot to plan."

Gerard came back with water and set it on the table before retaking his post by the door.

"Is Colin here?" Alice asked.

"No. He's—" I stopped myself, not knowing what I should say.

"Out looking for my husband," my mom said.

Gerard coughed and sputtered from the doorway. "Ma'am?"

"Alice has just as much right to know where her son is as these women deserve to know where their husbands are. We're in a secure location. Besides, she's my daughter's mother-in-law and Erin needs the support." Gerard didn't seem happy my mom was going to tell Alice what was considered top secret information, however, he didn't argue further. "Tom's helicopter lost radio transmission and GPS signal while en route to Camp David. There's concern an attempt has been made on his life. Colin and the rest of the teams have gone to retrieve him. They'll be back in a few hours."

Alice gasped, and I eyed my mom suspiciously, her tone was flat and matter of fact. I was beginning to wonder how much of my mother's confidence was a put on.

Alice's gaze slid to mine before she reached her hand out to me. "Yes. We have a lot to plan. And dresses to find. And flowers to order."

When Colin's mother pulled me into her embrace and wrapped her mom arms around me, they felt almost as good as my own mother's—almost.

"Everything's going to be fine, Erin. You'll see," she whispered.

"I hope you're right."

CHAPTER 28

"ALPHA TEAM, this is bravo team coming in hot from your south at five o'clock," Rocco's voice came over the comm in my ear.

"Copy that, bravo team. Last known . . ." I tuned out Zane while I relayed the last known GPS coordinates. "We're headed west. Eyes peeled."

"Roger," Rocco replied.

"I can't see a motherfucking thing through the tree canopy," Jax complained.

"Keep fucking looking," Zane barked. "Colin. Call in our location to Tex."

"Copy." I switched my radio to Tex's frequency. "Tex, this is Breeze, you copy?"

"Go for Tex." It was hard to hear him over the rotor blades even with ear-pro on over my comms.

"We're at last known. No sight. Do you have anything for us?"

"Has Rocco's team arrived?"

"Affirmative."

"I'm going to activate the subcutaneous tracking device.

You'll be on a fast-moving clock. Once it's active, the hacks will be able to locate him, too." Fucking hell. I didn't want to ask when the president had gotten a tracker implanted under his skin. "Twenty-four kilometers. North 39-39. West 77-27. Your time has started. I'll direct traffic your way when the rest of the guys land. Good luck."

"Copy that. Out." I switched back to the teams' comms and repeated what Tex had said.

"Roger," came from Rocco.

"Clusterfucking hell. Six minutes," Zane grumbled.

We had six minutes to get to the location Tex had given us. I took that time to check my weapons and extra ammo mags. I hoped to God when we got to Tom he was still breathing. It had been almost two hours since Tex had lost communication with the pilot. I didn't know how Tex had pulled off keeping this under wraps and I was a little afraid to find out. I always knew Tex was a whole lot of dangerous behind a computer but now, with a hundred percent certainty, I knew he could fuck some shit up and leave the US in shambles if he wanted to.

"I have visual on Marine One," Rocco said. "No movement. Switching to thermal. Three down. I repeat there are three down."

Shit. Three dead and cooling bodies. The helicopter Rocco and his team were in hovered over the downed Marine One.

It wasn't but a minute later a black rope dangled out of the side of the open door. "Cover," Gumby, one of the SEALs from Rocco's team said as the helicopter started to lower.

"Roger," I called back.

Pulling my FNH SCAR rifle up and to the ready, I watched the six men from the other team fast rope down. Once each of their feet hit the ground, we continued north and circled the location Tex had given us.

"Still can't see a motherfucking thing," Leo griped.

"Head five klicks north. We need to unload," Zane called to the pilot.

"Pilot down. Two SSAs down. He's not here," Bubba called in. "Repeat, not at this location."

It was a relief Tom wasn't among the dead, but both of the secret service agents were, which meant he was unprotected.

"Marine One took no fire. Fully functional," Rex called in.

"Repeat that?" Linc asked.

"No fire. Marine One was not hit."

Zane looked at me, and, in all the years I've known him, I'd only ever seen fear on his face one other time. When Ivy was missing, he was terrified. Now, he was a mix of red hot pissed and worried. The emotions didn't sit well with me.

"How they'd get into the box?" Zane asked.

He was asking about the bulletproof box in the cabin that the president sits in.

"Undamaged."

So either Tom let himself out or one of the agents unlocked it. Neither was good. The box being destroyed would've been the best case.

"We have blood—motherfucker," Phantom cut out.

"Rocco?" Zane called.

"Taking fire," he panted.

"Do you need backup?"

"Fuck no. We can handle this in our sleep. Out."

"Tex is in my ear," the pilot announced. "Both follow helicopters have been downed in a Pennsylvania field. No survivors. He said you have an hour tops before it's all over the news. He's doing what he can."

Marine One never flew without two follow helicopters. All the aircrafts were equipped with anti-missile and radar countermeasures. The fleet was guarded by eight hundred Marines, no one touched those helicopters unless they had special clearance. How in the fuck had someone taken down all three of them? Before today, I'd have said it would be impossible.

"How sure are we Gerard's clean?" Declan asked.

"He's clean," Zane answered.

"You willing to bet your life on it?"

"He's at HQ with my wife. I've already bet my life. He's solid."

Dec nodded and dropped the rope. The helicopter slowly lowered and finally came to a stop and hovered.

"Something's not right!" I shouted to Zane.

"You fucking think? The goddamn president is missing. There's not a damn thing right about this."

"What are the chances all three helicopters malfunctioned at the same fucking time?"

"None."

"Ready?" Dec asked.

Zane stepped forward, touched all of his equipment one last time, before he sat on the edge and wrapped his legs around the rope.

"Let's do this!" He was instantly out of the helicopter, fast roping down.

Five rifles pointed toward the ground, ready to provide cover fire if needed. Once his feet hit the ground. Leo went, Declan, Linc, and Jax followed. I took one last look around, making sure no one had left anything. With a silent prayer the president was holding on, I slid down the rope.

"Rocco, what's your twenty?"

"Counting the bodies," he came back.

"How many?"

"Fifteen. By the weapons and the rest of the gear they're well-funded. No patches. One guy has a tat on his forearm. Ace got a picture."

"What's it of?" I asked Rocco.

"A peacock feather."

"Same guys," I told Zane.

I'd seen the same peacock feather tattoo on one of the guys that had held Erin and me. The question remained, who did they work for? Greenwold? Militrix? Or the Omni? Hell, at this point I was almost positive they weren't mutually exclusive. All three seemed to tie together in one giant clusterfuck.

CHAPTER 29

"Jasmin. Gerard. May I speak to you both in the hall?" Garrett asked.

Jasmin stood and made her way to the door. "When did you get back? I thought you were in Pennsylvania?"

"Just now. Everyone else is still with Melody."

Jasmin and Gerard disappeared into the corridor with Garrett. The normally smiling, easy-going man looked haggard, almost as bad as Gerard, who hadn't moved from his post by the door in the last hour. Hadn't so much as spoken a word, as a matter of fact. The tension in the room was stifling. My mom, for all her tough talk earlier, was pulling into herself. She was still as polite as ever, but her voice was monotone. Not even the twins cheered her up.

"Is anyone hungry?" I asked.

Everyone shook their heads.

"Thirsty?"

Again, they didn't verbally answer, instead shaking their heads in the negative.

"Okay. Snap out of it. My mom was right. We should not

be sitting here breaking down. Olivia, how many missions has Leo been on since you've been with him?"

"A bunch."

"Violet? What about Jaxon?"

"A lot."

"Ivy?"

"Enough to know you're right. Zane would be pissed if he knew I was sitting here worried to death."

"Right. So snap the fuck out of it."

"Erin Lynn," my mom gasped.

"Mom. You've heard Jas drop the f-bomb about five million times."

"But, Alice—"

"Has a daughter in the Navy, a husband, and Colin is her son for God sakes. She's heard it, too."

"It's unladylike, dear."

"Maybe so. But it feels really good to say. You should try it. Call it stress release."

Ivy, Violet, and Liv all chuckled but it was Liv who spoke up. "Come on, Mrs. A. You should totally try it."

"Olivia, what would your mother think of you dropping the f-word?"

"I've heard her string a few curse words together," Liv informed my mom.

My mom cracked a smile and admitted, "So have I. The woman curses like a sailor."

"Come on, Mother, try it. Just shout it out. You'll feel better."

"Fuck!" Alice shouted at the top of her lungs, and I jolted in shock. "Fuck. Fuck. Fuck."

We all broke out in a fit of laughter at Alice's outburst, and when Jasmin and Gerard rushed back in the room to see why Colin's mother was yelling fuck, we laughed even harder. It felt good. The pressure that had been slowly building in my chest started to deflate.

"Fuck," my mom squeaked out.

"Mom. You can do better than that." I giggled.

"Fuck!" she screamed. "Fuck a duck!"

"What the actual fuck is going on?" Jasmin asked.

"Fuck," my mom repeated.

"What the hell have you done? You broke her. My debutante aunt is dropping the f-bomb."

"Fucker," Alice blurted, then quickly covered her mouth.

She and my mother were in stitches. They both tossed out obscenities and giggled like little girls. It was hilarious. The best thing I'd seen or heard all day.

"Never again do I want to hear anyone complain about my cussing," Jasmin announced. "If Robert and Asher's first words are fuck, I know who to blame."

I wanted to ask her why Garrett had wanted to talk to her and Gerard, but I didn't dare. The heavy weight had started to lift, which was a good thing because I didn't think I would have survived the elephant on my chest much longer.

Come on, Colin, where are you? Please come home safely.

CHAPTER 30

"Bubba, you got eyes?" Rocco asked his teammate.

"Crystal fucking clear. I found a deer stand, of all things. Let's hope this bad boy can withstand my .338. If not, I'm falling about twenty feet on my ass."

"Gumby, Ace, Phantom, you in place?" Rocco continued.

Three yeses came through the comms. We had an old hunting cabin surrounded. Rocco's men had the north and east covered and Dec, Linc, and Jax had the south and west. Leo had found a sniper's perch as had Bubba, the best long-range shooter on Rocco's team.

Rocco and I stood with Zane, hidden in the tree line, waiting for him to give the orders.

"Ready to punch some tickets?" he asked.

Eleven resounding yeses called back. I was more than ready. First, Erin and me, and now Tom. Someone was about to learn the meaning of a bullet is forever. It was a lesson a man only learned once if it was properly placed. With the reputation Rocco and his team had, they didn't miss. And neither did we.

"Leo. Bubba. Go."

The three of us hung back and waited, and two shots rang out, both just shy of the building. We couldn't strike the house and risk hitting Tom, but we needed to flush them out. Without eyes inside, we had no way of knowing how many there were or where they were hiding the president.

"Two tangos out the back," Linc called in before two more shots were fired.

"Both down."

"I see a peeker. Bubba, do you have a shot?" I asked.

"In three . . ." He never finished his countdown verbally, but when I got to one in my head, the man looking out the window crumpled from view.

"This is taking too long," Zane complained.

"Patience, brother." I placed my hand on his arm.

"Fuck that." He started to move, and I grabbed him with more force.

"If you rush in there and get—"

"Grenade out the door. Cover!" Leo yelled.

My body jolted, and I stumbled back from the concussion. Zane was on his ass next to me, but I couldn't see Rocco through all the smoke and debris.

"Rocco?"

"Good," he answered.

"Patience," I told Zane once again.

"They're filing out. I see five out the front door," Bubba announced.

"Six out the back," Jax counted.

"Pick 'em off," Zane ordered.

Once the three of us were back on our feet and the rapid gunfire from all around had begun to slow, it was finally our turn.

"I'm on point. Breeze, you're my second. Rocco, take our six."

We both acknowledged our roles and waited.

"Leo. Bubba. Lay down cover."

Zane took off in a sprint, and I followed. We were almost to the door when a hot searing pain hit my right bicep, and my step faltered. I swung around but before I could pull the trigger, the man who'd shot me fell sideways and hit the dirt. I'd seen a lot of fucked-up shit, but a head shot from a .338 Lapua at under five-hundred-yards took the cake. A large portion of the man's head was gone. Just gone.

We breached the door, and all hell broke loose. Men dressed in black were everywhere. Every time we'd take out a room full of them another wave came, like locusts, from the back of the house.

"Reload," Zane called out and he dropped behind what was a table but now had more holes in it than a sieve.

"Jesus. It's like a clown car. Where the hell are these fuckers coming from?" Rocco complained.

There was a lull, and, even though I had doubled up on hearing protection, my ears were still ringing, and my right arm was burning.

"There's a creeper coming in the door. I don't have a clear shot without hitting one of you. He's there in five, four, three, two, now."

I turned and fired two shots, he'd barely hit the dirt when I heard Leo in my ear. "You're clear."

"I'm runnin' low on ammo, Z. This needs to end."

I was down to my last hundred rounds, which sounded like a lot until it wasn't. Then you're left standing there with your dick in your hand getting shot full of holes.

Zane answered with a nod and began advancing into the next room. The entire place was torn to shit. The smell of gunfire hung thick in the air, coupled with the coppery smell of blood. I had to step over several men littered on the dirty cabin floor. They were everywhere. I'd seen fewer dead men in an Isis hideout.

Rocco motioned he was breaking left and moments later, he called out the all clear and joined us back in what I assumed was a dining room. Zane pointed to the only door that hadn't been cleared. He quickly opened the door, moving to the side as he did.

I internally groaned when I saw the stairs. A basement. My least favorite room to clear. Without being able to use explosives, we were sitting ducks. As soon as we started to descend the stairs, we could be picked off by whoever was down there.

"The famous Zane Lewis, I presume." A voice floated up.

I didn't recognize the voice, not that I would've been able to with the now constant pounding in my skull.

"Please, come down and join us," the man said.

"Not a fucking chance. Why don't you come up here if you're so eager to meet me?"

"You've gone through so much trouble and you don't want to watch the main event?"

A crackling sound filled the basement, right before an unmistakable sound of an electrical arc penetrated through the ringing in my ears.

"Holy shit," I muttered, just before a guttural scream came from below.

"Fuck this!"

This wasn't good. I knew Zane was gonna take the bait and go down the stairs.

Goddamn it!

Without a plan, Zane rushed the door. He couldn't fucking help himself. I hurried down after him and felt Rocco on my six. One hand was on my shoulder, and he used the other to point his weapon over the banister.

I damn near ran into Zane's back when he stopped short. I hadn't yet seen what had halted him and the moment I stepped to his side I wished I hadn't.

Tom Anderson was tied to a chair. His white, button-down shirt was torn open and covered in blood. His face had been beaten to a pulp. I had to blink a few times to recognize him. Three square electrodes were placed on his chest. How the sticky pads adhered to his skin with all the blood dripping from his nose, down his chin, and onto his chest was beyond me. A car battery sat on the floor at Tom's feet and the man held a cattle prod in his hand. A little over-dramatic, if you asked me. One or the other would've done the job. Using both on the president was overkill.

Zane hadn't spoken, hadn't even breathed.

Rocco had taken aim on one of the two men in the room.

"What do you want?" Zane finally spat out.

"Nothing."

"Nothing? All of this and you want nothing?"

"I already have what I came for. There's nothing I need from you."

"Bullshit. I don't believe, for a second, Tom would've told you anything."

"Tom?" The man chuckled. "Yes, I had heard you're a presumptuous prick that thinks he's one of President Anderson's *men*. One of the anointed few he's on a first name basis with. It's a shame you're so late. You missed all the good stuff."

Was that jealousy I'd detected? The man sounded positively envious that Zane and the rest of us were on first name terms with the president. Something all of us had struggled with, but something Tom Anderson had demanded. There wasn't a damn speck of pretense when it came to the president. Those closest to him, the ones he respected and trusted were asked to check the presidential title when speaking to him.

"Do it," Tom slurred.

My gut clenched, and I tried to work out what Zane was

going to do. He was the wild card. Then there was Tom. I wasn't sure if he was taunting the man into telling Zane something.

Goddamn clusterfuck of epic proportions.

"You have to know you're not leaving here alive," Zane told him.

I was taken aback by my boss's uncharacteristic calm demeanor. Zane Lewis didn't talk. He didn't negotiate. He simply walked into a room full of hostiles and started taking them out.

"I hadn't figured I would. Of course, the *hope* was I'd live, but there are somethings a man's willing to give his life for."

"And what is it exactly are you willing to die for?" I asked.

"Sometimes a reminder is needed. We are the whole of everything, in all ways, all places. No one is beyond our reach, not even the President of the United States."

"Omni."

"Do it," Tom slurred again, this time more forcefully.

I was done. I wasn't waiting for the fucking lunatic to light Tom up again. I lifted my gun and pressed the trigger—once for the kill, the second for good measure. Rocco's shot rang out, the second man hitting the concrete, and Zane moved to Tom.

"You ready?" Zane asked Tom when he cut his arms free.

"Get me the fuck out of this hell hole."

"Do you think you can walk?"

"Does it look like the fuckers broke my goddamn legs?" Tom asked.

"No."

"What's wrong with you? Why are you acting like a pansy ass asking a bunch of questions?"

I couldn't hold back my laughter. Zane looked properly chastised.

"What the hell are you laughing at? Took you long enough

to shoot the asshole. You know what these were for?" Tom ripped the electrodes off his chest. I winced when there were three bare spots and Tom's chest hair was left on the pads. "He shocked the fuck out of me. I'd take waterboarding any day of the week. How many teams did Tex call in?"

"Rocco's team is outside. Last I heard, Ghost and his squad were at the White House waiting, and Wolf and his men were on a plane."

"Good, he followed directions."

Tom started for the stairs, and my instincts were screaming for me to help the battered man up the stairs, but I didn't dare offer. Tom was cranky on a good day, right now, he was fucking pissed.

"We're coming out," I called.

"You're clear in the front," Bubba, a member of Rocco's team, answered.

"Back side is good to go," Linc returned.

"Leo. Bubba. Stay high. Everyone else, out front."

"What in the Sam hell happened up here?" Tom looked around the destroyed house.

"We met a little resistance, sir," Rocco supplied.

"A little? It looks like the war of 1812 in here."

We stepped out of the house in time to see all seven men: Linc, Dec, Jax, Gumby, Ace, Rex, and Phantom jog into what was left of the front yard.

"Jesus Christ," Dec mumbled when he drew close.

"What time is it?" Tom asked.

I moved my right arm to look at my watch and had to grind my teeth together from the pain. "Seventeen-oh-five."

"I told my Rissa I'd be home in time for dinner. You call in our ride or are we walking?"

"Three minutes until evac," Zane told him.

"What a long goddamn day!" That was understatement. "Good work today, boys! Appreciate you all coming out and working together. When I left instructions for Tex, I knew I'd chosen the right men for the job."

"You knew," Zane accused.

"I didn't know the how or the when but I knew something wasn't right. I knew they were taking me one way or another. I figured I'd rather get it over with. And now we know who we're playing with."

"What now?"

My question was cut off by the sound of rotor blades chopping through the air as the helicopter hovered overhead.

"You got two choices, tandem up with me," Zane shouted over the noise, "or in the basket!"

"Neither. Do you know who the fuck I am?"

"Yes, sir, I do." Zane's lips twitched.

"I'm a goddamn UDT. I may be battered but I'm not broken. There's no chance in hell, I'm going up in a basket."

"Hooyah!" Linc, Leo, Zane, and Rocco's team all belted out.

Jax and I shook our head. "Damn Navy SEALs and Hooyahs." I laughed.

"You know what we say to you Army grunts, right?" Rocco chuckled good-naturedly. "Follow us, we'll lead the way," he finished.

"That's because we're smart. We let the frogs draw 'em out and cover your asses."

"You're up first, Rocco." Zane cut off our banter.

Once Rocco was in the helicopter, then the president, I took my first deep breath since the whole ordeal started.

"You're next, brother. And when we get to Camp David, I wanna look at your arm. You good going up the rope?" Zane asked.

"Do you know who the fuck I am?" I said, using Tom's words from earlier.

Zane's face finally relaxed, and he smiled. "Yeah, brother,

I know exactly who you are." His hand landed on my left shoulder and he gave me a bone-jarring pound on the back. "You're one of the toughest sons of bitches I know."

I wrapped my left arm around the rope and when my feet were off the ground, I tangled my leg around the line, making a foothold. I glanced around the wooded area with dead bodies scattered about. Tom was right, it looked like a war zone. I thanked my lucky stars we'd made it through another battle, lived another day, and when the time came for the next one—we'd be ready for another fight. It's what we did. What we lived for.

CHAPTER 31

THIS WASN'T my first time in a helicopter, and each time I went up I swore I'd never fly in one again. It was worse today because I was already on edge. It wasn't that I got airsick, exactly, but I always got a little queasy. Alice was sitting next to me, happy as a clam, staring out the window as we flew north toward Camp David.

Gerard had received a call from Zane, and, within minutes, there was an executive helicopter on the roof of Z Corps ready to take us to my dad and the rest of the guys. We were told there would be a Delta Force team following us and not to be alarmed, it was simply a safety precaution. Gerard hadn't given us any information about my father's condition, and I hoped, for my mom's sake, he was okay. The past few hours had weighed heaviest on her. Yes, he was my father, and I loved him dearly, but he was my mother's every-thing. If she lost him, I don't know what she'd do.

The beautiful trees of the Catoctin National Park gave way to the retreat. I wanted off this aircraft and to find Colin. I needed to see for myself he was okay. That they all were. Looking around the cabin at Violet, Ivy, and Liv, I knew they were feeling the same as I was. Not to mention, Alice had been worried sick about Colin. Jasmin had stayed back with the twins, not feeling comfortable with them flying yet. She blew it off and said Linc would be home when he was done with his debriefing. But my cousin wasn't fooling anyone, she was just as worried. I think everyone was right, the babies had softened her, but not in a bad way. The boys had brought out all the best parts of Jasmin. Sure, she was still as brash as ever, but she seemed to show her emotions more. I liked it.

"Two minutes," Gerard mouthed.

He was the only one wearing a headset, staying in communication with the pilot.

I picked up my mom's hand and was rewarded with a tight smile. "Everything's fine."

For all the reassuring my mom had done today, she didn't sound fine.

My ears popped as the altitude changed, and it wasn't long before the pilot gently put the helicopter down. Gerard held up his hand signaling for us to wait, I'd say he had mere moments before five anxious women rushed him and exited whether he wanted them to or not.

The blades whined down to a slow thrum, and the door was opened. Seven men dressed in all black, complete with covered faces stood outside.

Alice stiffened beside me. "It's okay. Those are the good guys. They're just making sure we're safe."

She didn't speak but nodded. Gerard got out and helped my mother out before assisting the rest of us. My mother was straightening her skirt and otherwise making herself presentable. I knew it was a nervous habit, but with my nerves frayed I wanted to scream that no one cared how she looked. But I didn't. Instead, I took my mom's hand in one of mine and Alice's in the other. Gerard took the lead and started walking toward the Fieldhouse. We were halfway there when Zane, Leo, Colin, Linc, Declan, and Jax came into view. The six of them looked like tall, strong avenging angels. Violet, Liv, and Ivy walked ahead and were nearly jogging. I didn't dare let go of my mother and Alice. At first, I thought it was because they needed the support, but I realized it was for me. My legs felt like jelly, and my heart was beating so fast I was getting dizzy. He was safe. Alive. Sweet relief flooded my body.

But my dad was nowhere in sight. Which I told myself was because it was unsafe for him to be out in the open. However, I knew that wasn't the case.

Colin waited for the three of us to approach while the others broke away and were ushered into the house. I wanted to wrap my arms around him and pepper his face with kisses, but I couldn't my mom and Alice needed to be taken care of first.

"Did they task you as the one to give me the bad news?" my mom said to Colin when we stopped in front of him.

"Mother!" I scolded.

"It's all right. Tell me."

Colin's gaze slid to mine and his eyes told me everything I needed to know. It was bad. And he needed my help.

"Alice, let's let my mom and Colin talk for a moment."

I placed my mom's hand in Colin's and pulled Alice off to the side. The two of us were greeted by three of the seven-man Delta team.

Alice hadn't taken her eyes off my mom, and when Colin reached out for her just as she started to crumble, Alice let go of my hand and strode toward them.

I couldn't move. I didn't want to know what had caused my mom, the woman who'd always held her emotions in check in public, to break. It was bad, and I didn't want to face it.

Strong arms wrapped around me from behind, and when I started to struggle a familiar voice spoke, "I got you, Erin. Relax."

Fletch.

Even though Colin was holding my crying mother, and speaking to his own, his gaze hadn't left mine. He was silently giving me the strength I needed.

"Thank you. I'm fine now."

Fletch's arms loosened and fell, but I could still feel him standing behind me. Colin nodded and Fletch spoke, "Come on, he's ready for you now."

"I don't know if I am."

"Sure you are. You're the strong and brave woman who went toe-to-toe with Colin back in Texas. You survived being run off the road and then kidnapped. You're the woman who saved Colin's life. You can do this, too."

"I didn't exactly save his life."

"That's not what we heard. Word on the street is Colin needed his beautiful woman to come to his rescue. Come on, before he storms over here and kicks my ass for keeping his girl away from him. He needs you."

"He wouldn't do that."

"Oh, yeah? Then you're not paying attention."

We began walking, Fletch pushing me along, closer and closer to the bad news I didn't want to hear.

"Mama?"

"He's fine, little rabbit. Everything is fine."

"You don't look like you're fine."

True to form, Clarissa Anderson pulled herself together and dabbed her face with a handkerchief, one of many I knew to be in her handbag. "I *am* fine. And it's not polite to point out—"

"Stop, Mom. No one here cares. It's okay to show how upset you are."

Mom's eyes filled with tears again. "I can't. I'm afraid to go in and see him."

My mom's uncertainty triggered a deep strength I didn't know I had. She needed me to be strong for her. "Come on, we'll do it together."

I looked up at Colin and, for the first time, I noticed he'd changed. He also had a white bandage around his arm. "You're hurt."

"It's nothing, sunshine."

"But—" he shook his head, cutting me off. "Okay."

With Alice wrapped in Colin's embrace and my mother in mine, we walked the two women into the Fieldhouse.

My father was in the middle of the large room, pacing like a caged, wild animal. He stopped and turned to face us. Holy fuck. My mom gasped, Alice groaned, and I wanted to burst into tears seeing my daddy so badly beaten.

Dad saw Mom and he didn't delay, he stalked over to us, pulled her from my arms, and held her to his big, broad chest as she cried.

"Rissa, baby, I'm okay. Everything's okay." My dad's voice was gruff and thick with more emotion than I thought possible.

"Tommy," she cried.

"I'm safe. We're all safe."

Colin pulled me against his side and kissed my cheek. "I love you, Erin."

"God, I love you, too."

My big, strong soon-to-be husband wrapped both his mom and me in his arms and held us close. Thank God, everyone was safe, or so I thought.

CHAPTER 32

"I'M SORRY, sunshine, we have to debrief. It shouldn't take that long."

"We're fine. Take your time," Erin told me. "I'm just relieved to be standing here in front of you."

She tried her best to smile. "There was never a doubt I was coming home to you. Or bringing your dad home. This will be fast, your dad isn't going to let anyone take their time. He wants to get your mom home and soon."

"She was trying to be strong all day. I mean, she was strong, but you could tell the longer it went on, the more upset she was getting."

"And what about you? Are you okay?"

"I was scared," she admitted. "But after all of us talked, I was reminded I had to trust in your ability, trust you'd come home to me. Once I did that, it made the wait easier. But—" She stopped and sucked in a breath before she leaned closer and whispered, "I was afraid they'd kill my dad before you could get there. In my head, I was planning for everything I'd have to do to help my mom," she admitted.

"I'm so sorry you were scared. We weren't going to let anything happen to your dad."

"But sometimes shit happens, and you can't control everything."

She was more right than she knew. Shit did happen, bad shit to good people. But not this time, I tried to remind myself. This time the good guys won, and everyone came home.

"No, but we're good at controlling what we can. Thank you for taking care of my mom."

"You're welcome. Go talk to the guys so we can go home."

"Damn, I love it when you're bossy. Your forehead crinkles, and you look fierce."

"Are you saying I have wrinkles?" she mock-glared. "You have no idea what that comment cost you in expensive skin cream."

How in the fuck it was possible I was smiling at a time like this was beyond me. I would've thought it inconceivable that not even two hours after being in a battle for my life I could be this happy. But I was. And it had everything to do with Erin.

"Be back soon."

With one last, all too brief, kiss I headed to the other room where everyone was waiting on me. I passed by an agent standing at the door, and Tom's concerned eyes came to me.

"How is she?"

"Shaken up." His head fell forward, and I quickly added, "But you know Erin. She's her father's daughter. Nothing and no one is going to break her."

"First, thank you all for your hand in today's mission. As you're aware, the world will never know how you saved my life, kept peace and order in our great country, and risked your own lives in the process. Being the quiet professionals you are, I know you don't want the attention. But what you do have is my gratitude and that of my family.

"Wolf and his team are at the White House with Tex preparing the files I need. But before we get to that, we have a problem."

Tom stopped and tapped a stack of papers on the desk in front of him.

"All the information we have on Omni is right here. As you can see, it isn't much."

"Who?" Hollywood, one of the Deltas, asked.

"A secret fraternity made up of the most powerful men on the planet. The Omni doesn't discriminate. They have no country. Race, religion, region, or creed does not matter to them. Money and power are their currency. Today they sent a message, they're more powerful than the president. If they can get to me, they can get to anyone. Their plan was brilliant and beautifully executed."

"How'd they do it?" Coach, another Delta, asked the question we were all wondering.

"Remote control," Tom answered. "Tex pulled the maintenance report for Marine One, every two-hundred cycles she gets a full service and recertification. According to the last report, there was a faulty flight control module. It was replaced. This has Omni written all over it."

"You're saying Omni has someone inside the HMX-1 and they replaced the control module with one they had remote access to?" Zane asked.

HMX-1 was the Marine Helicopter Squadron responsible for the transportation of the president. There was going to be one pissed off Marine Colonel back at the Marine Corps Air Facility.

"Not only Marine One, but the two follow helicopters, too. Or maybe the whole fleet for that matter."

There was no missing the venom in Tom's tone. This

was worse than any of us could've ever imagined. And that was saying something, when it was just the NSA involved, and they were playing their spy games, it was a shitstorm. Now? We had entered into FUBAR territory —fucked up beyond all repair. If the Omni had infiltrated the United States government, we'd never get them out.

"How'd you get out of the box?" I asked, remembering the two dead secret service agents.

"I didn't get out. I was let out. And the two men on my detail who opened the door soon found they were expendable. You know what they say about honor among thieves."

Just as we'd assumed, the agents who'd gone with Tom were dirty. How fucking deep did this go?

"I need something from you, Zane. It's more than I should be requesting."

"Yet, you still are." Zane chuckled. "Whatever you need, it's yours."

"I need Declan and the Gold Team to track Omni."

Declan lifted his chin in acceptance and I wondered how his twin sister was going to feel about her brother being back in the field full-time.

"Done," Zane announced.

"What are we doing about Angel?" Linc asked.

"That's what Tex is working on now. I want all the intel wiped clean before I go public. There's one thing the US population loves and that's a good conspiracy, and I'm gonna give it to them. Omni has always had a veil of mystery surrounding them. They think they're safe because they work in the darkest recesses of the world. Not anymore. I want the world to know we're hunting. And I won't stop until Declan and his team have tracked each and every one of them down. Militrix and Perkins will be the first two Omni to fall."

"Excuse me. I'm sorry to interrupt," Erin stammered from the doorway.

"You're never interrupting, dear," Tom returned.

All the fine hairs on my neck stood up, and suddenly the mood electrified. A current pulsed through the room, and nineteen of the world's deadliest men stood stock-still. They all felt it, too. Erin hadn't moved or said anything other than to apologize, but it was the fear in her voice that had put us all on alert. Her arms were crossed awkwardly in front of her body, and I didn't know if she was holding something or trying to stop her hands from shaking.

Her head snapped in my direction, and she asked, "What's the color of the day?"

My hand automatically went for my weapon, so did the other eighteen men in the room, and I answered, "White."

Her arms uncrossed in lightning speed, and before I could blink or register what was going on, she'd popped off two rounds. The secret service agent in front of her fell against the wall, dropping his gun before he hit the floor. Everything happened so quickly I hadn't even noticed the man had drawn on her.

"Fuck!" someone shouted.

"Lower your gun, sunshine," I said as I jogged to her. "Where'd you get that?"

"Gerard needs a doctor. He's in the back hall by the pantry." She was still holding the gun out in front of her. "His lapel." She motioned the Smith & Wesson in the direction on the downed man. "His color is wrong. He's wearing blue."

As I studied the man on the floor's presidential detail pin, Ghost, Fletch, and Truck rushed past us. He was indeed wearing the wrong color. Every day the outside ring of the pin changed colors. Sometimes more than once depending on the threat level. Why hadn't any of us noticed? It was unacceptable. A huge fuck-up. An oversight that not only had deadly consequences but it would leave a lasting mark on Erin.

"Less than twenty-five feet. There's no time to aim. Grip and trigger control," she rambled. "I knew something was wrong when Gerard didn't come back right away. He never makes my mom wait. She asked for tea. He . . ." She waved the gun at the man on the floor. "Went into the kitchen after Gerard. He came back empty handed. The color is wrong."

For all the shakiness in Erin's voice, she was holding it together pretty well considering there was a man bleeding out in front of her and the complete chaos in the room around us. I tuned out everything going on around us, my only concern was Erin and getting the weapon out of her hand.

"Can I have the gun now, sunshine? You're shaking pretty badly, I don't want you drop it."

"No. It's Gerard's. What if there are more? I want it."

"Baby, there's no one else left in this building."

"But what if more come? I want the gun."

Her voice was coming out more and more high-pitched. She was going to be pissed as hell, but I didn't have a choice. I stepped toward her under the guise of hugging her and at the last second, I twisted the gun out of her hand.

"Colin!"

"You can have it back later," I lied. "Right now, you're shaking like a leaf and that's a dangerous combo with a loaded gun in your hand."

I clicked on the safety, shoved the weapon in the waistband of my cargos, and picked her up. Ignoring the pain in both my ribs and my arm, I carried her to a sofa and sat down.

"Is Gerard going to be okay?"

"I don't know, but if anyone can patch him up, it's Truck. Are you okay?"

"Is he dead?"

I smoothed the hair off her face and answered, "Yeah, baby, he's dead."

"I had to," she cried.

"I know you did. You did good."

Zane and my mom approached at the same time. While my mom sat on the couch next to us and took both of Erin's hands in hers, Zane remained standing in front of us.

"He has the feather tattoo."

Zane had snapped out of whatever funk he'd been in when we were in the basement and he was back to being the hardened warrior I knew him to be.

"Is Gold Team ready?" I asked.

"They leave tomorrow. How you holding up, Erin?"

"Okay," she whispered.

Zane crouched down to eye level and waited until he had Erin's full attention.

"You did what you had to do to save lives. Just like you did what you had to when you helped Colin. It takes a certain type of woman to be with men like us. There's no doubt you're exactly who Colin needs. It was a damn brave thing you did. Damn brave. I'm proud to have you as part of our family, Erin."

I couldn't have said it better myself. Erin's quick thinking and bravery was one of the numerous things I loved about her. There was no one in the world who was better equipped to be my wife, my partner, my teammate. And I'll spend the rest of my life making sure she knows how much I treasure her.

CHAPTER 33

Gold Team- Bahrain
Declan

"It's hotter than a mother," Brooks Miller complained.

"Better than freezing balls in the arctic," Thad Bench returned.

We'd been in country for less than a week, and acclimating to the over hundred degree, dry heat would take more than a few days. At least we weren't in full kit. Body armor acted like an insulator, raising the temperature another ten degrees, easily. While Brooks was not wrong, I had more important things to worry about. The team was meeting with a UN Political Affairs Officer. Zane's dossier was sparse, all I knew about the woman was her bullshit cover story. The most noteworthy notation was that her opinion was highly respected among the power players. We needed to play nice if we didn't want to be tossed out of Bahrain before we'd gathered the intel we needed on the Omni Group.

The cool air blasted as we made our way into a UN annex building outside of the US Naval Base. The furnishings around the room were as sparse as the report I'd received on UNOCT Tatiana Jones.

"Something smell funny to you?" Kyle Smith asked before I could comment.

"This ain't no normal UN annex, and before you ask, yes, I've been in plenty," Max Brown added.

A woman roughly my age walked into the lobby. Her high heels clicking on the tile floor announced her approach long before we saw her.

"Declan Crenshaw?" she asked.

"Yes." I stepped forward.

"Tatiana Jones," she introduced herself. "Sorry." She motioned around the room. "Budget cuts."

My bullshit meter was pegged into the red, but I didn't bother to call her out. Tatiana Jones was not my concern nor was her cover. We followed her into a small room that shrank considerably when five very large men entered.

"I've been briefed on the Militrix's transoceanic cabling contract. My divers inspected the area around the King Fahd Causeway and found no cabling." Tatiana sat at the head of the table, signaling for the rest of us to as well.

"Your divers?" Brooks cut in.

"Yes. Mine. The area is clear."

"If you don't mind, I'd like to take a look myself."

I hadn't worked with the team long, but Zane had promised they were solid, all coming from the same BUD/s class and having been on the same SEAL platoon together during their years in service, Brooks going off reservation and challenging Tatiana was not going according to plan. First, we didn't need a pissing contest, and, second, we didn't ask permission to carry out an objective. We simply accomplished our task, with none the wiser.

"There's no need. I have the utmost trust in—"

"Right. You may, but I don't. And, all due respect, I trust, but verify."

Tatiana leaned back and eyed Brooks.

"I know all about your verification process, Mr. Miller. I'm also well acquainted with men like you."

"Oh, yeah? And what kind of man am I, doll?"

"An overachiever. Demolitions expert. Divemaster. Low and high-altitude jumpmaster. Rappel Master. Fast Rope Master."

"Glad to see you've done your homework. Unfortunately, the work-up we received on you was only a paragraph. There was nothing listing your accomplishments."

"My accomplishments aren't important. The only thing that's imperative is you don't fuck up my op."

There were so many red flags waving, I was beginning to wonder what kind of shitstorm we'd walked into. This was supposed to be an easy in and out. Recon only.

"Well, Miss Jones. It is *Miss*, correct? We wouldn't want to get in your way. I'll take a quick look around this afternoon, and, hopefully, in a few days, we'll be on our way."

"It's actually none-of-your-business," Tatiana sparred. "I'll take you out there myself. Oh-five-hundred."

"You'll take me out?"

"Good to know all your combat tours haven't diminished your hearing."

It was by the grace of all things holy I was able to hold back my laughter. I didn't know what kind of shit Tatiana Jones was running, and I didn't want to know, but I liked her, she had spunk.

"What do you know about diving?"

"You're not the only one with special quals, friend. If we're done, I have shit to do. I was promised you guys wouldn't be an issue."

"There will be no issues from us," I confirmed. "Recon and out."

"Good. I have something scheduled in less than a week. I'd prefer you were gone by then."

"Ah. You're kicking us out of your country?" Brooks dramatically covered his chest.

Tatiana shook her head, not the least bit amused by his behavior. "With big egos, comes bigger mouths. Have a nice afternoon, gentlemen. Mr. Miller, I'll see you at the docks off 59th, slip fifteen."

The woman didn't wait for us to stand before she took her exit, excusing us.

"Damn, brother, I was having grade school flashbacks." Kyle chuckled.

"All that was missing was you pulling her hair," Max threw in.

"Mark this, assholes, if we had more time, I'd be doing more than tugging on Miss Sex Kitten's curly mane. Holy hell, those legs in those sky-high heels. Hot damn. And that mouth, she can throw some sexy attitude my way anytime," Brooks told the group.

"Keep your dick in your pants. Recon only."

"Copy that, boss."

"Brooks wishes he had time for a quick recon mission." Thad laughed at his own joke.

Please, God, get me out of this country in one piece. My first mission as team leader and I already have a man chasing tail. Zane wouldn't be happy. The faster we could figure out what was so special about the Gulf of Bahrain and why Militrix was in the country, the better. Brooks looked more than serious about getting to know Tatiana. And Tatiana Jones was absolutely not who she claimed to be.

I could feel the imminent shitshow revving up.

EPILOGUE

ERIN

"Are you ready?"

I finished adjusting the pearl necklace my mom had given me and turned from the full-length, mahogany mirror and faced my dad. I was mesmerized by the cheerfulness in his smile. It had been a hard six weeks, but seeing my father so happy soothed my nerves. I wasn't nervous about marrying Colin. I knew he was who I was meant to spend the rest of my life with. No, my anxiety came from the media circus that had surrounded the White House.

My dad had stood tall and proud in front of the American people and had blown the lid off the NSA's Angel program. On national television he'd explained that the privacy of millions of Americans had been trampled. His top advisors had begged him not to. But my dad believed in truth and above the truth was the constitution. He'd exposed the vice president's complicity, explaining that Mr. Perkins had known the program was running even after my dad had instructed that it be shut down. He'd denied it, of course, leaving his campaign scrambling to do damage control. Tex wasn't able to prove the vice president's involvement in my dad's or my kidnappings, but Colin and the rest of the guys were positive he not only knew, but had a hand in the planning. It was a mess, but, in the end, truth won out. I was proud of my dad, not only as a parent, but as my president.

"I am," I finally answered.

My dad stood in front of me and took both of my hands in his. "My beautiful, sweet daughter. I've heard that no father is properly prepared to give his daughter's hand in marriage. But I want you to know, I am. Today when I walk you to the man who will become your husband, I will do so with confidence. And not because I know he'll provide for you and love you and protect you with his life. It will be because I know you will do all of those for him as well. You'll provide him with the comfort and love he'll need to calm his restlessness. You'll cherish and appreciate him because he will adore and spoil you. And I know if the day should ever come again where you need to stand beside him, you will. All the lessons your mother and I have taught you about courage, honor, and bravery did not fall on deaf ears. We are so very proud of the woman you've become. *I* am proud." He squeezed my hands and smiled. "So, I'll ask you again, Erin Lynn, are you ready to go out there and get married?"

"Thank you, Daddy. I am now."

"I'll never tire of hearing you call me daddy."

"Everyone is ready for you," Gerard said from the doorway.

Thankfully, Gerard had made a full recovery, my dad had offered to transfer him to a less dangerous detail or to a different agency if he wanted, but Gerard had refused to leave my dad's side. I think he was relieved when Gerard wanted to stay. Now, more than ever, my dad needed people around him he could trust.

He let go of my hands but before he could lead us out of

the Lincoln bedroom, down the center hall, and finally into the Yellow Oval Room where Colin and my family were waiting for me, I needed to tell my dad a few things.

"Thank you for being such a great dad. I know I wasn't always easy, especially the last few years. But I want you to know, my behavior had nothing to do with you. It was me feeling . . ."

"Stifled?"

"Yeah, a little bit. Anyway, I'm sorry if my actions worried you, but I'm not sorry I pushed and rebelled. I think I needed to. There were a few things I did and said I regret, but only the things that hurt you and Mom. Other than that, I learned some stuff about myself, I grew as a person, and I found Colin."

"You should regret nothing, Erin. Live. Be who you were meant to be and never let anyone stop you. You are a force to be reckoned with."

"Thanks, Dad." I straightened his bow tie. "You sure do look handsome today."

"I know your mother is happy you agreed to postpone the wedding. She said my face would've ruined your pictures. I told her that you're going to be the wife of a tier-one mercenary, you should get used to black eyes. Your mother disagreed, and, smartly, I saw the light."

The thing was, in all the years my parents had been married, he'd always seen it her way. There were very few things Clarissa Anderson wanted for. If my dad could give it, he did.

I placed my arm in the crook of my dad's elbow, and we followed Gerard down the hall.

"Are you still scared?" my dad whispered.

"How'd you know?"

"I know my girls."

"Not anymore. You reminded me I was enough for him."

"Goddamn right you are, you're an Anderson."

"Actually, I'm a Doyle."

The large opening of the room came into view, and I saw a tall, beautiful woman in a Navy dress uniform standing with Colin's parents. The three of them smiled at me, and I recognized the woman right away.

"How did you get Keira here?"

"One of the many perks of being the president. When I request the presence of a particular sailor, no one questions my order."

"Thank you. They all must be so happy to see her."

"Least I could do for the man who saved my life."

"What about for the man who loves your daughter?" I joked.

My father stepped in front of the white runner that had been laid over the marble floor and faced me.

"For him? I would give my life."

Tears sprung to my eyes, and I didn't bother trying to stop them as they rolled down my cheeks. I knew my dad meant those words. With a wink and a smile, he walked me toward Colin.

My breath caught in my throat at the sight of him. If I'd thought he was a good-looking man in a pair of cargo pants and a T-shirt, he was absolutely man-of-the-year sexy in a tux. Zane, Leo, Jax, and Linc all stood beside him, looking handsome in their wedding finery. When my gaze slid to the other side of the aisle and I saw Ivy, Liv, Violet, and Jasmin all staring at their men instead of watching me walk down the aisle I couldn't help the laugh that slipped out. I couldn't blame them one bit.

My eyes finally met Colin's and the humor faded. I'd never felt so treasured from one look. All his focus was on me, everyone else could've disappeared, and he wouldn't have noticed. When my dad stopped in front of him, he still hadn't looked away.

My dad's deep chuckle echoed in the room, and the rest of our families followed suit.

"She's all yours, son."

My dad placed my hand in Colin's and stepped back.

"Damn right, she is."

One month later- Killeen, Texas.

COLIN

"Any word from Declan?" Fletch asked from across the table, throwing down his second full house in a row.

"Damn. Harley's gonna kick my ass if I lose anymore money," Coach griped with a shake of his head and a smile on his face.

"It's no surprise you keep losing, you suck at poker." Hollywood chuckled.

"Who wants another beer?" Ghost stood to go to the fridge.

After waiting for everyone's drink order, Ghost ambled off and I answered, "Yeah. He and the guys are still in Bahrain tracking the money. Tex gave them a good place to start."

"Tex, king of the dark web. Don't know how the hell he does what he does, but grateful he's on our side," Truck mumbled, throwing his cards onto the pile in the middle of the table.

We fell into a companionable silence as Beatle shuffled and dealt a new hand. The warm Texas breeze blew, and my mouth watered from the smell coming from the smoker. We still had a few hours until the women would be home from shopping, and the food would be ready, a few hours to sit around on the patio and bullshit with Fletch and his team. Ghost returned, set the beers down, and leaned back in his seat.

"Almost like old times," he mumbled.

"Better than old times," Blade corrected. "Old times means it was just us sad saps sitting on Fletch's patio wishing we had what we all have now. I think I speak for all of us when I say I like life better now."

Fletch looked around his old backyard, then to his teammates, and the pensive looked turned into a grin. "Yeah, you can say that again. Lots of good times in this backyard."

"I'll drink to that." Ghost held up his beer and everyone touched bottle necks. "What about you, Colin?"

"What about me?" Ghost motioned to seven bottles touching in the middle of the table and I lifted mine. "To the future."

Glass clinked, and brews were chugged.

"Hurry up and finish dealing," Truck instructed. "We have ninety minutes until the women get back. Let's see how much more of Coach's money we can take."

Sitting around the backyard bullshitting with the guys, giving them a little piece of their history, even if the present and future were better and brighter than the past meant a lot to me. The only thing that would make it better was Erin sitting on my lap. Not only because I loved my wife and hated being away from her, but she was a card shark, and I was losing my ass.

Two years later- Annapolis, Maryland.

ERIN

We pulled up to Linc and Jasmin's house, and I couldn't stop the fit of giggles.

"Who would've ever thought?" The front of their porch was covered in balloons. "I wonder whose idea it was to decorate the front of the house?" I asked.

In the two years since Colin and I had been married, a lot had changed. Children had been born, the guys had gone on countless missions, and my parents had moved back to Texas. The one constant was my cousin. Sure, in the beginning, after the twins were born, she'd softened a skosh. But the tiny bit she'd changed had taken nothing away from her badass demeanor.

"My guess is Linc. Sometimes I think he's the more sensitive one in their relationship," Colin joked.

I found that highly unlikely. Lincoln Parker was all man. Not that I'd say that to my husband, who was all alpha male himself, but there was no questioning Linc's manhood.

"If you'll grab Lexi, I'll get the presents," he continued.

Careful not to wake our daughter, I took the car seat out of the back and waited for Colin before walking to the house.

"Do you think you got them enough toys?" he asked, carrying a stack of boxes and had gift bags hanging from his fingers. "They're only two."

"You mean, *we*? And yes, *we* got them enough."

Colin was still shaking his head when we walked through the door. Thankfully, Lexi was a good sleeper because the house was utter chaos. Kids and toys were strewn about, adults weaved around the little ones, and laughter filled the space.

Nothing better.

"There you two are," Livie greeted. "Bummer, she's sleeping," she added when she peeked at Lexi.

"Sorry we're late. She went down for her nap early today."

"Oh." Liv laughed. "I see."

"The only thing you *see* is I was able to take a shower today without a bouncy seat in the bathroom with me."

Colin deposited our gifts next to the huge pile and was back at my side, taking the car seat from me.

"Where's Giorgia?" I asked about Leo and Olivia's first-born daughter.

"Already running around out back with Robby and Asher."

"Here, let me hold Francesca." I held my hands out and waited for Liv to pass me the baby she'd been cradling.

"Ready for another one?" Colin leaned down and whispered.

"Lexi is three months old. You're crazy," Liv answered for me.

"Who's crazy, *tesorino?*" Leo asked, joining us.

"Colin. He wants another baby."

"And? I'm ready to put another one in you. As a matter of fact, I think it happened last night."

"Nice." Olivia rolled her eyes. "We're done for a while. Giorgia runs me all day and now with Francesca here . . . just no. Don't even think about it, Leo."

"Yo!" Zane bellowed from the floor, his one-year-old son lying in front of him, struggling to roll over while Zane worked hard to keep him on his back.

Ivy, Jasmin, and Violet were nowhere to be seen. I was getting ready to ask where they were when Jaxon and Linc joined our huddle.

"The girls ran to the store," Linc said.

"And they left all the kids here with you guys?" I asked.

"Nope. That's why I stayed," Liv cut in.

"You do realize what we do for living, right?" Linc chuckled. "We hunt terrorists. We've survived in the worst conditions. I think we can handle seven children."

"Christ, what does your mother feed you?" Zane

complained. "How is it possible baby shit can be purple?"

Olivia and I had matching raised eyebrows in answer.

"All right, I'll give you Zane, he's a little squeamish when it comes to diaper changing," Linc admitted. "But the rest of us can handle—"

"Daddy!" One of the twins ran in the house covered in mud. "Robby pushed me."

"Shit. Where's your Uncle Jax? He was supposed to be watching you."

"Mason fell down. Dirt in his mouth," Asher explained why Jax wasn't watching him and his brother. Mason was Jax and Vi's son. "I got the hose."

"The hose. Shit. Is your brother wet?"

"Yes." Asher smiled.

Jaxon came in the back door holding a dirty Mason. A soaking wet Robby followed.

"Jasmin's gonna kill me," Linc muttered.

"So, seven kids, huh?"

Robby took off across the living room, dripping water as he went.

"Shit."

"I don't know how you do two. I'm done. One is plenty." Jax still hadn't moved from the doorway.

"Where's Gia?" Leo asked.

"Here," a cute little girl called out from the kitchen.

"Come here, *tesoro*."

Giorgia came into the living room and seven adults all muttered a collective oh, fuck. Gia's face was covered in what I assumed was icing from Robert and Asher's birthday cake.

Olivia and I broke out in a round of laughter.

"It's not funny," Linc growled.

"It kinda is," Liv barely choked out the words.

"Jasmin's going to kill me."

"No, she won't." I tried to assure him.

"Yes. She is. It's the twins' birthday."

"Is anyone hurt?" I asked.

"No."

"Then she won't care. Shit happens. Life happens. The only thing Jas cares about is that we're all together and her sons are smiling. Who the hell cares if they're a little dirty."

"Or wet," Liv answered. "For a group who's used to adapting and regrouping, you all sure looked panicked."

"Mission shift, boys. Kids out back, hose them off, and we'll clean up the kitchen," I called out. When I glanced at Colin, his lips were twitching. "What?"

"You're goddamn sexy when you're bossy."

"Is that so?"

"It is. And, tonight, I'm going to show you how hot I think it is."

"Looking forward to it."

"I love you, sunshine."

"Love you." I rolled up to my tiptoes and gave Colin a peck. Sadly, it was not the way I wanted to kiss my husband. One thing was for sure, over the last couple of years, even while pregnant and right after, our need and passion for one another had not waned. I wanted him now just as much as I did the first time I saw him. I kept my promise and loved him everyday like it was our last. Colin was a good man, a great husband, but an even better father. He loved Lexi beyond measure. Both of them filled me with so much love and joy I was busting at the seams.

The men left the house with all the kids minus a still sleeping Lexi and Olivia, and I went to the kitchen.

"You know he's gonna try to knock you up tonight, right?" Liv asked. "They're sneaky, all of them. It starts with a tough guy act, then they throw in the sexy smirk, they make their voices rumbly, and *bam*, panties drop. Careful, friend, don't fall for his tricks."

"I'm counting on it."

"Counting on it?" Liv laughed.

"We're working on giving Colin's mom the eighteen grandkids she wants."

"Your poor vagina."

"Mine? You've already popped out two. Leo walks by you in the hall and you wind up pregnant."

"He does more than walk by, trust and believe that."

The two of us laughed and cleaned up the crumbs and icing off the floor and counter. Luckily, most of the cake was intact. But even if it wasn't, it wouldn't have mattered. We were all together, the kids were happy, and life was good.

Sixteen years later

ZANE

"Eric, why is your sister crying?" I asked my son.

"I don't know, Dad. I guess she's still mad at me."

I looked at my son doing his homework and thought for the five-hundredth time how happy I was my boy was born first and he'd gotten my genes. He was tall, as much as it cost us keeping him in pants and shoes it was well worth it. He watched over his sister and it was necessary. My girl may've only been fifteen, but she was a knockout and looked like she was eighteen. I blamed it on Ivy, but my wife said it was my fault because Rose got my blue eyes. I had to disagree, they weren't mine, they were bluer and they sparkled like Ivy's when she smiled. Except, my girl wasn't smiling now. Something was making her cry.

"Why is your sister mad at you?"

With a heavy sigh, Eric put down his pencil and looked up at me. "Today after practice Rose was walking by the field and this asshole said it was a shame she didn't put out because she's the hottest girl in school."

My blood pressure spiked and, not for the first time, I wanted to kick a teenage boy's ass. I was going to have to talk to Ivy about this shit. I didn't want little pissants talking shit about my little girl.

"What'd you do?"

"Put him on his ass and told him if he ever talked about my sister like that again he'd be walking away with more than a bruised ego."

"Good man." I was damn proud of how my son handled the situation. "So why's she mad?"

"She has a crush on him. I guess that's why she was hanging out after practice 'waiting for me.' She wanted him to ask her to the dance."

"You tell her what he said about her?"

"Yes. And I told her, the last thing she wanted was to go anywhere with Pete. He's a douche and even if she doesn't put out, he'll tell everyone she did. I tried to tell her she doesn't want that kind of reputation."

"Not tracking why's she angry at you."

"Because I told her she was too good for asshole football players. And I've already put the word out if anyone dares to touch her, they'll be dealing with me, Asher, Rob, and Mason. Now she's really pissed and says she's going to be the only girl to graduate high school without a boy kissing her."

"I see no problem with that," I told my son.

"Neither do I. I don't want my friends talking about banging my sister." The growl that slipped out was unintentional. "Sorry, Dad, you know what I'm saying."

"You did good today. You straight? School going well?"

"Five by five. Counting down to summer."

With a pat on my son's back, I walked into the living room and went to the couch where Rose was crying.

"Sugar plum, look at me."

My fifteen-year-old did what teenager daughters did best and rolled her eyes. She hated the silly nickname I'd given her when she was a baby, but that was too bad, I wasn't stopping.

"I know you're pissed at your brother right now, but he's doing what he's supposed to do." I put my hand up to stop her rebuttal. "I want you to know your mom and I are so proud of the young woman you're becoming. You're smart and funny. And so damn independent you drive your old man nuts. You are also beautiful. I know you want a boyfriend. The only thing I ask is before you let any boy place his lips on yours, ask yourself if he's worth it. Is he worthy of your time, your affection, and the gift of you? If your answer is yes, proceed."

"How will I know?"

"You'll know. And the fact that you're asking, means you haven't met him yet. Because when you do, deep in your bones, you'll know he's the right one. Until then, you focus on you."

Not waiting for Rose to respond, I went in search of Ivy. Gone were the days of us living in the penthouse way up high above the city. Ivy had talked me into buying a house, complete with a white picket fence, down the street from Linc. It took months for the guys to stop giving me shit about it. I gave zero fucks I was the butt of their jokes. I was living the dream.

I made my way to the bedroom, finding Ivy getting ready for a shower.

"How was your class?" I asked.

Three times a week, she and the girls did yoga or Pilates or some shit. I didn't know what it was called and I think the class changed each time they went. What I did know was her ass looked fantastic.

"Jeeze. You scared me. It was good. Mason has a new girlfriend, and Vi hates her. Francesca has a boyfriend, and Leo has all but lost his mind, both of his daughters are dating. He's complaining Marco, Dante, and Nico aren't watching out for their sisters like they should be. Erin is freaking out that Colin's mom planned a trip to Florida and is taking Lex, Tommy, Max, and Ben for a week. Colin is—"

"Baby, I appreciate you giving me a rundown on everyone's kids, but I don't give a shit what Colin is. Though, I can imagine he's probably thrilled to get his wife to himself while his mom takes the kids."

"You'd be right. Class was good," Ivy said, peeling off her skin-tight spandex pants.

"Sore?"

"No."

"Good."

I yanked my shirt off and tossed it on the bathroom floor next to her discarded pants.

"The kids?"

"Occupied. After we're done, remind me to talk to you about homeschooling Rose."

"We're not homeschooling her."

"Yes, we are. Those little fucks at school keep looking at—"

"Zane. Do you wanna stand here and talk about homeschooling or do you wanna get in the shower and help me wash my back?"

Homeschooling was the last thing on my mind when she tore off the loose T-shirt and sports bra. Standing in only her panties, I took her in from top to toe and back again. I was one lucky son of a bitch. I'd never understand how I got so fortunate or how and why Ivy put up with me. And I wasn't asking.

"Shower, now." I stepped out of my pants and palmed my semi-hard cock.

"Can I take my undies off first, Mr. Bossy?"

"Only if you're quick."

Her thumbs went under the elastic, and ever so slowly she pulled them down. The minute they pooled around her feet, I was on her. I lifted her, and she wrapped her legs around my waist. Two strides and we were in the shower, two more her back was against the wall. And one single thrust later, I was home.

"God, I love you," she moaned.

"With every breath, I love you more."

Six months later

LINCOLN

Watching your child take the oath of enlistment is a surreal experience, watching your twin sons take it was exceptional. Overwhelming pride washed over me, and I squeezed Jasmin's hand.

I could still remember the day I swore in. I was running, looking for an escape, and serving my country seemed like the best option. It had been good enough for my brother, Zane, I figured it was good enough for me. When I went to BUD/s I wasn't prepared, not that one could actually prepare for the worst experience of your life, but I hadn't had a clue. I hoped I'd prepared my sons. Today both of them were swearing in to the United States Navy, and while I was proud as hell they'd joined, I was still worried. The world we lived in was a brutal place.

I knew Jasmin was thinking about the day she enlisted, too. She stood tall and brave next to me, just as I knew my little hellcat would. I also knew she shared my fears but would never show it. Not now, not in front of her boys.

"... so help me God."

Robert and Asher lowered their right hands and remained at attention while the other recruits filed out of the room. This was it. The busses were lined up, waiting to take those who were shipping out to the airport.

My sons turned, and Jasmin's quick intake of breath was the only sign she was affected.

"You guys set? You have your orders?" she asked.

"We have everything," Asher answered, not surprisingly. He was always the one to talk for the pair.

"Good. Come here and give me a hug so you can say goodbye to everyone else."

Asher stepped forward and pulled his mom into his arms. He was so much bigger than Jasmin, she all but disappeared. He kissed the top of her head and moved to his Uncle Zane. Jax, Leo, Colin, and Declan all waited to wish my boys well. Not boys, my sons, they were men now. Eighteen and off to start their lives. I'd tried to get them to go to college first, God knows they had the grades and athletic ability to go anywhere, but neither of them would hear of it. Asher was soaking up all the last-minute advice from the men who'd helped raised him, when I noticed Robert still hadn't said goodbye to his mother.

The two-minute warning was called, and we needed to make our way outside. My wife's stoic mask was firmly in place, while Violet, Ivy, Olivia, and Erin were all sniffling and wiping away tears.

Just when I was getting ready to kick Robert's ass for not talking to his mom, he stepped in front of her, preventing her from exiting the building.

"Mom."

Jesus, when had my son's voice taken on such a hard

edge? Where had the last eighteen years gone?

"You better hurry. There'll be hell to pay if your ass isn't planted in that seat in about sixty seconds."

"Mom. Look at me."

Jasmin, being the stubborn woman she was, shook her head. "Linc, tell him. They need to—"

"Look. At. Me."

Her eyes shot up to his, and I knew why she'd been refusing. There were tears.

"We got this. You know we do. You and Dad gave us everything we needed. In nine weeks, we'll see you at our Pass in Review. This is a walk in the park."

"I know," she clipped.

"Right." Robert smiled at his mom's short answer. "I love you, Mama."

Jasmin nodded.

"It's an easy day."

She nodded again.

"We'll be careful."

"Promise?" she muttered.

"Promise." Robert yanked his mom forward, and she collided with his chest. Her body shook, and Asher walked to the pair and wrapped his arms around both of them.

"I love you both so much. Watch each other's six. No matter what, you two stick together."

"We will," Asher said.

"Shit and damn. Now I'm crying. I don't freaking cry. Hurry up. Get to the bus."

Robert passed Jasmin to me, and she tucked in close, just like she'd done for the last twenty years. With a lift of their chins, my sons were boarding the bus to basic training.

"Good old Great Mistakes." I laughed.

"I miss them," Jasmin whispered. "Already, Linc. I fucking miss them so much I feel like my heart has been ripped out."

"I know you do, sweet Jasmin."

"What do we do now?"

"Now we get to sit back and wait."

"For what?"

"For greatness. For them to need us again. I figure we got at least ten years until they learn that just because you're men doesn't mean you don't need the guidance of the men and women that have gone before you."

"That long?"

"Baby, they're your sons, we may have to wait closer to fifteen."

"Are you saying I'm stubborn?"

"As they come."

"You trying to piss me off?"

"Is it working?"

Her pretty eyes narrowed as she caught on to what I was doing. At least she wasn't crying anymore.

"You guys ready?"

When I turned to reply to Zane, the significance of the day hit me. Not just my sons leaving but the families we'd created. Never would I have thought two kids growing up in West Virginia the way we did would have all this. For a long time I'd been afraid my brother would let his misplaced guilt keep him from finding happiness. Then Ivy had shown up and rocked his world. When Ivy was pregnant with Eric, I paid him back for all the shit he gave me when Jas was carrying the twins. If everyone thought Leo and I had been over the top when our wives were pregnant, Zane was worse, way fucking worse. And Leo, the overachiever that he was, had filled his home with two daughters and three boys. He would've kept going but Olivia announced she was done after Nico. Three little Leos running around was more than she could handle. Jaxon and Violet were the only smart ones out of the group and happily stopped after Mason. Erin, much like Olivia, gave up after her third boy in a row. She and Lexi were outnumbered in the Doyle house.

"We did it," I said, instead of answering.

My brother's gaze left Ivy and came to me. "That we did."

SIX MEN AND ONE WOMAN STOOD IN FRONT OF A GRANITE headstone.

"It's been a long time, brother," Jaxon started. "Twenty damn years since we've seen you."

"We kept moving forward, just like we promised. We didn't squander your sacrifice," Leo said. "Gia's getting married. I wanna hate the little fucker, but I can't. He's a good kid and loves my girl. His only problem is, he's in the damn Chair Force."

"Fuck off." Jaxon laughed. "I never heard you bitchin' about the Air Force all those years when I was saving your ass."

"Right. That's why your boy, Mason, went into the Army," Leo continued.

"I blame that on Jasmin. She got her hands on Mas and sold him on that human intel shit, and it was all downhill from there."

"Downhill?" Jasmin laughed. "You're full of shit."

"Did Rob and Asher get their orders? Are they splitting up?" Colin asked.

"They're both going to Virginia. The higher ups saw the value in keeping them together."

Zane was only half listening to his men's banter. This is what they did, what they promised each other. Visiting Eric Wheeler's grave was not the time nor the place to mourn. Some might think it disrespectful standing in a cemetery laughing and joking with a dead man. But not them. Eric had lived and died a hero. A man worth celebrating, a man worth remembering. And they did remember. His memory would live in each of their children. The families they were all afforded by Eric's sacrifice.

The fuck of it was, Zane still harbored guilt. Now it wasn't the guilt over the men he'd lost, but knowing he wouldn't change anything. Eric giving his life for his team meant that fourteen souls were born into this world. Grief and loss had turned into happiness and family. Over the last twenty years, Eric's light had never dimmed; it was still shinning upon them, breathing life into their families. And at the end of each one of the days, Zane and his team knew family was all they had, the families they'd created, and the bonds they'd forged.

The laughter began to fade as the time came to leave. Each one touched the headstone as they made their way to leave. Zane lingered for just a moment, allowing the grief of Eric's absence to soak in.

"Miss you, brother. Every fucking day. Rest easy." With a slap of his palm on the cold granite headstone, Zane left.

Long Live the Brotherhood.

*

BE SURE TO READ ALL THE OTHER BOOKS IN EDWARD'S RED Team series and be on the look out for the new GOLD Team books coming soon!

If you haven't read all of the Red Team books yet, you can get them for a special price in the Red Team Box Set!

Also, if you enjoyed seeing Susan Stoker's characters in this book, check out *Romancing Rayne* and find out all about how Rayne and Ghost's honeymoon in London went!

ABOUT THE AUTHOR

Riley Edwards is a bestselling multi-genre author, wife, and military mom. Riley was born and raised in Los Angeles but now resides on the east coast with her fantastic husband and children.

Riley writes heart-stopping romance with sexy alpha heroes and even stronger heroines. Riley's favorite genres to write are romantic suspense and military romance.

Don't forget to sign up for the **Riley's Rebels** mailing list to receive a **FREE COPY of Unbroken** and stay up to date on releases, sales, and giveaways.

Riley Edwards Newsletter –
https://www.subscribepage.com/RRsignup
Add Riley Edwards on Goodreads
http://geni.us/goodreadsre

There are many more books in this fan fiction world than listed here, for an up-to-date list go to www.AcesPress.com

You can also visit our Amazon page at: http://www.amazon.com/author/operationalpha

ALL the below books are in Kindle Unlimited!

Special Forces: Operation Alpha World
Denise Agnew: Dangerous to Hold
Shauna Allen: Awakening Aubrey
Shauna Allen: Defending Danielle
Shauna Allen: Rescuing Rebekah
Shauna Allen: Saving Scarlett
Shauna Allen: Saving Grace
Brynne Asher: Blackburn
Linzi Baxter: Unlocking Dreams
Jennifer Becker: Hiding Catherine
Alice Bello: Shadowing Milly
Julia Bright: Saving Lorelei
Julia Bright: Rescuing Amy
Victoria Bright: Surviving Savage
Victoria Bright: Going Ghost
Victoria Bright: Jostling Joker
Cara Carnes: Protecting Mari
Kendra Mei Chailyn: Beast
Kendra Mei Chailyn: Barbie
Kendra Mei Chailyn : Pitbull
Melissa Kay Clarke: Rescuing Annabeth
Melissa Kay Clarke: Safeguarding Miley
Samantha A. Cole: Handling Haven
Samantha A. Cole: Cheating the Devil
Sue Coletta: Hacked

Heather Long: Guarding Gertrude
Heather Long: Protecting Pilar
Heather Long: Covering Coco
Gennita Low: No Protection
Kirsten Lynn: Joining Forces for Jesse
Margaret Madigan: Bang for the Buck
Margaret Madigan: Buck the System
Margaret Madigan: Jungle Buck
Margaret Madigan: December Chill
Rachel McNeely: The SEAL's Surprise Baby
Rachel McNeely: The SEAL's Surprise Bride
Rachel McNeely: The SEAL's Surprise Twin
Rachel McNeely: The SEAL's Surprise Mission
KD Michaels: Saving Laura
KD Michaels: Protecting Shane
KD Michaels: Avenging Angels
Wren Michaels: The Fox & The Hound
Wren Michaels: The Fox & The Hound 2
Wren Michaels: Shadow of Doubt
Wren Michaels: Shift of Fate
Wren Michaels: Steeling His Heart
Kat Mizera: Protecting Bobbi
Mary B Moore: Force Protection
LeTeisha Newton: Protecting Butterfly
LeTeisha Newton: Protecting Goddess
LeTeisha Newton: Protecting Vixen
LeTeisha Newton: Protecting Heartbeat
MJ Nightingale: Protecting Beauty
MJ Nightingale: Betting on Benny
MJ Nightingale: Protecting Secrets
Sarah O'Rourke: Saving Liberty
Victoria Paige: Reclaiming Izabel
Anne L. Parks: Mason
Debra Parmley: Protecting Pippa

Debra Parmley: Split Screen Scream
Lainey Reese: Protecting New York
Rose Smith: Saving Satin
Jenika Snow: Protecting Lily
Harley Stone: Rescuing Mercy
Jen Talty: Burning Desire
Jen Talty: Burning Kiss
Jen Talty: Burning Skies
Jen Talty: Burning Lies
Jen Talty: Burning Heart
Megan Vernon: Protecting Us
Megan Vernon: Protecting Earth

Fire and Police: Operation Alpha World

Freya Barker: Burning for Autumn
KaLyn Cooper: Justice for Gwen
Aspen Drake: Sheltering Emma
Barb Han: Kace
Reina Torres: Justice for Sloane
Stacey Wilk: Stage Fright

As you know, this book included at least one character from Susan Stoker's books. To check out more, see below.

Delta Force Heroes Series
Rescuing Rayne (FREE!)
Rescuing Aimee (novella)
Rescuing Emily
Rescuing Harley
Marrying Emily
Rescuing Kassie
Rescuing Bryn
Rescuing Casey
Rescuing Sadie
Rescuing Wendy
Rescuing Mary
Rescuing Macie (April 2019)

Badge of Honor: Texas Heroes Series
Justice for Mackenzie (FREE!)
Justice for Mickie
Justice for Corrie
Justice for Laine (novella)
Shelter for Elizabeth
Justice for Boone
Shelter for Adeline
Shelter for Sophie
Justice for Erin
Justice for Milena
Shelter for Blythe
Justice for Hope
Shelter for Quinn (Feb 2019)
Shelter for Koren (June 2019)
Shelter for Penelope (Oct 2019)

SEAL of Protection Series

Protecting Caroline (FREE!)
Protecting Alabama
Protecting Fiona
Marrying Caroline (novella)
Protecting Summer
Protecting Cheyenne
Protecting Jessyka
Protecting Julie (novella)
Protecting Melody
Protecting the Future
Protecting Kiera (novella)
Protecting Dakota

SEAL of Protection: Legacy Series

Securing Caite
Securing Sidney (May 2019)
Securing Piper (Sept 2019)
Securing Zoey (TBA)
Securing Avery (TBA)
Securing Kalee (TBA)

New York Times, USA Today and *Wall Street Journal* Bestselling Author Susan Stoker has a heart as big as the state of Tennessee where she lives, but this all American girl has also spent the last fourteen years living in Missouri, California, Colorado, Indiana, and Texas. She's married to a retired Army man who now gets to follow *her* around the country. She debuted her first series in 2014 and quickly followed that up with the SEAL of Protection Series, which solidified her love of writing and creating stories readers can get lost in.

If you enjoyed this book, or any book, please consider

leaving a review. It's appreciated by authors more than you'll know.

www.stokeraces.com

www.AcesPress.com

susan@stokeraces.com